I0555973

Mission Critical

Daniel Greene

Clink
Street

London | New York

This book is dedicated to my friends and family without whose support this book would not have been written.

Chapter One

Clifton looked down at his watch again as the delayed 17:10 train sped through the deserted platform. He noticed the merging of colours into streaks as the train sped by out of the corner of his eye. Greys, greens and blues in sweeping brush strokes as if across a canvas. Irritably he rummaged through his dispatch bag that he used for work and laid his hand on the book that he had been reading.

Not before long his train pulled into the station, there was no screeching from the brakes which used to signal the imminent halting of the train. Today with the new modern carriages the train came to a more controlled gentle stop, there was no apparent mechanical noises only low-tone humming that was similar to the modern electrical cars promising a new way of transportation for the future. A few more people had joined him on the platform. Clifton hated train travel because of the lack of control over your destination or the timing getting there. The carriage was packed which was not unusual, which left Clifton suffering with claustrophobia. He used to stand in the alcove carved out by the doors to take full advantage of the sense of freedom from the main carriage. With each station stop he would take full benefit of the cool air that flooded onto the train as the doors parted. He sucked in as much of the fresh air that he could before being once again sealed within the tin box.

Standing for the full thirty minute ride into Central London was not comfortable, especially when everyone was aggressively clamouring onto the already crowded train. The inevitable call sounded up and down the carriage from the doors from one disgruntled commuter, "Move down!"

The sea of people within the carriage waddled a few inches each creating the smallest of gaps which was no larger than for a seven-year-old child, yet at least two rather slender young men in business suits managed to drive their way into the gap.

Clifton thought to himself that this mode of transport was not even fit for cattle, let alone human beings! The alarming chimes resonated out of concealed speakers around the carriage and the doors began to slowly slide across in the hope of connecting in the middle. There was a sudden cram of people at this point as they pushed their bags into the train which had previously been hanging outside of the doors over the platform. Clifton had hated this before when he was a daily commuter, he was sophisticated and although he did not wear the sort of suits that was fashionable with the City Boys he had style but more importantly manners.

After a while Clifton found solace in reading on his journey. This gave him the escapism he craved from the claustrophobia of the train. Since using his time on the train for reading he had discovered that he could go deeper into the jungle of the carriage and actually get a seat at the start of his journey. Here he could be anyone living the adventures he dreamed of from the comfort of his seat. The escapism allowed him to travel to places that he had never been before and evade the chaos around him. Today he was reading the George Orwell classic *Nineteen Eighty-Four* which he had picked up from the airport WH Smiths a short while ago.

Clifton felt the alert vibration of his mobile phone in his right hand breast pocket. It was a text message from Philippa.

"Really sorry to do this again but I won't be able to make it this evening. Something at work has come up. Have a great time P."

Clifton returned the phone to its locked screen and replaced it to his pocket without a reply. "Fool, this is the third time she has stood you up," he muttered to himself as he rubbed his forehead in the uncomfortable stuffiness of the train. He was annoyed as he had made special arrangements for a wine tasting evening at his club for the pair of them to enjoy.

As the train pulled into St Pancras Station Clifton carefully placed the worn leather bookmark into the centre of the page, closed the book and prepared to leave the train. The hoard of people gathered at the base of the escalators waiting to be transported from the depths of the station to the cathedral like vaulted glass canopies which made up the roof structure. Clifton did not have the patience for the herding at the escalators, all that was missing from the station's concourse was the sheep dog.

It was only three flights of stairs to the surface and besides it all counted towards his daily goal of three thousand steps a day. Since starting his new job as a Project Architect for the construction of a data centre of a Social Media giant MyLife Clifton had begun to feel as though he was not as fit has he had been before where he walked nearly two hours each day to work. This was now replaced by a car and train journey. Clara had shown Clifton how to use an application on his mobile phone to calculate his walking and running distances.

At first Clifton had been rather impressed that such a device could collate all this data but then he began to see a more sinister use for the device as he realised that it was actually tracking his movements through Global Positioning Satellite mapping. Although it was done with the best of intentions he could not help but feel as though it was just another system built to monitor people and gather data on them. Clara and Clifton had been friends for well over seventeen years and had first met at University. She was studying to become a structural engineer as Clifton had been studying to become an architect.

In their second semester the university had thrown them together as the architects and the engineers were given joint projects so that they could experience what it was really like working collaboratively within a larger team. Clifton and Clara hit it off from the start. They shared the same principles and worked extremely well in delivering their combined projects. They often met up outside of university for exhibitions, art fairs and meals. They both found it slightly amusing that having both travelled all the way to Bath for their first picked university and ended up partnering with someone whose family home was a stone's throw away from each other.

As time passed after they had graduated they had drifted slightly apart. Clifton had taken a job in London following his degree and Clara had decided to stay in Bath taking up a job with a medium size practice of engineers. They had both loved and lost in life by the time they were in their early thirties.

Clara had fallen in love with a colleague after a few years of working. They used to work late into the evening many nights and eventually started seeing one another. Over time they had purchased a small but cosy cottage together. One day returning home from a two day business trip to Belgium she found him in bed with one of her close friends.

She had contacted Clifton and had asked him what he thought she should do. His advice had been to tell her to do what her heart and head told her to do. Whatever Clifton was he was not going to direct someone else's life choices. They had spent about two hours on the phone talking before Clara through floods of tears finally concluded that whatever the future brought she would never be able to trust her boyfriend again. She had then left Bath and returned to her family home in Hertford.

Clifton had met Chloe through a friend. Their first meeting was at Alexandra Palace on a warm sunny May afternoon. Clifton was sitting on one of the benches on the main terrace looking out over London twiddling with the zip on the cool bag that he had brought with him which had all of the picnic food he had made. Every time a double decker bus pulled up at the stop below he would lean forward in the chair trying to see who was getting off and if Chloe really looked like her MyLife profile account picture. He waited for about ten minutes longer than the time they had agreed over text messages. He checked his watch again and then his mobile phone. There was no clue. He began to wonder if she had come, seen him there and then decided to walk on. Anyone's first date nightmare.

He was about to get up and leave when he felt two hands covering his eyes from behind. A soft voice sounded 'Boo! I've got you!' and she had got him hook line and sinker. He was bowled over by her. She could argue like no one that he knew, she was passionate but distant. He always felt as though she had been concealing something.

As their relationship went on there were times that Clifton would ask after her sister and she would look at him confused before he would explain how he thought that it was this weekend that she had gone to visit her sister in Bristol. As time went on there seemed to be more misunderstandings over events and places which started to make Clifton suspicious until one day at a Saracens rugby match Chole told him that she had been seeing someone else and that they were going to make a go of things. Clifton felt as though the ground had been ripped out from under him. He felt angry but strangely more so with himself. He had allowed himself to be deceived all this time. Everything made sense now. The lies, the times she was away and the poor recollection of stories told.

He did not notice when she left the seat after telling him, he was blind to the match being played out in front of him and all he could think about was how stupid he felt for loving her so much. He vowed there that he was not going to let anyone again make him look this foolish. It had cost him some short-term relationships but he felt that it was better to be direct and know where you are rather than be manipulated and fooled again.

Clifton pulled out his phone from his pocket as he walked down the stations concourse and wrote a message to Clara, "You know what I'm going to say don't you… You were right, Philippa has cancelled again so I have a plus one if you are up for a spell of wine tasting?" It was a long shot but everything had been pre-booked and arranged. "Sorry I would love to come but I am in Sheffield at the moment for an interview. Sorry to hear that she has let you down again."

Clara was moving away to Sheffield and had started the search for a new job. Clifton knew that this was a good move for her but he also felt a sense of loss that relocating friends create. It would be fine at first he thought with visits and such but like all distances they won out and in the end he would mourn the loss of one of his closest allies.

The day wore on and at such late notice Clifton was struggling to arrange for someone else to take Philippa's place. "Right," he said to himself, "no more of this online dating. Next time I want to meet a real person in the traditional way. I am going to enjoy tonight regardless of who is or isn't there."

Clifton got off the tube at Green Park Station and made his way out past the Ritz Hotel. He noted the glamour of the place. Freshly planted window boxes garnished the sills of the perfectly formed windows into another lavish world. Looking ahead there was a vagabond stretched out on the pavement without shoes. The soles of his feet were black. Clifton thought of him wandering the streets barefoot and how it was possible that this type of poverty was possible in the twenty-first century. He also wore a pair of tatty faded blue jeans which were stained with marks and what appeared to be dried blood. He has a black coat bleached grey by the sun. The grey scraggly bearded face looked up at him with honest green eyes. "Spare change sir?" Clifton gave an apologetic smile and while shrugging said "Sorry, I do not carry any change."

Like many City Dwellers Clifton no longer carried cash around with him. Everything was paid for either by cards or mobile phone touch technology. The West End was a diverse place, there were all walks of life, the young, old, the rich, poor and every type of definition or categorisation that you could imagine all was within a stone's throw. The City certainly was an assortment of all things. Before he knew it Clifton had passed the grandeur of the Fortnum & Mason clock which he used to joke with Clara was a Waitrose for kings and queens. He was shortly standing in one of the many gem like grassed squares of London facing his Club. It was grand with its Corinthian colonnade. Regal in its appearance with the five flags raised outside with the crescendo to the Union flag at the centre.

Checking that his tie was straight and that his top button was not showing over above the Windsor knot, he proceeded to climb the stone staircase, climbed by so many others that they dipped slightly in the middle, to the welcoming entrance. He was greeted by the concierge as the doors were drawn open, "Good evening Sir. May I have your membership number?"

Clifton smiled and nodded, "Good evening George, Yes I'm here for the wine tasting evening. I am very sorry but my guest will be unable to join me tonight." As he relieved his membership card from the inside compartment of his wallet.

Beaming back a similar smile George answered, "That is no problem at all, I will let them know in advance before you are seated. If you care to take a seat in the Library a member of Staff will let you know when we will begin."

He made his way up the striking staircase and wondered about the history of the place and whose footsteps he was following in of yesteryear. The library had a tall ceiling and the only gaps in the bookcases which ran around the perimeter of the room from floor to ceiling were the doors into the library and a window that overlooked the grassed square where he had been standing just a moment ago.

How wonderful this room was with the smell of leather-bound books and the pages of knowledge contained within. He sat in one of the many green low back Winchester leather chairs feeling that they were built to tease a sense of comfort without being so. He had never really liked these types of chairs however in the library with a good bourbon these chairs were magnificent. The soft leather both supported and hugged the lucky occupant to sit in them. He began to page turn a Sam Willis book about the *Glorious First of June* before a friendly face appeared to let him know that they were ready to begin the wine tasting.

Clifton made his way into the main dining room where the event was taking place and took his seat at one of the six circular tables that had been laid out in the lavish room.

Clifton watched as others came into the room and took their seats wondering what they did and who they were with. In front

7

of him there were three glasses, a large silver chalice-shaped table piece was placed in the centre of the table. Clifton looked at is as if to make a study of it. "That is the 'dump bucket', said in a kindly French accent, "it is important to expectorate when tasting wines. You want to taste the wine rather than drink it, however I suspect we will be mostly drinking tonight."

His features stretched and a broad smile swept his face. "I understand that your guest will not be joining us this evening?" Without waiting for a reply he continued, "That just leaves us more to taste now, no?" He gave a friendly elbow nudge.

The tables began to slowly fill and strangers exchanged introductions and pleasantries. The French sommelier raised his glass and with great delicacy made three chimes ring out from the glass with a teaspoon.

"Ladies and gentlemen you are most welcome. Tonight we are here to have an introduction to wine tasting. I want this to be memorable and more importantly fun! If you have experienced wine tasting before they will usually lecture you in wine and it will go, flit," raising his hand over his head in a combine motion, "over your head. So tonight we shall play a game. Here are the rules.

Each player will be given a series of three flights of three wines each to taste. There will be no label and the wines have been removed from their host bottles so you will be judging them purely on the appearance, age, scent, palate and quality.

Each flight will share a common theme however one of the wines within the flight will stand out on its own for a variety of reasons."

Grinning in a playful way he continued, "This could be grape variety, or wine making technique. I want you all to start having a conversation about your experience, what it tastes like, how it smells, is it new world, etcetera." Picking up a glass and raising the contents to his nose and inhaling a deep breath he resumed, "This will be a methodical assessment, one that a professional wine maker would use when tasting the wine."

The three uniform bottles arrived at Clifton's table and their contents were shared out around the table, each with slightly more than necessary for the task of tasting alone.

"Within the first flight I would like for you to identify Les Grandes Chailées from Condrieu AC Northern Rhône Valley France, my home country," the sommelier said, almost salivating at the thought of the taste. "The Les Granilites from Saint-Joseph AC Northern Rhône Valley France and lastly Le Cigare Blanc from the Beeswax vineyard, Arroyo Seco AVA Monterey Country Central Coast California USA."

Clifton swirled the glass as he had seen in films and began to inspect and interrogate each of the three glasses before him. On the sheet of paper in front of him he began to make notes about each glass, beginning with the appearance. Raising the glass up to the light and slightly tilting the glass he forensically examined the colour and fluidity of the wine in the light. Others in the room saw this and began to replicate the action. "This should not be necessary for the white wine," the sommelier announced, gesturing with his glass imitating what was now happening around the room, "This is more for the red grape variety where you are looking for tannin. But there is no harm in appreciating the wine and its appearance."

The first glass that Clifton held up appeared clear and bright, it had a lemon-green colouration which reminded him of a summer trip to Regents Park with Clara some years ago. Taking in a deep breath, the wine revealed a cleansing sensation of freshness with hints of something more earthly. He closed his eyes to fully appreciate the glass and shut out other distracting sensations.

"You may be detecting a mineral characteristic from this wine which could have something the do with a degree of reductive taint from the wine having matured in a bottle under screw cap." The sommelier's voice drifted around the room.

Peter who had introduced himself earlier was sitting to Clifton's left. "I have absolutely no idea about wine tasting, but this is jolly interesting and a great opportunity to learn before you look like a fool in a restaurant!" Clifton nodded and smiled politely without making any comment. The truth was, he thought to himself, that apart from here it was unlikely he would get the experience of such wines anywhere else.

Clifton was not from Peter's world of inheritance and title. He he worked hard to be seated at this table and although he hid it well he did sometimes feel as though he was a file and rank solider sitting in the officer's mess. Peter enquired into what Clifton's line of work was. "I work as a Project Architect for Mission Critical Systems buildings, data centres. Basically everything that is on the internet needs somewhere physically to exist and as businesses expand data centres offer them the ability to store large amounts of their data and systems off site."

Changing the subject, Peter continued with a telling slur – leaning forward in almost a conspiratorial way. "This wine is hard to identify… The fruit is there but it is rather lean. The perfume really dominates but there is certainly orange in there as well don't you think?"

Clifton nodded in agreement, "Yes and an undertone of thyme and beeswax, I think we have found our Californian. It tastes slightly heavier than the other two." His eyes widened as he noticed the elegant young lady who was sitting opposite him.

She began to speak in a soft voice with a hint of an American accent, "Yes this definitely is Le Cigare Blanc. The closure is a screw cap with metallic seal, the wine is a blend of 48% Grenache Blanc, 44% Roussanne and 8% Picpoul Blanc. You could use it as a rather fetching accompaniment to chicken or any white meat including lobster or fish in a rich beurre blanc sauce."

She wore a navy blue dress which wrapped itself around her bodice to her waist where the material turned vertical and cascaded down in a crescendo of pleats from the knee to her ankles. The top section was overlaid with lace detailing creating a seductive curtain to her skin beneath. The dropped neck line revealed an Amulette De Cartier necklace, the thirty-nine brilliant cut diamonds sparkled in the light with the movement of her body. Its simple elegance of its polished curves matching the wearers. The natural stone at the centre almost emulated the sun's rays in a wavering pattern which extended to the diamond band at the perimeter. Her earrings shaded behind her soft wavy brown hair imitated the gem which hung around her slender neck.

Clifton gave a sideways smile and raised his glass, "It seems that you know your wine well for an introductory session?"

She lowered her head and slightly blushed. "Yes, well you see my father owns Sandhi Wines in Santa Barbara. As a child I was brought up touring all of the different vineyards in Bordeaux and Australia."

She leaned into the table and lowered her voice, "Can I tell you a secret? I really came here tonight to stake out the competition! My name is Amelia, I don't think that I have seen you here before?"

Unbeknown to Clifton, there were other wine families in the room. The journey through the cellar continued with magnificent clarets including Vosne-Romanée Pinot noir and a Marion's Vineyard Pinot Noir. The conclusion of the evening saw the sommelier serving dessert wines including a delightful Vin Santo from Tuscany Italy and a rather sickly sweet Château les Mingets. Swirling the final glass Clifton inhaled a honeysuckle perfume mixed with pineapple and peaches; there was a slightly lingering aftertaste of vanilla. He couldn't help but be contented in his environment and gazed across the table at the young girl in the blue dress smiling to himself as if in a daydream fantasy. He looked down at the notes that he had been making throughout the evening. Even at this stage Clifton could clearly see how neatly the handwriting has started and how through the course of the evening the text had become more and more incomprehensible and unrecognisable against the flat edge of the lined page. "Successful evening," Clifton coughed turning to no one in particular with a grin. He spent a further thirty minutes speaking to the others on his table while not losing eye contact with the girl in the blue dress. It was in his nature to be the last one out of a room. He had begun speaking to Peter who was explaining that he ran a small group of hardware outlets, and wished to expand but was not sure in which direction to go.

Clifton thought about this for a moment. As a part-time job before leaving for university he had worked in a large hardware shop, which he well remembered and learnt much from. He felt slightly embarrassed in present company that stating as much would lead to ridicule. His idea was bursting out of him but he had to consider how to deliver it without revealing how he had come by the knowledge.

"Well, have you considered leasing equipment directly to the contractors rather than selling? In a lot of instances contractors do not want to spend out the capital cost of purchasing equipment when they will only need it for a set period of time. In this you will also have some assets which you could offset to acquire further loans to expand the business." Peter and Clifton discussed this in greater detail in the bar afterwards, although Clifton was unlikely to remember any of it. He found that he was far more sociable and alive with thought and creativity although inebriated. The only trouble was remembering it all once sober. The girl in the blue dress came into the bar area and Clifton looked over, almost forgetting Peter was standing next to him. "Will you excuse me one moment?"

Before Peter could respond Clifton was making his way over to the girl. Their eyes met and she smiled revealing a set of perfect pearl-like teeth, "Hello again, so how did you find the wine tasting and the competition?" Clifton said.

"Erm, very informative and interesting to see the New Zealand Marion's Vinyard Pinot Noir." Suddenly Clifton was looking at the back of a young City boy in a slim fit grey suit and red tie. He had short cropped hair and a poor attempt at a beard.

"Darling, there you are! Sorry I'm so late you know how it is."

She looked a little hesitant, while Clifton composed himself and she introduced him.

"This is my boyfriend Terrence," opening her palm towards Clifton, Terrence placing his right arm around Amelia.

Clifton extended his hand, to Terrence, "Alex Clifton, please to meet you."

Terrence nodded and exchanged pleasantries. Before Clifton knew it, Terrence had guided Amelia away to a more secluded section of the bar. Clifton looked over at the backwards clock, a quirk of the place that hung over the bar and decided that it was time to head home before he missed the last train. To the best of his knowledge he left very gracefully given all that he had to drink and did not stumble once, not even on the escalators which he felt that he flew down at the station at St Pancras.

Silently, slightly swaying he looked up at the tiny illuminated orange stars that were the LED lights of the information board. He fought to make the constellations of stars form into letters, which appeared as a blur to him. In the morning of course he could read this clearly but at this time of night and with this level of intoxication the whole board seemed to be swimming in an electrical amber glow.

He raised his hands up on his right eye as if to form a telescope, oddly this seemed to help make some sort of scene of the board. He then felt a guiding grip on his right shoulder and at the same time he recognised a familiar sounding voice from his past. "Alex, how the hell are you?" Dropping his hands to his sides as an attempt at a considered motion he turned, almost pulled around by the grip, in the same way that a kitten is plucked by the nape of its neck and freezes.

He started to recognise the features of the face before him. "Lockridge!" Clifton exclaimed, "Crikey I have not seen you since College. I'm well thank you for asking, I have been at a wine tasting event this evening." At this point Clifton took on the pose of someone swigging from a bottle as a visual accompaniment. "How are you? What have you been up to?" he said, extending his hand to meet Lockridge's outstretched arm. Lockridge was a tall man with the broad shoulders of a rugby player with a wave of short cropped golden hair. He wore a suit with a green Barbour Hereford Wax Jacket which seemed a little out of the ordinary, given the time of year and the likelihood of rain. Unlike most of the other commuters standing at the platform Clifton noticed that he was not carrying any form of luggage which was the usual give away of the Financial Sector City worker, who often had no luggage or who walked around with a clutch type case.

"I've just come back from China," Lockridge said, "I've been working there for the past three years with the Diplomatic Service."

"That must have been amazing" Clifton retorted, attempting to compose himself. "Fantastic architecture our there don't you think? Did you manage to see the Beijing Airport? From start to finish it only took four years to build compared to six years for Terminal five at Heathrow. It was also designed by our very own Norman Foster for the 2008 Olympics. It is one of the world's largest and most advanced airport buildings in terms of experience, operationally and sustainability. Oh and of course the 'Bird's Nest' Stadium which looked phenomenal for the games however I have heard that since the Olympics it has become somewhat derelict?"

"Yes," said Lockridge in an almost dismissive way. "I saw plenty in China." There was a change in the air, almost like a dormant volcano becoming active. The rails at the station became alive with the vibration and the distant clattering of the train became louder and louder as it drew into the station.

"Ahh this is my train," Clifton pointed in the general direction of the carriage. "Excellent," said Lockridge, "my train also, which station are you going to?"

"St Albans," Clifton replied.

"That's mine also" Lockridge placed his hand on the small of Clifton's back to usher him along as he boarded the train to a vacant seat. Clifton seemed enthralled at the coincidence. Within one stop at Kentish Town, Lockridge and Clifton had caught up on the latest from the old boys. "So you are reading *Nineteen Eighty-four*?" Lockridge queried, raising an eyebrow.

"Yes," Clifton replied, "I brought it at WH Smith at Stansted. It was a buy one get one half price. The Richard and Judy Book Club or something like that. I thought that it was about the Berlin wall falling but I think I was slightly confused as I was also buying a John Le Carré novel at the same time."

"Wait a minute," Lockridge jumped in, "the Berlin wall came down in 1989."

"Exactly, this is what happens when you try and buy books at four o'clock in the morning!" Clifton replied.

"Listen." Lockridge seemed to change personalities to a far more intensive character. Leaning in and lowering his voice, he said, "We know that you are working on the data centre in Ireland for the social media group MyLife." Clifton had slightly glazed over, he was aware of what was being said to him but it was as if through a pane of frosted glass. How did – suddenly as if a hand wiping away the ice he thought to himself – how did Lockridge know what he was currently reading? It would have been unlikely that he would have mentioned it before. Clifton looked down at his brown leather dispatch bag which was secured by its buckle. He knew that he was still rather the worse for wear and that it would have been highly unlikely after attempting to read the information board that he would have taken out the book to read a few pages, especially in present company. Clearing the mist from his mind Clifton said, "Yes I'm there every other week, on site." Now it was Clifton's opportunity to be analytical as he began to quickly drift back into sobriety. "Who is this 'we'? The Diplomatic Service?"

Lockridge sat up straight, "No that was my last assignment, I am currently with the National Cyber Security Centre. You have probably heard of us from that incident with the ransomware taking over the National Health Service computers in early 2017?"

Clifton thought for a moment, "Yes I remember that, it didn't seem all that bad in the end." Lockridge leaned in once more "Well, it was a bit more serious than we let the public believe. All of the medical records we duplicated and downloaded. Since then we have defeated several threats. The next generation of warfare will not be fought by troops on the ground, but in cyberspace. Every large company that you can think of has at some point been under attack by cybercriminals or State-sponsored saboteurs."

"Was the British Airways computer melt down that left thousands of people stranded for days really a failure of systems in India or was it cyberterrorism?" Clifton enquired.

"Yes that was another ransomware threat. In that instance British Airways had no choice but to pay. As it is not a publicly owned company they did not have any duty to inform its passengers the reason for the delay. It was something that they were never prepared for. Think about it with information flowing so fast, the various duplicates of information stored at various locations and with the growth of mega data centres for cloud computing the threat is substantial and growing at the same rate as data is being produced. More data has been created in the past two years than in the entire history of the human race. It is estimated that by 2020 over 6.1 billion smartphones will be used globally, each one packed with data capturing sensors.

"There have been whispers of an extremist group who call themselves F5."

Clifton interjected, "Refresh?"

"Precisely," Lockridge continued. "They deal in the most sought after commodity.

Information.

Think about it, how much personal information is there about you out there online. If you have a MyLife page what details are there, birth date, occupation, photographs of you and your family, business contacts, known associates listed as 'friends', what you eat, your political views, where you have been and what you have recently purchased online. Now on its own these trinkets of information do not seem to mean much but when you add more of a profile to that information think what the value that would mean to businesses, governments, law enforcement agencies, political groups and fanatics.

"It has been difficult but GCHQ believes that they have intercepted a message from F5 activating its sleeper cells within Western Europe. We have very little to go on as the messaging services are encrypted from end to end. Sometimes we get lucky and information is broadcast by accident or the encryption is broken by an algorithm.

Think of it this way, these messages are flying from tree to tree like birds in the night. We are on the ground trying to capture the birds to hear their song but we are looking blindly up into the night's sky. When we do succeed in breaking the encryption we are quick to analyse the communication. The problem is of course is determining the fact from fiction. As with every intercepted message its authenticity has to be ascertained by an analyst to determine if we are looking at the real thing or not. Or more to the point if we are being deliberately led to believe that this information is correct to send us on the wrong trail."

Clifton looked apologetic "I'm not sure that I can help you, this all seems very sophisticated and complex. I have no experience in analysing data."

Lockridge carried on, ignoring the comment. "As you are working on the latest MyLife data centre you will have access to the places that no one else will. You will be our fly on the wall so to speak."

Clifton looked Lockridge squarely "I would be extremely surprised if MyLife were at any risk from this F5 group. They have some of the most sophisticated systems around."

Lockridge looked at the floor of the carriage, "We have reason to suspect that F5 is a sub-set which has infiltrated MyLife. We need proof though before we can take any action, the scale of this is global, which is why we need you on the inside."

"And what if I say no? This could be considered a conflict of interest and I would be in breach of my non-disclosure agreement," questioned Clifton.

Lockridge smiled, "Think of it as services rendered to your country and every other country with the internet and if that is not enough I believe that complaints can be raised against you and your firm via the Architects Registration Board. I understand that a single complaint to your professional body could be very challenging for you and your practice?"

Clifton narrowed his eyes, "Is that a threat?" "Think of it as encouragement. Help us help the wider society that is after all what you believe architecture is about?"

"And where have you read that?" Clifton asked almost defeated.

Lockridge stuck up once again "Information is a powerful tool old boy, everyone has a digital fingerprint, even you. In your case you have a CoNet profile, a digital curriculum vitae, giving information about everything you have written, business contacts and where you graduated. I see you decided to study in Bath as opposed to studying further afield?"

"There was more variety in courses in the UK and besides the courses have to be accredited by the Royal Institute of British Architects to be accepted, sorry, but when and if I find out anything how exactly can I pass it on? I can't exactly email you can I?" Clifton queried.

"You are travelling tomorrow to Dublin on flight FR203 from Stansted." Lockridge said in a rather matter-of-fact way. "Once you clear security you will feel compelled to buy something from the Hugo Boss store in the duty free area. The less you know now the safer you will be if you are picked up.

"I have to level with you, there is a significant risk that you may encounter counter-intelligence agents if you raise their suspicions. If you make your way onto their radar you have no links to the government or us to you, as most things in this world you will be on your own. You understand why this is necessary for us to have deniability."

The train began to slow as it approached the station. Clifton began to adjust himself preparing to depart the train as the tannoy sounded. "The next station is St Albans." As Lockridge and Clifton stood in front of the doors Clifton asked over his shoulder, "Aren't you worried that everything that you have just told me could be overheard or recorded?"

Lockridge had switched personalities once again back to his welcoming persona. "Look around you Alex." Examining the carriage Clifton could only see four others; a couple who could not have waited until they were home were deeply engrossed in a loving embrace, a teenager completely shut out to the world with black Beats headphones connected to a brightly illuminated iPad screen, and a businessman balancing a laptop computer on his knees attempting to reply to the deluge of emails that plagued his days and nights.

"A train is an ideal place to talk," Lockridge almost whispered into Clifton's ear. "Everyone is only interested in themselves. You are moving at approximately eighty miles per hour so any listening devices would only pick up the background noise, half the journey is underground which rules out data tracking or satellite. This is one of the few places that you can truly be off grid."

The train slowed and Clifton and Lockridge made their way to the doors. As they parted Clifton filled his lungs with the cool night air. He stepped down onto the platform and began to walk down towards the station exit noting the tapping sound of his own footsteps created by his black Oxford shoes. The events of the last half an hour sinking in. Turning to ask Lockridge one further question he stopped realising that he was quite alone on the platform.

Chapter Two

The journey to the airport seemed almost like a daydream. It was four-fifteen and there was a blanket of mist over the ground. Trees stood tall with their branches silhouetted against the opaque background. As the morning voice softly introduced the next symphony on Classic FM, Clifton could not help but be preoccupied with the previous evening's events.

Dawn was breaking and there was a freshness of the pending new day ahead. Pulling up the slip road from the M11 the backdrop of screening vegetation drew back like a curtain to reveal Stansted airport rising out of the surrounding landscape.

Clifton was not sure if this was to the credit of the architect or a fortunate result from the grading of the road. It seemed to be perfectly situated in the landscape, not of the surrounding vegetation but crafted to assimilate neatly within it. He glided the car into the orange short-stay carpark as on autopilot and parked, making sure to take a mental note of its position within the expanse of the parked cars.

It had taken him a quarter of an hour once to find the car as it had been so well disguised amongst the rows of other parked cars. With a confirmation flash of the indicator lights he wondered when and if he would see his car again. He tried the handle of the car just to make sure that it was indeed locked before he left. Clifton made his way from the carpark into the airport through the glass tunnel which rose up to the podium level. It was much busier than usual and he quickly concluded that it must be the school's half term holiday which would account for the number of children at the airport at this time of the morning. Clifton walked briskly through the concourse. Some children were riding on the pull along suitcases, and others were being carried on their father's shoulders. A young couple in front were rummaging around in their backpacks attempting to separate their toiletries into a single small clear plastic bag which was now required at every airport before security.

Clifton searched in his pocket for his mobile phone which had his boarding card saved, another thing that Clara had shown him how to do. Looking dead ahead he could see people queuing at the gates, scrambling around in bags trying to find their boarding cards, which they had left until the final moments of arriving at the barriers. To the right was another set of gates which were slightly concealed by their angle of approach. These gates had far fewer people at them which was why he always used this side to clear security. He looked down at the small screen of his phone and scrolled through the menus until he had his boarding card while he habitually followed the purple graphic line which has been stuck to the granite floor pavers. He reached the gate as an athlete reaches the finishing line. He made his way through the maze of handrails until he reached a smaller queue of people at the conveyor belt. The din of the rollers and the calls from the staff, "Please remove laptops and other electrical equipment from your bags and place them in a separate tray. If you have any liquids in your luggage please remove them and place them separately in the tray inside a sealed plastic bags provided."

One young family standing to his left at the conveyor belt were struggling with two young children. One of whom was starting to have a tantrum about losing his ride on suitcase to the security checks. The other was blissfully asleep in a pushchair. Their mother was trying to quickly get everything in the tray and had not put the liquids into one of the plastic bags. The older man on the opposite side of the conveyor belt wore blue plastic gloves and handed her a spare plastic bag while reciting, "All liquids into the bag and placed separately into the tray." You could tell that he had spent most of his life at the airport as his actions and speech had become automated and almost chant like. He had black combat type trousers and a light blue shirt with epaulettes with various cards hanging around his neck on a black necklace. His hair was silvery grey and he was well tanned, indicating that he made the most of his time away from his conveyor belt. His eyes looked glazed and although he was performing a function it was clearly just that. Purely a function, the character and joy had long since left him in the years of the repetition. As the trays came around on the conveyor belt Clifton began to remove his belt and watch. This had almost become part of his airport ritual and Clifton had worked out the most efficient system for getting himself through this part of the airport. He ordered his possessions neatly in the tray before him.

His dispatch bag placed to the left of the tray with his laptop removed, shoes to the right with belt to the furthest right and watch placed south of the shoes. His jacket was folded and then placed carefully over the top of the shoes. He pushed his tray forward onto the belt and it began to roll up the ramp towards the x-ray machine. A second tray whirled around at his knees which he took out and placed his cabin bag in taking care to remove his toiletries, which were already in an airtight plastic bag from previous trips. His laptop computer was placed at an angle leaning up against the short side of the cabin bag. He then moved the tray forward onto the conveyor belt before one final pat down to check that he had not forgotten to remove any metallic elements which would inevitably set off the alarm in the arch and lose him precious time with a more thorough search.

The older lady on the other side of the security arch wearing the same uniform as the man behind the conveyor belt beckoned Clifton through with her blue gloved hand as his possessions made their way up the conveyor ramp. As he made his way through the arch he could not help but notice the rapid movement of blue shirts on the opposite side of the conveyor belt.

The child from earlier was now on the secure side and was playing with the spring gate of the further bag search area. It seemed that he had packed a plastic sword for his travels in his ride along suitcase. Whether it would be accompanying him on his forward journey was being debated between the blue shirted security officer and his mother.

Clifton waited and looked for the trays that contained his belongings to come through the machine on the secure side. Sometimes a tray would appear and be reassigned to a second conveyor belt for further inspection, as had happened to the families cases, however Clifton's did not seem to be appearing anywhere. There was a young woman wearing a black Bershka Gingham Cami Bralet top and tight fitting maroon trousers which matched her hair. She pushed past Clifton to retrieve her case from the tray now descending down the runners of the conveyor. He knew that she must have been behind him in the queue before as he would have definitely of noticed her in front of him. He tried to examine the line of trays on the opposite side of the plastic partition to see if any of his items were in there for further investigation. It had happened to him only once before when Clifton had accidently packed a pen which doubled as a screwdriver. On that visit the security officer had deemed that the screwdriver part could be considered as a weapon despite the head only being two centimetres long and it was disposed of to his disappointment.

He looked down the line of trays and none of them looked familiar to him. Then he recognised his jacket in a tray that was just appearing out of the machine, followed by his cabin bag making is way down the slide. As the trays drew nearer he noticed that although everything was neatly packed into the tray the order of the articles had changed. Still the same black gloss Oxfords he was used to wearing, even worn slightly at the edge of the outside of the heel. Only he noticed that the right one was completely flat like when the shoes had been re-heeled or were new and needed breaking in. Restoring his belt, watch and shoes, which he double knotted as they would regularly come undone if he did not. He carried his jacket over his arm. The watch strap and belt seemed to have a newness rigidity about them.

Clifton did not have time to inspect his belongings more closely and quickly went about swinging his dispatch bag over his shoulder and extended the handle of his cabin bag and headed towards the duty free area. As he walked down the hallway amidst the holiday makers and business visitors' two people seemed to stand out to him. There was nothing physically which stood out about these two, it was more something that was missing. Who travels to an airport without any luggage? One was a male wearing a black baseball cap which had a light brown suede leather visor that had been curled and was pulled down low over his sun-glassed eyes. He had a leather jacket with a rounded high collar and a dark grey polo shirt beneath which was tucked into a pair of dark blue jeans. The shoes stood out most of all to Clifton as they were a cross trainer rather than the 'All Star' plimsoll shoes which were currently fashionable.

His companion was a tall women with long blonde hair beneath a similar baseball cap, probably around thirty-five with piecing blue eyes, which Clifton found hard not to fall into. Although she was beautiful there was a Germanic hardness to her features. They seemed to be watching him but without looking directly at him. Perhaps these were his contacts?

Clifton was not sure whether to look at them or to keep them in his peripheral vision. He remembered what Lockridge had said to him the night before, his contact was to meet him in the Hugo Boss store. After all these could be plain-clothed customs officers or worse, agents of F5. Clifton tried to push all thoughts of espionage and spies out of his mind as he knew the more he thought about it would begin to show on his face and he too would begin to look suspicious. An airport is the last place that you would want to look suspicious in this period of heightened security. With the recent cyberattacks the threat level had been raised to severe which meant that an attack was highly likely.

He needed to make sure that he was safe but would not allow himself to become paranoid about it. Suddenly he was swept into the rotunda which displayed all of this morning's flights on the large curved array of screens. His flight was showing but the gate had not yet been assigned. Clifton decided to walk at the pace of the majority, knowing that any rapid movements in an ocean of wading people would draw unnecessary attention to himself.

He wandered through into the main terminal where he was surrounded by shops and stores that he had become well acquainted with over the past year of regular travel. Only a fortnight ago he had purchased some books from the WH Smith that he was now walking past on his right hand side. So much had changed and yet stayed the same. He was now living the lifestyle of a John le Carré novel character. There was something exciting that also made Clifton's stomach churn as he knew not all of the characters made it out at the end of the story. As he passed the newspaper stand he noticed the headline on the *Independent*.

"MyLife social media giant in storm after Chinese ads revealed ahead of the forthcoming German election." Clifton pulled out his phone from his pocket and click on the news application. The screen illuminated.

The German Chancellor Angela Merkel gave a statement yesterday as investigations gathered pace into China's use of MyLife to meddle in the forthcoming German elections.

German officials have been pressuring the social media company which divulged details of more than 3,000 election advertisements apparently paid for by Chinese-linked operatives against the West.

MyLife, used by over 70% of Germans of voting age, revealed earlier that the Chinese propagandists have spent over £100,000 on advertisements in the run-up to the German elections. It is estimated that the blanket coverage was enough to reach millions of voters. The social media giant revealed that Chinese agents assumed false online profiles on their platform to organise rallies and inspire people to vote for the Social Democratic Party who are against putting limits on social media.

A source from MyLife publicised earlier this week that they have closed hundreds of fake Chinese-based accounts that had bought 3,000 political and social advertisements for £75,000.

On Thursday, the social media mogul and founder of MyLife, Ethan Thomas announced that the company will share the 3,000 advertisements with the German Federal Intelligence Service investigators who are looking into allegations of Chinese meddling in the Federal elections.

"The Party cannot accept this fabrication by the western media. This attack was definitely not carried out by China and we resent these wrongful allegations," The Beijing spokeswoman Chen Li said on a conference call, as quoted by state-run news agency. "China would not involve itself in something like this."

MyLife technicians managed to locate the source of the purchased advertisements which are linked to the infamous "troll factory" based in Zhongguancun in the Haidian district.

For more on this and other news select 'top stories'.

He powered down the screen and slipped his phone back into his pocket. He could see that he was gaining on the Hugo Boss store and pulled out of the crowd as if a car departing from the motorway. He wandered in casually with one hand guiding his wheeled cabin bag across the highly polished tiled floor in front of him. "Good morning sir, how can I help you today?" a cheery wide-eyed sales assistant sung. Clifton was suspicious of anyone who could be this cheerful at this time of the morning, it was not normal in his opinion.

How do I answer that question, he thought to himself, I cannot exactly say 'Hey I am your contact. Surprise!' He had not been given any passwords to say or anything to identify himself to the person he was supposed to meet. Looking around there were no other customers in the shop so it seemed unlikely that it was going to be anyone else. Unless of course they had not arrived yet or had been picked up by other agents. He had no idea and was over-thinking this. The sales assistant could see the look of confusion on his face searching for an answer. Eventually he broke out into a smile and muttered something incomprehensible about ties. The assistant still with a beaming smile suggested that he looked at the cufflinks. Clifton's shoulders dropped with relief and he confirmed with a nod making his way over to the tiered display.

The sales assistant stood behind the display and produced a small rectangular box and, with a click, revealed two ocean blue cufflinks with a bright silver framing. "I think that these would suit you for your trip," she said in a confident, alluring Italian accent, handing them over to Clifton to examine. "Thank you," Clifton said looking into the blue gem of the cufflinks, "but I do not have any double cuffed shirts for my trip sadly." Offering the small box back to the assistant.

The assistant made no attempt to take them from Clifton. "I think that you will find that there are some double cuffed shirts packed into your cabin bag, Mr. Clifton." She looked up at him with big brown eyes. His eyes slightly widening in confirmation that this must be his contact. She continued "Now these cufflinks are very special, along with some of your other effects that you are wearing. These cufflinks have two USB data storage devices contained within them." She demonstrated how to pop out the blue gem to reveal the USB connection on one side. "This one has software pre-loaded onto it so all you will need to do is to find an inconspicuous USB data port within one of the cabinet's servers in the Point of Presence colocation room. You will need to think about its hiding place carefully as there will be maintenance technicians looking at these servers all of the time. Digitally the device is camouflaged so it will not be detected by the servers systems. This is where the fibre network cable comes into the data centre. Once connected this device will be able to monitor the incoming and outgoing data packages. The other device is a clean sixty-four gigabyte device for any information that you feel will be useful to us for analysis. To conceal the device just push back into place and they are undetectable.

"Your watch has a homing device implanted on the back of the casing so that we can keep a track of you. I'm afraid that it is a copy of your Mondaine white and black Evo watch, not the original, which will be returned to you in all good time."

Instinctively Clifton looked at the recognisable face with its red second hand passing around the black rectangular lines, he could not detect any difference other than the strap that did not fit quite as comfortably as usual.

Out of nervousness Clifton blurted out, "I'm rather disappointed it doesn't fire a laser or something like that if I'm being honest"

She looked at him with dead eyes. "You need to take this very seriously. There is no room for fooling around."

"No, of course not. I'm sorry."

The sales assistant continued "We have also hidden a master key which will bypass locked security doors to the data centre into the heel of your right shoe. The compartment can be opened by twisting the whole heel ninety degrees. The heel is made from solid fibreglass so that there is no sound difference from one step to another. This will also protect the key from being detected by any metal detectors. Now this is important, the key will open doors however any doors with door contacts will detect that the door has been opened and will sound an alarm. We have been unable to clone a swipe card for the security devices operating the electronic locks however at this stage of construction we are hoping that the commissioning is incomplete. This is our best opportunity to get on the inside before commissioning is complete and the site is handed over becoming one of the most powerful data centres in the world with the ability to monitor all kinds of personal data."

She placed the cufflink box into a Hugo Boss bag and put an imaginary item through the till so as to not raise any suspicion from anyone watching from outside of the shop. Clifton looked solemn and then smiled as he turned to leave the shop considering who might be watching. "Have a safe trip sir," she called out after him.

The reality and severity of what had just been divulged to him hit him as he walked in contemplation through the departures lounge, only pausing to scroll through the departures board for the gate number for his flight. He made his way to gate fifty and sat down on the cold metal bench seating facing the stands where the planes were parked. The dawn had already broken as the warmth of the rising sun stretched across the concrete. This was not his world he thought to himself; he consoled himself that he would just get the job done, plant the device that he had been given and carry on as normal. There was no higher authority that he could go to protest about his task, no one would have believed him if he had. In any case if he did speak to anyone he knew that it would only give Lockridge the reason he needed to destroy Clifton's career.

It was highly unlikely that anything would come of this anyway, it was probably some analyst with an over-active imagination, he reassured himself. It was nothing to worry about. A sense of relief swept over him as he began to appreciate the grand scheme of things happening around him. Just then a voice sounded over the public address system informing passengers that the gate was now open and that boarding had commenced.

Clifton gathered his luggage and proceeded to the Priority boarding queue that his secretary has insisted on booking for all of the office's flights. He scanned his phone against the reader at the check-in desk and handed his passport to the Swissport receptionist. She thumbed through the pages until she found the one with the photo of Clifton. Studying the photo she scanned his face for the similar features before her. "Thank you Alex," she said handing the passport back to him. He did not care for the familiarity of the use of his first name by someone that he had not been introduced to. Easing into his way towards the doors he made his way down the staircase where there were already a few people at the base of the stairs waiting to go airside.

It was chilly in this waiting area and Clifton pulled his jacket closed. Another person joined the queue forming on the staircase. "Good Morning!" A deep hearty voice came out of the gloom of the enclosed staircase. Clifton looked up towards the friendly looking round face that was looking down on him over the top of some thin spectacles.

"Good morning Jim, we have to stop meeting like this!" Clifton chuckled while offering out his hard towards the older man.

The older gentleman took his hand in his bear-like clasp. The had met a few times before on their journeys to and from Dublin. They had first met when on a delayed flight due to a panel in the cockpit needing to be replaced. Unlike the underground trains it seemed to be quite accepted to speak to your fellow plane passengers while there was a delay. They had struck a chord with one another complaining about the lack of information and the annoyance of the delay to the day ahead. It was also this trip two months ago that they had exchanged names.

"It's good to see you too, how have you been?"

"Oh you know busy as usual. I haven't seen you the last few times?"

"Yes I was ill towards the start of the month with this nasty tummy bug which keeps you grounded. If you catch my drift. Apart from that I have been mainly in the office covering for a colleague who caught then same bug but after I returned. I think it has been around the whole office now"

"Goodness me. Thankfully I have been quite lucky so far. Keep taking those vitamins though! Tell me what is it that you do again?"

"I'm in software. I go around some of the leading firms and we basically see what systems they are using, run some analysis of what they are doing with their current software and systems and see if we can make things more efficient using different strategies and software."

"You said software quite a few times there – I take it that your company sells software?"

"You've summed it up pretty much in a nutshell. What business are you into?"

"I'm an architect, currently my practice is engaged in the new MyLife data centre just to the west of Dublin"

"MyLife wow that must be huge. I'm on MyLife, well, when I say I'm on it , and I use the term 'on it' in its loosest form, I don't really put anything up there but I like to see how other people are getting along and things like that."

"So rather than social media you are using it as social stalking?"

"Ha, yes I see what you mean. Well I guess I don't really like confrontation really. So many times you see friends falling out or arguing over such frivolities. It's so sad."

"I see what you mean but don't you think it depends on how you use it? I mean I will put a tick against something that it positive and basically ignore anything that I disagree with – but to be honest it's only the soap box people who get on my nerves and then thankfully most of my friends are not that sort anyway."

"Soap box people?"

"You know, Hyde Park with its Speaker's Corner on a Sunday morning. It's traditionally where any member of the public can go to get up on their 'soap box' and give speeches or have debates exploring their views. Originally the area had been the home to the Tyburn Gallows, every condemned man had the opportunity to make a last speech before the inevitable. Some would confess to their crimes while others would plead their innocence. It was seen at the time as quite a social event, a bit like bowling or going to the pictures is today. It was not until sometime in the late 1800s though that the Government passed an Act allowing free speech in that part of Hyde Park." Clifton was interrupted with a knock coming from the outside door. Then it opened revealing someone dressed in a high-visibility orange suit. "Can I see someone's boarding card please?"

Someone nearer the door presented a creased piece of paper to the man who studied it for a second before opening the door fully and asking everyone to follow him.

"Looks like time we were off, are you at the front or back this time?"

"Erm wait a second let me check." Scrambling around in his pocket for his phone, he swiped the screen to see his boarding card.

"Entrance through the front door."

"Ah I'm rear door – have a safe flight and see you soon."

"You too… have a good day" Clifton was stuck over what else to say as to repeat 'have a safe flight' would seem odd.

There was the usual ant-like army working in procession, a multitude of purpose-built vehicles scuttled across the concrete. There was something very satisfying about watching the trucks darting around in their choreographed display. Eager to deal with the next incoming aircraft that was yet to draw into the awaiting stands. There was a peace and tranquillity to the order of it ,which was suddenly shattered by noise which was reminiscent of a ship's foghorn alarm. Recognising the sound Clifton quickly reached for his left inside jacket pocket to stop the alarm clock on his phone which had been pre-programmed to sound at six o'clock in the morning every morning. He fought to silence the noise as quickly as possible. One of the other passengers who was waiting behind him gave a friendly smile. After all it was only six o'clock in the morning, the day had just begun.

The boarding was fairly quick as only two-thirds of the seats were taken. He made himself comfortable and began to read his book through the safety announcement which he had heard dozens of times before so its effects just washed over him. The distraction would get him through the take-off, which he had eventually decided was not as bad as the landing.

The noises of the plane grew louder as the plane taxied towards the runway. As the surface changed from concrete to tarmac Clifton felt a jolt in the plane. He could feel the plane turning at right angles to the runway, it suddenly lurched forward in a burst of acceleration. The plane made its charge down the runway and the cabin started to rumble with every imperfection of the tarmac's surface. Clifton felt the cabin change to a steep angle as he tried to focus intently on the sharpness of the printed text against the organic texture of the paper page. As the light of the sun travelled across the pages with the turning of the plane, Clifton wondered to himself how anyone could get the same sensation from an illuminated screen.

The use of electronic reading devices had increased dramatically. He had first noticed this on his morning commute into London. It had started with the hand-held Blackberry devices in 2009, then it evolved into smartphone devices in 2011 and by 2013 most Londoners were on the tube and buses reading or watching videos from tablet devices. How could anyone experience the writing through a screen? You were not able to caress the slight embossed typeface of the printed text or smell the pages, or even run your hand over the corner of each crisp page. There was something enchanting about reading a virgin book that no one else had read. Clifton took great care not to bend the spine of the books that he read, sometimes forcing himself to read at slightly odd angles to prevent creases forming on the spine. He always grimaced when he saw people bending the covers over to read page by page. It almost felt like he was witnessing an assault on the book.

The plane had now levelled out and Clifton looked over the Irish Sea. He could see the newly installed ocean wind farms which were located just off from the Blackpool coastline. There was a small white wake against the carpet of deep blue sea that was being cast by a small tug boat as it manoeuvred one of the pylons into position. When looking at the scale of the tug against the whole array of wind turbines it really hit home to Clifton just how much had been invested in sustainable energy.

He was admiring the symmetry of the arrangement of the wind turbines before he noticed something quite out of place. What he could see resembled something that looked like a double arrow head, almost black, pointing west and flying below the plane by some distance. It was definitely man-made as it was far too angular and large to be anything from the natural world.

He quickly wondered what it could be, if it was a concept stealth plane being tested or a drone of some kind scanning and maintaining the wind farm. He then recalled a recent news programme special on the BBC. They were interviewing the creator of this solar powered drone which was financed by the social media group MyLife. The designer explained how the double arrow head shape helped the aircraft to maintain altitude for extended periods of time requiring next to no maintenance. It had a wingspan to rival that of a commercial Boeing 737–800, the very same aircraft that Clifton was currently travelling on. MyLife had make the plane enthusiasts' dreams become a reality by financing the whole project. It had all started with him creating a page of the concept on his MyLife account. The programme's narrator explained how their aspirations were both aligned in the idea of allowing internet connectivity to desolate, isolated areas where the idea of the internet was only for the extremely rich.

For governments around the world it was not possible to justify the high expense of full fast internet infrastructure coverage to such remote areas outside of towns and cities. The drone however can beam the internet down onto the planet from any location like a satellite. The philanthropist ideal was to bring the internet and connections to people who would otherwise not have access to it. But why would it be flying around the United Kingdom's coastline?

He began to suspect something more sinister, maybe the plane was actually being used as a snooping device. Monitoring what people were communicating outside of the MyLife social media forum. After all information is the most desired commodity in the twenty-first century, as Lockridge had said. Clifton shook his head and thought how silly all this nonsense was. It was more likely that if it was indeed the MyLife drone that it was being put through further testing. If it were to come down for any reason then sea was a far safer place for a crash landing than over land.

Soon tiredness began to overwhelm him and he drifted off into a fitful slumber. His mind drifted over recent events, work and friends. He thought of Clara and how much he would miss her once she relocated.

Suddenly Clifton felt as though he was reversing at great speed from the images in his mind and becoming more aware as he awoke with a start. The airhostess had pushed the food trolley into the row of seats causing him to wake. At first he was annoyed and was getting ready to vent the irritation that was welling up inside of him. Then he heard the softest Irish accent, "I'm so sorry Sir, you look as though you could do with a cup of coffee," she said in a matter-of-fact way. The first thing that he noticed about her was the gleaming white friendly smile, set between two rosy lips. She had green eyes and soft brown hair which had been plaited, forming a crown braid with two whispers of hair that had broken away to soften the formal style. Instantly he had melted, and agreed that a coffee was just the ticket. It probably was not the best coffee he had sipped through a plastic topped paper cup, however having it prepared by such a beautiful woman certainly make it taste all the better.

The voice of the captain came over the public address system. "Cabin crew please take your seats, landing in ten minutes." As the hostess made her way down the cabin collecting the empty cups and wrappers. Clifton smiled at her looking into her deep green eyes as he handed her the empty cup and complimented her on how nice it was. As she took the cup he felt something being placed into the palm of his hand. He fought not to register surprise and slid what felt like folded paper into his trouser pocket.

Looking through the port windows of the empty row opposite Clifton could see the Wicklow Mountains rising out of the horizon. It reminded him a bit of the mountains that surrounded Ballater in Scotland where he had spent many a year in the summer in his youth. The mountains flowed down to an array of road networks, houses, fields, coastline and ocean.

Observing how quickly the ground was rising up towards him, Clifton quickly sought solace in the text printed on the back of the seat in front which gave an abbreviated food menu. The plane seems to hover just above the runway before seemingly falling forward down onto the tarmac with a screech of the tyres. The wings unfurled hidden flaps and the plane rapidly decelerated. The older lady sitting across from Clifton crossed herself saying a silent prayer as the Ryanair landing jingle played over the speakers of the public address system. The plane coasted across the runway and towards its stand. The captain's voice flooded the cabin once again. "Welcome to Dublin, please remain seated until the plane has come to a complete stop. Please make sure that when leaving the plane that you have all of your personal belongings with you and please also refrain from opening the overhead lockers until we have stopped as baggage may have become dislodged during the flight. The weather is about sixteen degrees Celsius and it looks as though the sun will be with us for the rest of the day. We hope that you have had a pleasant flight and we look forward to welcoming you on your next Ryanair flight soon."

Clifton looked out of the window once again and caught a glimpse of one of the infamous Dublin hares which live on the grounds of the airport. Clifton was eager to open the folded paper in his pocket but decided that there were too many prying eyes on the flight. He would have to find somewhere private to read the message. The plane pulled up into its stand and the doors opened. People began to slowly depart, politely letting each row empty before moving onto the next. Clifton made his way down the cabin towards the front door where the brunette airhostess was. Now standing up he could see her fitted white shirt tucked into a dark navy skirt with the Ryanair yellow cravat around her slender neck. She smiled making him involuntarily blush, quickly diverting his eyes and head towards the floor in shyness. Being typically British he mumbled thanks as he left the aircraft to the airhostess, in the same way that people thank the bus driver when departing the bus.

Clifton walked briskly down the stairs and into the reception area and immediately headed for the gents so that he could read the message in private. He walked straight into a cubicle and secured the door hanging his dispatch bag on the back of the door and pushed his flight bag into the corner of the cubicle. He reached for his pocket and pulled out the folded paper between his tweezer like fingers. Very carefully he began to unfold the paper until the message was fully revealed. "At arrivals turn left towards the escalators and head upstairs to the departures. Leave by the nearest exit and look for a black Skoda Octavia for your contact."

Clifton screwed the paper up into a ball and dropped in into the toilet pan flushing it so that no one else could read the message. He left the cubicle, washed his hands and headed towards the passport control and onto his rendezvous. As he cleared passport control he headed towards customs and began to get nervous that he had come this far without being followed or was he being followed, he could not tell which made him more anxious. The customs officers looked up at him over their computer monitors, however he maintained looking ahead, and kept the same quick pace to avoid suspicion despite the beads of sweat that had broken out across his forehead.

The white screen door retracted to reveal the arrivals lounge. There was a small group being held back by a cordon holding welcoming signs for much loved family members, and also taxi drivers with the name of their clients on book-sized sheets of acrylic. He turned left to face the escalators. Taking two steps at a time he was quickly at the first floor level in the departures area. Turning around he could see an exit to his left which he went through.

He took a gasp of the brisk fresh air as the automatic doors parted, being reminded of his commuter train journeys. It was a bright sunny day, Clifton had wished that he had his sunglasses with him. He had neglected to remove them from their hiding place in his car. He raised his hand up to his brow to offer some shade for a clear view of the drop-off zone. He could see various cars pulling up and others moving off from their set down positions.

Then he noticed one vehicle making its way meaningfully towards him at a more rapid pace than the surrounding vehicles. It was indeed a black Skoda which drew up alongside him with a 'taxi' sign on its roof and side doors. Clifton noticed that the signs were printed onto a magnetic sheet so that they were removable at a moment's notice. The front passenger window was winding down as the car came to a stop, an Irish voice called out from inside the car "Mr. Clifton, pleased to be meeting ya. I'm Derek. Let me help ya with d'ose." While indicating to the bags that Clifton had set down on the pavement.

Chapter Three

The sales assistant watched Clifton like a bird of prey as he left the shop. She walked around to one of the displays so that she could see the entrance without any obstructions and fondled a pile of tee-shirts pretending be arranging them. The Beatles song, 'She Loves You', gently played in the background from the Lacoste store across the way. She kept up the charade for a short while by folding and unfolding the tee-shirts, scrutinising the slow march of people that passed by outside the shop.

One of the airports legion of cleaners made their way into view. She was pushing a trolley with one hand and had a broom in the other. She stopped for a moment and peered into one of the recycling receptacles which sat at the ends of the benches which separated the recycling from the non-recyclable waste. She pulled the broom towards her and balanced it against the side of the trolley before opening the front panel of the general waste receptacle and removing the tied in bag placing it neatly into the compartment of her trolley and in one movement pulling out a new liner bag, opening it and tying it into the receptacle.

Her radio was clipped to her waistband with confused radio chatter resonating around her, warning those that she was approaching and to get out of the way. The sales assistant could see that the cleaner had a black wire just showing as she leaned forward behind her hair. She wondered for a moment if this was an undercover airport police officer, before deciding that it was more likely that the cleaner was in fact listening to music on small earphones wearing the wire beneath her shirt to conceal the fact. Besides she was doing too good of a job of cleaning. An undercover officer would not be paying that much attention to cleaning as they would have felt it below them even to be doing such work.

All seemed to go silent for a second, her reactions sharpening and her heartbeat quickened, sensing something was coming. A 'bong' noise echoed around the canopy as a female voice sounded over the tannoy "If something doesn't seem right, report it to a police officer. See it, sort it." There was a quiet pause before the ambient sounds returned to their former volume.

The avenue of shops turned a corner a bit further down from this store where, in the centre of the avenue, there was a brand new bright yellow Porsche Carrera displayed on raised pedestal. There were two enthusiastic youngsters dressed in business attire each wearing red sashes with white text saying 'Win a sports car today!'

She could see that they were both trying desperately to catch the eye of the passengers who swept by, in an attempt to sell them raffle tickets to win the car at ten pounds a go. Most people were walking straight past although a few middle-age men did pause around the car with coffee's in paper cups in one hand and the handles of flight bags in the other. When they were approached by either of the youngsters they would smile politely shake their head and walk on.

A group of guys who she estimated were in their early twenties then went past the stand. Maybe on some sort of stag weekend, the sales assistant thought to herself. They stopped and gathered around the car admiring its sleek lines as it gently rotated on its platform, with the spotlights above shining sparkles from the pristine paintwork. They did not seem to have much luggage between them, carrying sports holdalls. They all wore the same sort of clothing, trainers, jeans and tee-shirts with some indistinguishable writing on them.

The blonde girl with the red sash and fitted dark navy blue skirt and jacket approached them with her clipboard and tickets, while her male teammate walked around to the other side of the stand trying to speak to a lady who was standing there next to the car.

The group of guys were chatting with the female sales representative for what only seemed a few minutes. Maybe only three minutes at best, before they were parting with their hard earned cash. She worked quickly and handed out the written tickets to each of the six gathered around her.

The sales assistant scoffed to herself thinking it was easy money. It was unlikely that anyone from the party of six would actually be in a chance of winning the car.

The whole set up reminded her of a travelling carnival where grifters would hone their skills on impressionable minds. Young males were the ideal target as they are easier to part with their cash, especially to a young beautiful woman. They would usually be either trying to impress another girl or show off in front of their companions, and if one were to buy a ticket, it was sure enough that their cohorts would buy them also, not wanting to be left just in case there was the slimmest possibility of beating the bank and taking home the prize. In this case it would probably be worse if one of them won the car as every gathering would remind the group of the fortune of one of them but not all of them.

She was interrupted by the sound of a rhythmic tapping of luggage wheels over the tiled floor, as the wheels found the grout line creating a 'click' sound as they rolled over sounding almost like the marching of steps. With the changing pace it sounded like a small old-fashioned steam train making its way down the tracks, clattering along to a rhythm. She turned her attention back to the entrance of the store. The occasional person slowed their pace to gaze longingly at the displays and to visually delve into the delights of the store. Another would stand just outside and then take out their phone. Yet none of them did in fact enter into the shop. The products that furnished the displays and shelves were exquisite, bringing whole level of style and sophistication to the parade of shops. The pricing being the only factor which discouraged so many of the people outside from entering the store.

Once the assistant was sure that Clifton was out of sight and would not come back she reached up to her lapel and carefully removed the pinned name badge before placing it gently on the top row of the keys of the keyboard of the till. She did a quick sweep of the store with her eyes and saw a business man hovering over some the wrapped shirts.

She tapped her nail against one of the keys on the keyboard deciding what to do next. He looked up towards her while pointing towards the stack of shirts within their cellophane and asked if she had any of the blue shirts in a sixteen collar with double cuffs.

Not wanting to arouse suspicion she smiled and walked over to him and began to thumb through the shirts that were there. "I'm afraid that we only have available what is out on display" she said, smiling to herself as she had the foresight that if the size sixteen was not there that the next question would be could she go and look in the stock room.

It was the last shirt in the towering pile and she slid it cleanly out from underneath the others without making a single one wobble. Before she handed it to him she made a quick study of the spread collar which seemed to be this year's fashion.

She went to walk away before pausing and turned towards the gentleman again. "Excuse me," he looked up from the shirt catching her eye once more. "Are you intending to wear a tie with that shirt? Only if you are the spread collar won't suit. Those shirts there with the forward pointing collars would be much better with a tie."

He looked over to them, smiled and thanked her for her assistance. She walked back towards the till takin up her sentry post She watched him while he put back the original shirt and brought over the one with the forward point collar in the same cotton sea blue.

Panic struck her as she realised that she would have to process it through the till. She kept her nerve and smiled which she tried to work out what to do. There was nothing in front of her which seemed to look obvious so she pressed the return button on the keyboard. The screen came alive and asked for a card swipe.

This cannot be the credit card at this time. She thought to herself. As I have not yet scanned the item. There was a white card with a black magnetic strip resting along the edge of the keyboard. She swiped it up and down quickly hoping that this was what was needed. The screen then flashed to a new page and asked for the items to be scanned. She held the shirt over the desk which had a convenient recess where bar code scanner was housed. There was a beep from the till. The screen then instructed her what to do to ensure that all security devices had been removed.

She studied the packaging but there was nothing there which seemed to resemble a security tag so she carried on with the on screen prompts guiding her through the process. He paid using the credit card pad and while she placed his receipt and shirt into a bag. She wished him well on his flight and he started to leave the shop when the alarms started ringing forcing him to return to the desk.

Damn she thought, there must be a security tag in there somewhere. She inspected the packaging and saw that the reverse of the barcode sticker had some form of printed chip which resembled something from a computers motherboard. She peeled off the sticker and returned the shirt to the bag. Apologised profusely and escorted the gentleman towards the exit by looping her arm into his and smiling.

Now alone in the store, without ceremony, she walked casually to the back of the shop and into the secluded staff room making sure that the door was closed behind her and that she would not be disturbed from any prying customers of the shop. She pulled out the wheeled chair from behind the desk and sat down at the computer terminal. She proceeded to access the computer with little effort before removing its hard drive, which also happened to control the shop's security cameras. She removed the umbilical-like cabling and yanked it out of the connection and placed the metallic silver box into her handbag which she had placed below the desk earlier.

She stood up from the chair, letting it roll back slightly across the vinyl flooring and placed her bag on the chair. She started by removing the glasses that she had been wearing and the Boss uniform suit jacket which she had taken out of one of the staff lockers in the corner of the room. She replaced the jacket with a short sand-coloured one which had been neatly folded within her bag, shaking it before hand to let any creases that would have formed in the time it was in the bag fall out.

Taking a scarf out from the pocket of the jacket she rolled it around itself and tied it into a bandana around her head tying a knot at the nape of her neck. She removed the hair clips which held back her hair and let it fall out of the ordered bun so that it now rested on her shoulders. In her other pocket she pulled out an iPhone 8 and powered it up leaving it on the table. The white Apple logo filled the black screen as it loaded. She continued unpacking the contents of the bag until it was all on the table in front of her for, laid out like a surgeons tools. When the phone was ready she typed in the password and went to the menu to check that she had her boarding card saved.

Once she was satisfied with her clothing she took out a small compact mirror from the bag which she set up on the desk. She spent a short time changing her makeup, removing the thick eyebrows which had been painted on and playing with blushers which gave her a much more bronzed continental appearance from her earlier pale complexion.

By the time she had finished and removed her green-coloured contact lenses she did not resemble the sales assistant that had spoken to Clifton in any detail except for the dimples when she smiled which she could not disguise.

She looked around the room, checking that she had gathered up everything that she had come with and placed it all precisely into her bag. She pulled out a burgundy-coloured passport document to check that all was in order. She had followed the plan to the letter so far but if anything was going to let her down it would be this as it had been the only thing that she had to depend on someone else to procure. The golden five-pointed star set within a spoked cogwheel surrounded an olive branch to the left and an oak branch to the right identified it as an Italian passport. She flicked through the pages and studied the photo. The resemblance was uncanny, it was like looking into a mirror. The document of course was a fake but so professional that it would fool any customs officer. There were two stamps with associated travellers' visas to make it look all the more authentic. The issue date on the passport was for March 2013. The passport was pristine and without a single crease. The cover still retained its waxy finish. It would have been suspicious for a document of that age to appear as if it had just been issued, in reality it had. She went about artificially aging it quickly by folding some of the pages, flexing it in the palms of her hands and rubbing the cover with the elbow of her jacket before it would be scrutinised.

Satisfied that the passport document would pass and examination she moved towards the door, passing the shop's delivery door, deliberately heading towards the shop floor once again. She moved swiftly but meaningfully as she passed the locked changing room on her way out of the shop. She used a passing caged delivery trolley full of cardboard boxes which was being pushed from WH Smith to mask her exit from the store into the sea of travellers, making their way towards the awaiting gates and beyond.

It took two hours before anyone found the body of the young female sales assistant who was locked in the changing room.

Her body was discovered by her colleague who had wondered where she was, as it was very unusual for her to have left the cash desk unattended. Concerned she had taken it upon herself to search the store, finally finding the body of her friend who was more like a sister to her than a colleague.

She had turned up early than usual for her shift with the intention of bringing her close friend and confidant breakfast in the form of a latte coffee and buttered croissant. Fiona had been out with Kevin the night before and she had coached her in first date etiquette. She was keen to know if he had called already, if there was likely to be a second date and what was the latest airport gossip.

Now she sat shivering with shock on the store's seating area too traumatised to speak, holding Fiona's name badge between her fingers, which she found on the till on her arrival.

Detective Chief Inspector Hamilton Musgrave had been called to attend the crime scene by the airport police. He had had been told that a body had been found in one of the stores and that it was being treated as a murder at this early stage.

He had not only thought that it was strange for someone from his section to be requested to attend a murder case but also that they should specifically request such a senior officer, especially at such a major airport, which should be more than capable of dealing with a case such as this internally.

He mused that there must be more than meets the eye which was the only explanation as to why he was being summoned in particular. He had departed directly from his house rather than heading into his office in Piccadilly, only to have to fight his way back out of the city once more.

On his way to the airport he used the hands-free to call his team back at Foxglove House to see if they had any further information that they could give him en route. He spoke with one of his detective sergeants who give him a short briefing on what who had made the call to SO15, his section, and why a senior officer had been requested to attend.

After hearing all that the sergeant had to say Musgrave started to create an ideas map in his mind which he could utilise as most normal people would do a sheet of paper or whiteboard. In days gone by Criminal Investigations Departments used to use screens or pinboards to attach photos to and create spider-like webs of connections to help them solve cases similar to those seen on dramas like *Midsomer Murders*. Technology of course had moved on as it inevitably does, and today it was all PowerPoint presentations and interactive boards. However Musgrave would create a similar type of nexus of information in his mind about a case and let his subconscious work out and calculate the curious links.

It was not long before he was on Terminal Road and passing the short stay carparks. Not knowing the proper procedure for police parking at this airport, and driving an unmarked car he decided the best thing to do was to go into the first of the short stay car parks which in this instance was the red zone carpark. He was yet to make contact with the lead officer on the case at the airport and thought it best to meet them inside.

As he got out of the car he noticed the Stansted Javelins mobile sculpture by Peter Logan gently dancing in the warming air currents. There remained a slight chill from the cloudless night before but it was setting itself up to be a glorious day which made situations like the one he was about to walk into all the more tougher.

On his arrival the front of the store was adorned with police blue and white cordon tape, which moved gently with the recirculating air. It was starting to get warm beneath the over-sailing canopy.

Although the airport was internal, this area with its arcade of duty free shops formed a sort of 'Market Street' for passing visitors to the airport before the gates. There was everything you could image here like a condensed shopping centre. The only real difference was the waiting area which sat it its heart which was filled with row upon row of seating tied together. Musgrave could smell the strong scent of coffee from the 'Joe and Juice' restaurant as he walked past it which made him yearn for a good coffee and breakfast which he had inadvertently skipped rushing to take the call out.

The area was completely locked down. The parade of shops looked like something from a catastrophe film. Half-eaten food with cutlery left as if dropped in a hurry and half full glasses of juice were left abandoned at empty tables. The advertising screens and departures boards continued to flicker while all else remained still.

It was the same morbid aftermath scene that Musgrave had become all too familiar with after a major incident. The only difference this time was that there were no personal belongings left behind. No abandoned luggage or clothing. It was possible to hear the din of passengers clattering somewhere in the distance in the airport beyond. It was as if there was an invisible screen between the two worlds. One in which a murder had been committed and the other the continuation of life with the repetitive clattering of suitcase wheels on the floor and conversations being held in multiple languages.

There was a police century who was stood guard outside the Boss store. He was armed with a SIG Sauer 516, the weapon of Counter Terrorism Command (CTC), held across his chest in readiness, since the threat level was increased the airport police had CTC working alongside them. He had a further two weapons, comprising a yellow toy-like taser fastened to his chest body armour and a Glock 17 pistol in a drop-leg thigh holster. He wore dark navy combat fatigues and baseball cap with black and white checker band, which identified him as a police officer. In a rapidly changing world, Musgrave remembered when policemen had worn shirts, ties and tunics in similar fashion to the guards at the Royal Households, however now modern police resembled something out of special forces, far more combat prepared and militaristic.

He did not care for it, he preferred tradition and thought that the old style uniforms inspired confidence and respect, but for operations which were sensitive then plain clothes officers were definitely the way to go in his opinion. Far more discreet, which brought its own advantages in live operations. Musgrave identified himself as he approached the front of the shop by flashing his warrant card. The sentry nodded and shifted to the side granting him entry to the shop.

Hamilton Musgrave had been a police officer all of his life. He had been to one of the top five secondary schools in the country and furthered his education at Reading University, studying for a Bachelor of Science with Honours in physiology. On graduating he had signed up to the police in a surprise move away from his family's expectations of a career as an importer of fine wines. He had excelled during his training and had been put on the rapid promotion scheme which saw him as a DCI at just thirty-eight.

He had moved from the Criminal Investigations Department at the City of London Police as a detective in 2001 to SO12 Special Branch with the Metropolitan police, where he had excelled and was promoted to Detective Sergeant following an investigation into a shoe bomber. In 2006 Special Branch merged with SO13 Anti-Terrorist branch to become the Counter Terrorism Command SO15. Musgrave was promoted again to Detective Inspector during the transition which also saw him and his team deployed around the world in direct response to terrorist related incidents and international operations.

On scene nothing seemed to be out of place on the shop floor. All of the displays and racks of clothes were neatly ordered in size and were pristine. Not an item of clothing was out of sync. Whatever had happened to the young sales assistant had been done by a professional without any struggle or mess.

The victim's distressed colleague was sitting on a cushioned bench which was usually used for trying on shoes. She had her hands around a polystyrene cup of tea while also clutching a fist full of dampened tissues which the attending inspector had handed to her. Streaks of tears showed on her cheeks. She was rocking gently backwards and forwards trying to process the shock. The inspector was sympathetically taking down her statement. The shock of the seeing her friend so still and with the colour drained from her lifeless body was taking its toll on the young apprentice.

As Musgrave approached the inspector, turning, gave an acknowledging nod and gave her notes to the female sergeant hovering behind her to finish. "Musgrave, Counter Terrorism Command, please do not let me interrupt things here."

The inspector drew him away from the apprentice so that their conversation could not be overheard. "No," she firmly said, "I think that we have everything that we need from her for the time being. She didn't actually witness the incident but she is helping us with our background enquiries. I know who you are by the way, your reputation precedes you. I'm Inspector Sarah Waters." Placing out her hand which Musgrave shook while making a single nod of the head type bow.

"Thank you," Musgrave responded and quickly turning to the point in hand, not wanting to associate with any form of praise or flattery, "I was told that you needed our assistance?"

"This does not look like anything that I have seen before, there does not seem to be any clear motive for the death. This morning at a similar time to when we believe the murder took place we had not one but three knocks on the watch list. The two may not be connected however I have asked for SO15's involvement as this may be terror related. We will start in the staff room as there is nothing to see out here. Forensics have been all over this area and they have not been able to locate the weapon that was used for the murder. The forensic pathologist has said that it was a shape weapon, possibly a stiletto - long slender blade with a needle-like point. As you can imagine this is a very busy airport with lots of people coming and going. You could have at least a dozen of more fingerprints on the cash desk alone."

Making their way to the back of the shop they passed by the scene of crime forensics officers in their paper jumpsuits uniforms, purple latex gloves, white masks, protective glasses and blue plastic over shoes.

Standing just inside the door way Musgrave and Waters looked over the shoulder of the last forensic officer who was stood over the body of the deceased taking a photos of the scene. There was a small yellow triangular marker with a number three printed on it. There were a few of these dotted around the shop which were points of interest of the officers and would be further scrutinised and recorded.

Waters and Musgrave could see that the body had been unceremoniously dumped into the changing room. The small size of the cubicle had contorted the body as it had tumbled in there. Her arms lay around her head, her hands open. There were no markings on her bare forearms which would typically indicate signs of a defensive struggle.

The officer who was taking the photos then looped the camera over one shoulder so that the camera was behind his back and leant forward pulling on some tape which had been applied to the edge of the door leaf in an attempt to lift what he suspected to be some fingerprints.

Another officer worked in an area with denoted with a small triangular marker with the number 5 printed on its face. A black circle drawn on the floor with magic marker encompassed what looked to be a footprint, barely visible against the vinyl floor of the staffroom. The remaining ghosted step looked to be an imprint of a high-heeled shoe. Waters turned to Musgrave. "Look at her shoes. She's wearing flats. Most of the girls here in the retail side do because of the long hours on their feet. You just could not do it in heels. Whoever these belong to they are not someone who works in retail."

In the staff room at the desk there was a plastic evidence bag with what resembled a jacket folded within.

Waters sat on the corner of the desk and looked towards Musgrave who studied the room with his arms folded across his chest. "So this is what we know so far," this Waters stated. "Our deceased, Miss Sophie Lane, nineteen years old and only daughter, arrived for work at three o'clock this morning. She was dropped off by her father who, works as a haulage driver and was on his way to work.

"She entered the main terminal on the podium level from the Southern entrance and walked up the ramp to the ground floor where she purchased a latte coffee at the Costa coffee shop at the front of the airport and then made her way to this room to open up.

"There are two methods of entry to this store. The first you came through and the second is that door behind you," she said pointing towards the steel door.

"It has a card reader and fingerprint recognition. The security here is high as you can imagine, being such a sensitive environment. Deliveries can be made by either way but this route is more secure and only operates when the concourse is open to the public as we don't particularly like deliveries mixing with boarding passengers. We do not have a record or any deliveries being made to the store this morning, no delivery guy can get in here without a member of staff being present. We considered if card cloning was possible but even if they had a duplicate card to access, the fingerprint recognition should of kept the door locked.

"We have checked out everyone who has access to this door in the past week, only two three people and one of them was Sophie. The rest all have alibis for the time of the murder which was estimated at being between four and six. We can be more precise once a post-mortem is carried out."

Musgrave studied the door momentarily, "Do you think it could have been held open intentionally or possibly she was tailgated into the store?"

"It's possible that someone could have tailgated her through the door although they would have had to have been standing almost on top of her. There's no evidence of a struggle on the shop floor and the body relocated to the changing room. We believe that the murder took place inside the changing room, if you were thinking that she was forced to open the door by someone else.

"The door is also alarmed to prevent someone holding the door open. See the door contacts here in the leaf and frame. If the system detects that the door is open for anything more than ten seconds it sounds an alarm which has to be reset by us.

"At this moment in time I believe that the assailant came into the shop through the front door in plain sight."

"Is there any available CCTV?" Musgrave questioned.

"There is CCTV in the store but someone has removed the hard drive which stores all of the recordings," she replied indicating to an open bay of the table mounted server. "There will be CCTV coverage from our own CCTV systems of the main piazza and other retail units will have their own CCTV which may offer us some clues. However the cameras are not supposed to be positioned so as to see into any other store, but it happens. I have placed a request for the release of any CCTV that covers the store and its surroundings immediately."

"Would the store's CCTV be backed up anywhere remotely? Some of these stores have a central location that feeds in CCTV from all over the place to be monitored by one central hub," he asked in hope.

"We may be in luck. Speaking to the area manager on the telephone the system does have a remote back up, however it is not continually streamed. It is sent as separate data packages pushed each hour."

"Have you contacted the service provider to see what can be retrieved?"

"We are onto it but I am doubtful. The chances are that the last received package came after the hard drive was removed. I would suspect that they would have neutralised the CCTV before any crime could be captured on it."

"Before I ask you who was knocked on the watch list is there anything else that you would say was unusual?"

"One other thing, her name badge was found on the keyboard of the till. Not broken, fully intact whether she removed it and put it there or if someone else removed it we cannot tell. We are sending it for testing to see if we can pick up anything from it."

"Right, so who was picked up on the watch list?"

"Yes," she said while pulling a smart phone from her pocket and scrolling through the images on the screen. "We have three; one male and two females. They were picked out with the facial recognition cameras at the security line. Two with a yellow warning, IC1 male about six-one, IC1 female five-five and the other with an amber IC2 female five-eight. The amber being one Giulietta De Luca from Milan. Her alias used in the United Kingdom is Julia Milani."

Musgrave studied the faces, it was difficult to make out the male's face with the baseball cap, however he could recall seeing the second female's face in mug-shot photos on file.

"Do you know who they are? We are checking their boarding card details to get names, address, and card payments, etcetera. It is quite possible that they are travelling with false papers." The inspector put her phone back into her pocket.

"More than likely," Musgrave stated. "We will find out of course. Will you please send those onto me," he said, indicating to the phone before it disappeared from view. "Have you notified next of kin yet?"

"Not yet, I didn't want to be closed out of this one. This is my airport and my crime scene."

"I can fully appreciate that. I am not here to upset the applecart and I will keep you fully up to speed of our departments' findings."

"That's not good enough. It has to be an equal share operation. I have a good team here, they are really good and close-knit. Anything that happens here everyone knows about it."

"I will see what I can do. You do know the score of course, once it becomes a S015 investigation we have a closed books policy" Weighing up the situation Musgrave continued, "However given the circumstances and for the benefit of the investigation how would you feel about a secondment to S015 for a short period of time?"

"If that is what it takes to keep this investigation. I want to bring my team with me."

"That will not be possible. What you learn you can only share with S015 officers and only those who I will tell you that you can talk to. We run a very tight ship and we cannot afford any leaks in this department. This cannot become public knowledge especially since we have had three knocks this morning.

"This is the start of something big, mark my works. We will run a cover story, something like a jilted lover or something to that effect.

"One more thing, apart from your team in the immediate area how many people know about what has happened here?"

Waters took no time in thinking before replying. "As I told you before everyone knows everything that happens here, it is a very close community."

Pausing to think for a moment Musgrave started again. "We need to contain this here. The whispers going around will have already mentioned that there is a body involved. The cover story should put the whispers to rest but for heaven's sake do not let any of your team post anything about this on social media.

"I have seen everything I can here, you can come with me to 'the House'. I will leave your team to liaise with mine before this is cleared up and this area reopened."

Bemused Waters questioned, "The House?"

"My team do not operate out of a police station. It would not be secure and far too public. We have a separate secure residence in London off from Piccadilly, Foxglove House, often affectionately shortened to 'the House'.

"It is discreet and has alternative entrance and exit onto Jermyn Street which takes you to the underground carpark on Bury Street."

Musgrave scanned the staff room one more time before leaving when his eyes met with this morning's newspaper which had been left on the desk. Always someone who wanted to be kept up to date with the latest information he could not resist skimming the front page article.

"Cyberattack causes chaos in computers across the globe," was the headline of the *Times*.

The world's biggest cyberattacks disabled computer systems across the United States, Britain, China and Russia yesterday in another ransomware attack freezing computers of government officials.

Experts said that the ransomware which struck Silicon Valley before spreading to Europe, could be an outbreak of Revolve, a new type of virus that affected the NHS hospitals a few months ago. In all instances the hackers demand payment of £2,000 in the internet currency Bitcoin exchange for unlocking machines. Russian intelligence sources said that it has all the hallmarks of Isis sabotage although the identity of the hackers remains unknown.

The attack which has targeted key institutions did not come through previously thought medium, email or a file buried within a seemingly innocuous document, but through posted media on MyLife. It is reported that these posts were uploaded by a robot account which promised a lottery style chance of winning a luxury ocean cruise.

While most organisations focus their security on training their staff to be vigilant on opening suspicious email attachments and direct attacks on computers, hackers have already evolved onto a new sort of attack specifically targeting social media accounts, which people unconsciously trust

Whitehall officials are concerned that the unknown hackers, thought to be state-backed, are using social media sites, such as MyLife, to break into Defence Office computer networks. Once a single individual is compromised the attack moves at breakneck speed through the network of friends, who are also colleagues in many instances, leading to what one official described as 'a disturbing situation where the entire department could be at risk'.

While more is now known about the methods of attacks officials are worried about the limited ability to spot the problem. The Defence Secretary declined to comment on the *Times*' findings.

SecureCom, one of the UK's leading cybersecurity companies commented that phishing via social media was the fastest-growing method for hackers. 'Rather than simply using phishing emails to access a network, attackers are using MyLife accounts to gather intelligence. For example merely observing the posts of acting service personnel hackers can locate and monitor troop movements or more worryingly actively engage in conversations in an attempt to find out military intelligence'.

Chapter Four

"Good morning Derek," Clifton said as he strode over towards the boot of the car. The boot lid popped up and before Derek could reach the back of the car Clifton was already manhandling his flight and dispatch bag into the boot. Derek met him and held out his hand. "Please to meet ya, so how was the flight over?"

"Not too bad. Thanks for asking, a typical Ryanair landing – no nonsense. One minute I was looking out at the sea and the next moment there was the coast and the next we were braking hard on the runway." Taking Derek's hand in a firm grip and shaking it once while smiling.

"I see ya brought the weather with ya."

"Thankfully it's forecast to be dry all day today although it's supposed to get a bit cold tonight with the clear skies."

They parted and walked around to the doors. Derek jumped in the driver's seat expecting Clifton to sit in the rear of the car however he was surprised when Clifton joined him up front in the passenger's seat and fastened his seat belt without instruction.

"So we are just in time for the first Guinness Factory tour group," Derek said with a smile.

Clifton looked quizzical and before he could answer Derek interjected "Ah, I'm jus' playin' with ya. I'm gonna take you to and from the site and anywhere in between as required. My number will be sent to you in a mo' so you can call me as ya need me."

As if on cue, Clifton's phone vibrated in his jacket pocket. "So you are effectively my 'minder' while I am here?" Clifton retrieved the phone from his pocket and saved the number into his list of contacts under 'Derek'.

"T'ink of me more as a representative, so." Derek pulled away from the departures area set down area and followed the road down the ramp towards the traffic lights amongst the buses and hire cars.

Derek turned on the radio to a local talk show which was airing a debate on the principle of the introduction of separate water charges across the country. Following a Dáil vote of 67% it was highly likely that the charges were going to be scrapped and that those who had paid the charges would be fully refunded. "Mr. Coveney declared Dáil at the debate on Wednesday night that the finalised deal on water charged will be a 'victory for sensible politics'. But also stressed the requisite for future investment in infrastructure after many years of under-investment."

The host of the show retorted with the comment "But isn't this what it is all about? If we don't start charging people for what their actual usage is it will be unfair to those who use the least. We cannot risk significant fines from the European Union if we don't face up to the obligations of the framework directive."

"But there is an opportunity for exemptions to apply," came back the other voice, "on such grounds as having medical conditions or particularly large families. With over 90% of households telling us that they will not pay for water as it is a necessity something needed to be done to address this which will satisfy everyone. Micheál Martin has told his party that the population will see that charges have ended and that the party has stayed true to that commitment."

During the ride to the M50 the only two voices had been those on the radio. The silence in the car made Clifton feel slightly uncomfortable so he decided to begin a conversation. "So what is your opinion on this, do you think that it is fair to have the same water charge throughout the country?"

Derek thought for a moment before he answered. "Well the way's I see's it we'll end up paying for it one way or another. It's jus' gonna be added onto another tax under a different name. I don't t'ink t'at we should have to pay for water, you need water to survive but the pipe infrastructure is so old now, it has to be maintained and supported somehow.

"See ya' got some which will have a tap runnin' all the day long because the taps broken but they can't afford to get it fixed. So what do ya' do in t'at situation? If they had to pay a rate it would be astronomical."

"Are you are local to Dublin or do you have to commute in from the suburbs?" Clifton asked moving away from what could be considered a contentious subject.

"Well t'at's an interesting question, to be sure," Derek answered while looking straight on at the road ahead. "I'm not really a taxi driver, you know, however to answer your question t'is week I live in Blanchardstown, which is to the North West of Dublin, with my wife. Who I have been married to for the past thirty-two years. Lovely lady, we met at my cousin's wedding – friend of my sister's cousin, no relation. We have two children, a boy, Lorcan and a girl, Eva, who are twenty-eight and t'irty – in that order."

Clifton chuckled to himself wondering how much of the back story was true and how much was a work of fiction. He mused that for any story to be truly believed there had to be an element of reality for it to be tangible.

As he thought through this he looked at the driver's left hand and there indeed was a worn golden wedding band on this third finger. It made sense of course. There would be no point someone who did not have children to pretend that they did as a person without children would not have the same experience of life as a person with children.

He thought back to the airport and the child at the security area. It seemed logical that a child would have packed what was important to them however their parents would not necessarily have assumed that this included a plastic sword. It was that kind of small detail or antidote which could reveal a lie from a truth but what about a half truth.

The car carried on at a steady pace. Clifton noted the differences between the road signs comparing them to the ones at home. The standards were pretty much the same however there were subtle differences which stood them apart. He noticed the traffic was beginning to get busier and the taxi moved across to the inside lane which had been painted red. "It seems that you have the same problem here that we have in the UK," Clifton said to Derek, "none of the German cars seem to have indicators fitted as standard!"

Derek laughed and replied, "Ah you see people don't use t'em because they don't want to wear t'em out!" They both laughed as the car swept under the bridge.

Dereck led the rest of the conversation, "So is t'is your first time to our green and pleasant land?"

"No, I'm over here quite a lot really monitoring the progress of works on site."

"Have y'a managed t' see anything other than planes of glass and construction sites on your trips?"

"All bits and pieces really, those that I can fit around my visits. It would be a shame to come all this way and miss out on everything that it has to offer. I am still to do the Jameson's Whiskey factory tour. Which I hear is a must see, especially with the factory taste tours. I'm just worried that I would never want to leave!"

"The brewery was founded by ya man John Jameson about two-hundred years ago and expanded very rapidly. It grew so big ya know that they used to refer to it as 'a city within a city'. T'ay had all sorts inside those walls; saw mills for t' barrel making, a forge for the ironworks. The water for the distillery comes from two wells dug beneath the site believed to be ground water flowing to the Liffey. Tell me have you been to Phoenix Park yet?"

"Er, yes. Yes I have, very briefly though. I did manage to see the president's residence from a distance, the American Ambassador's house and the monument to the Duke of Wellington."

"Ah, I bettin ye' didn't know he was Irish did ya? His real name, before it was lorded up, was Arthur Wellesley – the stylish version of Wesley. His family was from County Meath, up the North-West of Dublin. He enlisted in the British Army and spent a few years as an MP in the Irish House of Commons but made a name for himself in India. Proving himself there as the new man about town he was appointed as the representative of the British government in Dublin with a fancy title Lord Lieutenant."

The conversation ended and Clifton opened his dispatch bag and pulled out last week's copy of *Building* magazine which he would read to keep himself informed of the current news within the construction sector. Keeping up with his Continuing Professional Development programme included reading articles and keeping up to date with developments in the construction industry. The first few pages were from a masonry company of the name of Keystone who had probably funded this month's issue of the magazine. Each month a different manufacturer would have a case study documenting their products and where they had been used. A lot of the photos accompanying the case studies looked like architectural pornography. He skipped through the pages of sales patter and stopped at the news section.

The header read: MyLife appoints team to Masterplan new residential village campus next to its Headquarters in Silicon Valley.

MyLife has announced that the design team, headed by Concept Studios Architects, who will be Masterplanning a new village to the adjacent Headquarters campus in Silicon Valley, California. The social media giant invited the team from the top practices around the world to redevelop the former forty-six acre former industrial site that the social media group acquired last year.

According to MyLife, the Meadow Campus neighbourhood will provide long needed community services, including infrastructure such as schools, nurseries, sports facilities, retail units, transportation and housing.

"It is an exciting opportunity to be able to collaborate with MyLife, whose innovation in networking and social media extends to urban ambitions for connectivity in the Valley area," said Concept Studios Architects partner Emma Miller, who leads the firm's California office. "The Meadow Campus Masterplan creates a sense of place with a diverse programming that responds to the needs of the Silicon Valley community," she added.

The housing element is described as critical to the overall plan. It will be comprised of 2,500 new houses with at least 25% of those being offered at a lower rate to assist first time buyers and MyLife employees. By providing affordable housing in the scheme the design team hope to control the growth of road traffic in the community.

The technical team have also been working on a driverless car share scheme using the new MyLife drive system thus allowing for almost continuous shared shuttles around the town, which is estimated to reduce carbon emissions by 15% overall.

Some are concerned about the use of driverless cars however they will only be operating within the MyLife campus for the first phase of the Masterplan. The cars can be pre-booked and use satellite navigation as well as the new Beta version of MyLife's drive system which has yet to have been able to be hacked as earlier trials highlighted this risk which brought the attention of the worlds press to the risks associated with driverless cars.

The diversity of the housing is also intended to encourage the San Mateo County Government to develop a new East-to-West transportation corridor. The development will have a transit hub at the heart of the campus.

As Clifton read through the articles his mind started to wander. Was what he was about to do ethical? He worked for the contractor who was working for MyLife and he was being sent there to plant a device so that the Government could intercept F5 information. Was there truly a greater good and was he really doing this action in good conscience? His loyalties were torn between what he felt were his duties to his work and his duties to his country. Lockridge really had him over a barrel in any case. If he did not do what he was told his career, which he had been building up for years and sacrificed so much to achieve, would be over.

The data centre construction site that they were travelling to was located to the south-east of the Town of Clane, situated in the County of Kildare. The River Liffey travels to the south of the site and continues its twisted route through the rolling countryside connecting the Town to the Ryder Cup Village, where Clifton was staying at the K Club and then onto Dublin.

The car rolled up to the entrance gate where there was a small silver gatehouse with two permanently stationed guards which on rotation with another two team of guards were active twenty four hours a day. Derek and Clifton could see one of the guards looking out from his control point through two inches of BR7 ballistic rated glazing, enough for an assault rifle firing 7.62 calibre rounds. Derek stopped just in front of the steel road blocker which had been freshly painted with black and yellow chevrons. Derek wound down the driver's window and pressed the call button on the intercom. The intercom must of only rung once before a cheery voice replied. "Morning, are you here to drop off?"

"Yes I'm here with your man Alex Clifton, the architect. Can you let him in, he's come all the way from London without any breakfast can ya believe it and he's starvin'!" Derek spoke into the metal panel. Clifton kept his eyes on the guard.

"Does he have his pass with him?" came back the voice from the intercom.

Derek looked towards Clifton has he retrieved a plastic card from his dispatch bag and held it up to the window.

The voice can back over the intercom. "Tell him to place it on the card reader and the bollard will go down. Wait until the light goes green and then it'll be safe for you to go through to the main site office where he can get some food."

"T'anks a million, God bless!" Derek said as Clifton handed him the pass card to make the bollard drop.

The landscape works to the site were all but complete. There was a three metre high fence that ran around the entirety of the site. Some 12,000 linear metres of screen fencing around the entire perimeter. There was a ten metre boundary set between the external fencing and a two and a half precast concrete wall which resembled something from a military base. The concrete was screened from the outside world by rapidly growing vegetation which was to, in time, disguise the wall. Only artillery would be able to penetrate through this perimeter at ground level. Clifton had thought that this was probably overkill when the security advisor had first suggested it however the MyLife had stressed the importance of keeping people out of the site.

He looked out of the window as the car swept through the entrance roads. There still some construction going on towards the last phase but the piles of earth and the yellow jacketed army that had been here for the past nine months were eroded to only a few persons making their way up to the main campus building. In total there were five buildings planned for the site. The first phase consisted of the landscape and securing the site with security barriers, fencing and gatehouses. The second phase was for the main data centre building. The building resembled something of an alien spacecraft. Its size was immense. The plan was arranged so that there was no clear definition from the front or the back. From the air it was possible to make out the series of small triangular fins forming an overall circular shape. From the approach the building looked rather striking using insulated precast panels for its external cladding. Windows to the outside world were not easy to spot, however they were set within the recesses of the triangles. This reason for this being twofold. Firstly, in internal space would receive indirect lighting so they would not suffer with glare and overheating, and secondly from a security perspective not having easily accessible glazing meant that the risk of attack from a vehicle was a lot less.

Invisible from its elevation but from the air was a services gantry which ran the entire length of the roof following the circular shape. As the car wound its way through the landscape

Clifton could feel the designed sweeps which were developed to control the speed of the traffic within the campus. To his left they were passing one of the eight attenuation reservoirs located around the site. These were used to cool the server halls inside the data centre buildings. The reservoirs were steeply banked and very quickly went up to a depth of up to five metres. Around the edges of the ponds there was wildlife planting and newly planted trees which were being staked into place. To his opposite side Clifton could see the array of solar panels following the curvature of the road. The collection of angled panels formed a canopy where which carparked beneath. During the winter this would keep the cars sheltered from the rain and allow staff to access their cars in the dry. In the summer the shading provided much relief after a long day at the office stepping into a cool car than a sweat box. There was a second check point in front of them and Clifton flashed his card at the two guardsmen as Derek stopped the car and wound down the window once again.

"Site operatives," said the larger of the two guards, both of whom were decorated in bright orange personal protective equipment and sunglasses. He raised his arm directing them towards the portacabin which had been the contractor's home for the last few months. Derek pulled up into the first available parking space and turned off the ignition.

"So where do we go from here?" Clifton enquired.

"I'll leaves you now to do what you have to do and I'll come back at six o'clock to pick you up again unless you call me first."

"Great ok," Clifton said.

"Yes, all ya need to do is call as they say and I'll a come-a runnin!" Derek said while he smiled tilting his head to one side.

"Right ok, I guess I'll talk to you later."

"T'anks see ya'all later on then."

Clifton walked into the site office entrance and greeted the security guard in his usual fashion as he approached the first one in a line of four glass tubes in front of him. The reception was split into two areas, the non-secure side and the secure side. To pass through to the secure side a visitor would have to have a security swipe card which would open the initial set of sliding doors.

Clifton fumbled in his dispatch bag and located his swipe card which he kept in the front compartment so that it would be easily accessible for his frequent visits. Swiped the card through the reader and waited for the confirmation beep and for the light to turn from red to green which indicated that he could enter the glass portal.

He stepped into the portal, sliding his cabin bag in closely behind him and put his card into his pocket. He turned at right angles so that he was no longer facing the door into the secure side. The small screen in front of him lit up into life and began a strobing blue light to indicate that he should place his finger on the reader. As he placed his index finger into the reader the blue screen turned red but continued to strobe while the open door to the unsecure side rotated closed. Once inside the tube the outer tube rotated to a ninety degree position preventing progress or retreat from the device. Clifton hated the claustrophobic encounter each time.

Despite the whole process taking less than a minute to complete it always felt like longer and he always feared becoming trapped mid-cycle in the revolving tubes. As he waited patiently for the reader to turn green Clifton considered what would happen if the reader gave a negative reading. Not wanting to tempt fate and become stuck in the tubes he had never carried out such an test of the system. Just then the reader light stopped strobing and turned a friendly green colour and the whooshing sound of the revolving tube started up to complete the opening for his exit.

It was not unusual for Data Centre cliental to require security for their sites which would seem extreme to most other commercial properties. Two years earlier Clifton remembered a smaller site based in an Enterprise Zone where the Client's security operators had insisted in installing iris scanning devices to open and close doors. This was introduced after it was found that staff were frequently sharing their own personal security cards with other staff members who had lost their own. By lending their card to someone else it meant that they could have access into areas that they were not supposed to and steal information. In one instance looking through the security logs one staff member, Peter Jenson, had been in and out of the point of presence room twenty-eight times in one afternoon. This was something that definitely had to be controlled. Biometric security was becoming very popular over other forms of security because it was simple to use and it was unlikely that the device to open the door would ever be lost.

He stepped out and headed towards the main office area to drop off this things and set up his hot desk. He thought it would be best to do everything as he would do naturally on any other visit. Before setting about getting his Personal Protection Equipment, PPE, out of the dry room he stopped at the tea point and took a cup from the adjacent cupboard. The coffee machine on the worktop had a vast array of caffeine based beverages. Clifton had tried absolutely every single option and had noticed that whatever button he pressed, whether it be a latte, cappuccino or a mocha the resulting coffee would still tasted of brown water.

After drinking his cup of brown water with a satisfying gasp he went to the dry room to change into his PPE which he changed into quickly.

As he was getting changed he had removed the key from the compartment in the heel of his shoe and had placed this inside his right trouser pocket to keep it safe. Keeping the key in his site boots would not be practical. He placed his mobile telephone in his vest pocket facing forward, which to the untrained eye resembled one of the site radios. Because the site was so vast the way the construction staff communicated to each other was through radio. Only the team leaders were supposed to carry a radio but procession being nine-tenths of the law meant that quite a few operatives had radios who were not supposed to.

He adjusted the cuffs of his shirt and checked that the cufflinks were still there – concerned that they may have dislodged during the journey. Losing a cufflink was always something that concerned Clifton however he had never lost one yet. He was tempted to test the mechanism for releasing the USB device from its cufflink mount but resisted the urge it in case it were to ping out and break so he left it as it was.

Involuntary he said "check" out loud before making sure that all his belongings were packed into his locker, closing the caged door and putting the padlock through the holes and twisting the combination back to 0,0,0,0 so that it would be extremely hard to guess the actual combination.

He made his way to the end corridor where the heavy steel service door would lead him down a utility metal staircase to the haul road and track which ran around the perimeter of the building. He met two mechanical subcontractors on the staircase making their way back to the office. It was common to wish people walking towards you 'good morning' or 'good afternoon' as a passing pleasantry – even if it was the first time you had even seen this person. At first it had been quite a culture shock to Clifton who knew that if he was to greet any strangers walking the streets of London it was likely that he would either have been ignored or would have been snubbed and regarded as some sort of peculiar individual. He admired the kindliness of the local culture. In London everyone looked scared, people looked at the ground as they walked around. It was not possible to make eye contact with anyone on the underground let alone talk to them. When had this happened?

Clifton thought to himself – in all the years he had been working in the City he could not remember it being any other way. He had befriended a fruit and veg stool holder and would speak to him every day, even when it was raining. Putting the world to rights and concocting ideas which they could present to *Dragons' Den*. Before Clifton left working in London Tony, the vender of the stall, was taken ill and replaced with someone else. Clifton had always regretted not being able to say goodbye but other than the stall he had no other way of contacting him. He then considered how ironic it was, all in all he had probably spent more time every week talking to Tony that he would do with any other family yet he undoubtedly knew less about Tony than any of this other friends or colleagues.

As he made his way along the compacted track path he mentally checked off all of his equipment as he would do before going anywhere. Boots, vest, gloves, glasses, hat, phone, pen, clipboard, wallet and keys.

Unlike his other visits Clifton noticed that there for far less contractor staff on site in yellow jackets and far more people walking about in the orange MyLife PPE paraphernalia. The faces in the office area had looked different also. He had only recognised a handful of the Contractor staff still there greeting them with his usual welcome.

It was well observed that all of the MyLife employees wore some form of product placement. It had been suggested jokingly that it was a company policy that everyone had to sport some form or another clothing, brandishing the company's logo. Unlike other data centre operators who preferred discretion for security purposes MyLife were big on their branding, which could be seen throughout the facility, even down to the small embossing on the trays in the canteen which had the infamous ML letters embossed into the shiny orange plastic.

The employees of MyLife did not have a specific uniform that they would wear however you would always be able to pick up on the corporate branding whether it was in their attire coloration or the overriding theme of the abbreviated 'ML' symbol and the two colours orange and navy blue. This often made Clifton think of the McVities Jaffa Cake packaging.

It was rumoured that the blue and orange colour selection for the branding was inspired by art, specifically the impressionist movement. The orange and blue combination formed complementary colours. Monet's 1872 *Sunrise* painting had oranges forming the sun and light reflecting in the clouds and water amidst the obscure bluish landscape. Writing in 1888 Monet was reported to of written, "colour makes its impact from contrasts rather than from its inherent qualities... the primary colours seem more brilliant when they are in contrast with their complementary colours."

It had remained an in-house secret who had come up with the MyLife branding and design, however whoever had knew how powerful these two colours were combined were, how much brighter they made everything seem and how easily identifiable the branding would be, albeit not next to McVities Jaffa Cakes.

Clifton walked through the management suite which was comprised of a large open-plan office space with glazed pods forming cellular offices in the centre. The glazed partitions were switchable glass which allowed controllable privacy to the room with the flick of a switch by making the glass turn from transparent to translucent instantly.

It was remarkable technology and something quite new to Clifton. A thin layer of liquid crystal is sandwiched between two layers of polyethylene terephthalate or PET films which are coated with a dusting of metal deposits. The film is then further layered between two ethylene-vinyl acetate or EVA and encased within a cavity between two pieces of toughened glass. When an electrical current is introduced to the film the liquid crystals within the build-up align turning the glass from translucent to transparent.

The small voltage required to switch the glass and keep it running far outweighed the carbon footprint of any other technologies including electronic blinds. There was also no maintenance to perform and no wear and tear due to over use. Which tended to be the reason that blinds had relatively short lifetimes.

The walls were covered with monitors displaying different information which rotated ever so often. It was a combination of information relating directly to the usage of MyLife with a map of the world and tiny pin pricks of light denoting someone logged into the site. You could almost tell from the map the difference between day and night because of the pattern displayed on the world. Other slides were more akin to the traditional motivational posters that you used to see in office with bold text and bright colours. Although these ones seemed to be more propaganda related than motivational with their doctrinal slogans. Clifton wondered the extent of the conditioning that these sort of systems had on the employees over an extended period of time.

Clifton could really start to see the building starting to take on its own life now. He thought how remarkable it was to think that only a short time ago this wall all just a green field and now he was standing inside the most advanced data centre on the planet. As building begin it is like a phoenix rising from the flames. There is destruction of the natural world, fields are dug up, and trees are removed. Earth is scrapped away by the tons. Then a working platform is created, foundations are laid.

The structural frame which forms the skeleton of the building is erected and the scale is realised by its neighbours as the building begins to reveal itself. The roof is laid and the external cladding skin is added. Walls and internal corridors form the arteries for later habitation and pedestrian movement around. Services are installed and the building takes its first breath. Scaffolding which has been supporting the building is slowly dismantled allowing the building to take its first steps unaided. That smell of fresh paint lingers in the air and soft furnishings are added. The building completes its creation and becomes its own living organism and just as vulnerable as any human being and destined to one day be demolished and die.

Clifton made his way down into the data centre spaces below the administration area above. It was very much conceptually like a traditional factory with the office areas overlooking the production area hierarchy. It also meant that the heat produced in the data hall spaces could be reused to heat the floor above.

As he made his way down the showcase intertwining spiralling helical ramp set within the sky lit atrium. As he descended into the workings of the space the atmosphere changed quite dramatically from a high end office environment to a much more secure clean space almost like a labyrinth of laboratory spaces with exposed pipes ducts and cable routes running along the walls and across above the rather wide corridors.

A typical corridor of any building type would be around two metres to allow for two wheelchairs passing but on these projects the corridor widths were extended to well over four metres to allow for all of the ducting and pipework to run in tiers from the soffit height down. There was a small maintenance zone allowed for to get mobile scissor lift up into so that future cables could be laid and pulled through. Huge valves with handles as long as a person's forearm connected pipe which were larger in section that the most generous dinner plate.

Cables sat in trays organised by colour and appeared like spaghetti looms branching off on trays which resembled train tracks. Clifton was reminded of going to a shop many years ago in London's Kings Road, Chelsea, where they had a small brass train which ran around the shop well out of the reach of any customers, which ran on a track which circumnavigated the store, transporting money, receipts and messages from the front of house to the back of house. It was fascinating watching the small train clattering around just below the high ceiling and the organisation of the track with all its branches allowing the train to travel to all parts of the store. It was quite a spectacle, sadly lost to the depths of time and maintenance costs.

He approached the first set of double doors and tried the handle. The handle turned but if felt as though it was disconnected. He tried again pushing against the door but there was no response. He looked over towards the card reader mounted on the wall next to the door looking to see if the LED lights were flashing green and red indicating that the door lock had not been connected yet.

The LED was red showing that the door was secured. Clifton considered waiting for someone to go through the door and he would follow them through, but if it was a MyLife employee rather than one of the, rapidly becoming sparse, construction team there would be questions as to why he was attempting to access that space. He looked around causally to see if there was anyone around within sight and looked up towards the corner of the room where usually there would be cameras mounted to give them the best range. The camera was there but the wires were hanging down showing that it was not yet wired up.

He felt for the master key and placed it in the lock. It fitted perfectly which was a relief. He wondered how they had come by such an item and then thought that they must have approached the ironmongery supplier who supplied the cylinders to the locks as there was no other way of duplicating this type of key without the specialist cutting machines. The door opened with a slight spring and Clifton walked though hiding the key once again. He took a deep breath and proceeded on his mission.

Most of the hardware for the data centre would be modularised cabinets that would arrive at the campus pre-fitted out, so that it simply just a case of taking the cabinet out of its protective shipping packaging, locating the cabinet in the correct position and connecting it up. The facility had the capacity to have up to four deliveries taking place at any one time. Which would equate to approximately two hundred and fifty-six cabinets. The turnaround time from a cabinet being unloaded, unpackaged, located and connected was paramount for the logistics of the campus.

A fully loaded sixteen and a half metre articulated lorry could be processed within a little under three hours. To speed up the process the location of the cabinets was predetermined and they were delivered from the loading area to their final location by an army of intelligent robots. The cabinets would be connected to the data centre by a specialist installation technician and the day to day maintenance of the data hall, which resembled something like a digital farm with its acres of cabinets neatly lined up row upon row, would be maintained by a different technician who nursed the servers and replaced parts as required. The cabinets were also intelligent and would report back to a central point any faults or if the server was not performing to its optimum capability. The technician would be sent to that particular server amongst the sea of racks and either attempt to fix the issue or completely swap out that server blade in the way a farmer tends his crops.

Clifton was in the delivery area now. It was quiet with no one around. One of the sectional doors was open and Clifton went to investigate. As he approached he realised that a trailer was in fact docked and he was looking into the darkness of the inside of the empty lorry trailer. He jumped up and down on the levelling system as if to test it for any sign of movement. There was none. He moved onto the operations area which housed the control area which was like the bridge of a ship to the data centre. Everything was controlled from this room. He tried the handle of the door but it was locked. Tried to look through the glazing into the room but there was some sort of film applied to the glass making it almost impossible to see into the space. This must have been a change directed by MyLife as this was not something that Clifton had remembered designing into the scheme.

It began to dawn on him how secure this place was coincidently by design. The most sensitive spaces was set deep within the bowls of the building. All the secondary support systems were location around the perimeter. If one system were to go down then a backup would instantaneously come online and if that were to fail then yet another backup system would come online like a life support machine. He began to fiddle with one of the cufflinks, spinning the toggle clasp and then realising the importance of not losing it stopped at once.

He was now in a large open space which was three storeys in height. At the centre of the space was a series of large water tanks, almost cathedral-like in scale with a metal elephant gantry mezzanine which ran across the top suspended from the soffit above. The space was filled with various degrees of whirring noises which was deafening. Clifton could see some people in the distance wearing their PPE and ear defenders looking at some gauges and indicating towards some read outs on the panels around them. They were oblivious to his presence. Clifton decided to avoid any contact in case it he was stopped prematurely, and walked up to the nearest cat ladder access point and climbed up to the mezzanine level so that he could walk above them unnoticed. As he made his way across the grating he told himself not to look down as, despite the knowledge that it was not possible to fall through the grating, when you are four metres up in the air and you can see the floor below you through a grating that is only three millimetres wide nothing prepares you for the vertigo. As he got to the middle of the expanse of the mezzanine, he pulled out a handheld torch to get a better look at something up at high level which looked like incomplete fire stopping material. As he removed the torch from the Velcro packet of his vest it slipped through his fingers. In a panic he tried to catch it mid fall, only flicking the edge of it causing it to spin rapidly in the air and bounce through the grating mesh. 'Shit,' he muttered to himself as the people from below looked up to see where the smashed torch had come from.

Chapter Five

"Can I have one medium flat latte please, what are you having?"

Waters did not have to think twice before responding, "I will have a medium cappuccino if there is one going, ta."

"And also a medium cappuccino, both to go please." Musgrave ordered some drinks from the coffee shop before leaving the airport. It was well past time for what would have usually been his third cup of coffee of the day. The machine hissed steam into the milk jug amid the raucous sound of coffee grinders and someone hammering out the spent grains from a previous caffeine creation.

"You must have been contacted rather early this morning I imagine to get here when you did. Did you get a chance to get anything to eat?" Waters was looking at the array of pastries behind the curved glass counter.

"Sadly no, I did not get a chance but it's like that some days. When there is a fast moving case there isn't time to get too concerned about food. I find that I am also sharper without it, like the hunger drives me forward.

There was a calorie restriction study carried out by Italian scientists in 2011. It all revolves around the production of a protein in the brain which is stimulated by less calorie intake and that is linked to memory and learning.

Further tests carried out showed that caffeine also was beneficial, not only acting as a stimulus but also in the production of the protein made in the body. Think about it this way, with an aging population Alzheimer's and dementia will double within a generation. If we look after ourselves better not only can we perform better now but we will continue to perform well into the future."

The young girl who was serving behind the counter wished them both a safe flight, letting it fall off her tongue rhetorically. Musgrave thought better than to correct her and smiling politely gave a slight nod as he collected the two paper cups and handed Waters her cappuccino. He took a handful of sugar sachets from the counter without counting them, then went back and while retaining one between his fingers dropped the rest back into the pile. He tore it open and poured in into his coffee making sure it was thoroughly stirred before throwing the wooden stick into the waste receptacle. It did seem a waste of material just to be discarded so wastefully but he really could not think of any other use for them.

Musgrave started on the journey back towards Foxglove House with Waters sitting in the passenger seat. The quickest way back would be to go around the M25 towards Watford and to cut down the A1. It was almost a straight line into London that way. As they travelled down the M11 the mid-morning traffic was taking the place of the rush hour morning stream. Waters tried to make some small talk in the car but Musgrave put the radio on, subtly indicating to Waters that this was not the time to be talking but to be thinking.

They followed in the steady flow of traffic for about half an hour before pulled over to the exit lane at the Junction 23 South-Mimms and headed south onto the A1 in the direction of London. He was mentally running through case files in his mind considering motives and any past precedents which he could relate to the facts. Sarah was looking out of the side window watching the green landscape merge into streams of colour as the car sped along. They sat in silence but for the soft playing music coming from the car's radio. The music gently faded out and a well-spoken relaxed female voice interrupted the silence with the credit of the piece from Ludovico Einaudi.

The female voice was suddenly replaced by an automated tone. "Incoming call … Incoming call."

He looked down at the small screen that was built into the dashboard console which was now pulsating with an illuminated telephone icon. There was a green receiver and a red rejection receiver underneath the icon. Musgrave had never used the screen to answer a call, and then questioned if it was even possible as he always used the controls on the steering wheel. The name of the called then flashed up underneath the telephone icon displaying the name of the caller "Emily Musgrave."

He hesitated for a moment, and then he pressed the green receiver button icon with his thumb on the steering wheel. "Hello Emily, I'm a bit busy at the moment. Is everything alright?" It was unusual for Emily to call her father at all let alone during working hours.

She had become so accustomed to him being busy and not able to hold a proper conversation. It was something that he knew that he had to work on but when he was on a telephone there was usually so much going on around him that he could not dedicate his full attention to the conversation which usually meant that he would either not fully remember the conversation or he would give inconclusive answers to questions, predominately replying "Well what does your mother think?" in an attempt to delegate the decision-making to his wife. He tried to make sure that when he was at home he was actually there and not replying to emails and taking calls – although it was quite difficult. Sunday lunch was almost the only time when they ever spent quality family time together.

This was usually when Emily would spring any requests and also when she knew that her father would be most susceptible to agreeing to do something. The week before last she had convinced him that she wanted to take up hockey. He had not been too sure about the whole thing as he was concerned that she may get injured but then realising that when he was her age he played county rugby and well. He gave her his blessing and they talked for the remainder of the afternoon about training, equipment, where she could practice and with an upcoming birthday what stick would be suitable.

She was a typical fifteen-year-old and although deep down she loved her father dearly it was her role as an adolescent to make his life as difficult as possible.

"Dad the police are here and they are going through everything in the house… I think that they are looking for something but they haven't said what."

"Honey is your mother there, put her on if she is please."

"No dad she's gone out to get the food for tonight. I wanted to stay here and catch up on some homework."

Thoughts rushed through his head. It was unlikely that his daughter would miss the opportunity to go out of the house, which she had so often referred to as her 'prison'. She was a fine student and often would hit the books straight away when arriving home from school after a glass of orange juice and a few Maryland cookies. She would have completed her homework long before he would have ever arrived home from a day at work. He had regretted not being there more when she was younger and supporting her with her education but Elizabeth, his wife, had been an excellent mother and had played both parents roles when he was out trying to make the world a better place for his family.

It was more likely that she wanted to stay behind and spend time going on MyLife and chat to her friends. Musgrave was thankful that she was at an age where she did not have any serious boyfriends. An all-girls secondary schooling education had been a godsend in seeing to that.

Boyfriends were going to be a whole new future chapter of anxiety that would be the source for many a sleepless night with worry when it happened and he fretted about those days yet to come and how he would protect his daughter without seeming to be the controlling parent he was.

To him she would always be his little girl no matter how old she was. He would always remember the time when he caught her attempting to hide the evidence of a broken china tea cup. She had been told not to play with the fine china but she was determined, just like her father, and one day when she had been playing tea party with her stuffed animals one of the cups had fallen slipped and smashed. She was so upset and knew what she had done was wrong. Musgrave could see how sorry she was and that she had made a feeble attempt to repair the cup with Plasticine.

"Your mother is going to be very cross when she finds out about this isn't she?" he remembered asking her.

She nodded slowly muttering nonsense between tears.

"Well this cannot happen again can it?"

She shook her head most adamantly and looked at him with those sad little eyes.

"I can see that you are sorry and that it won't happen again. Don't tell your mother."

He then took the pieces in his hands and she had hugged him so tightly. He had replaced the cup before anyone had realise what had happened. From that moment he knew what his responsibility was as a parent.

"Can you find who the officer is in charge and let me speak to them please?" he said in a professional way with Sarah in the car listening.

"Ok dad," came the short reply. He could her the soft conversation over the speakers of the car as it cruised down the road. He picked up on some kind of confrontation and raised voices in the background and the speakers made a loud clattering noise as if the source of the call had been dropped. He could hear Emily calling out to him. "Dad, Dad, they are taking me away, help me!" He desperately called out after her in vain hoping that she could hear him but it was likely that she was too far away from the phone to hear the response.

There was a loud cracking noise as the line went dead and a single tone sounded around the car indicating that the call had been terminated. Silence then filled the car as before the music began to slowly fade back to an audible level. His mind raced as he tried to imagine what was happening at the other end of the phone. With his window to the situation closed with the termination of the call he could only fear the worst. He knew then at that moment someone was trying to get to him through his daughter, but who? The question bounced around in his head of who would have the power and audacity to do something like this.

As he thought his foot pressed heavily on the accelerator of the car. He reached towards the dashboard without thinking and flicked the switch that brought the car out of its sombre cruise into a blue flashing illuminated chariot. The siren kicked in and the traffic in front of him moved across to free up the road ahead. He accelerated to one-hundred miles per hour in no time. Forgetting that Sarah was in the passenger seat he went into parental mode, nothing else mattered accept his daughter. He used the scroll wheel on the iDrive to go through his phone contacts and he found Barnet Police Station. He called the number in desperation and asked to speak to the superintendent. They had trained together at Hendon and had remained friends. Although James had risen in rank to become a superintendent he was only in control of the area of the London Borough of Barnet. Whereas Musgrave, although technically a lower rank, was playing a far greater role in country wide protection.

It seemed to take a long time to get thorough the various receptionists, secretaries until the voice of the superintendent answered the phone. "Hamilton how are you, is this a pleasure or business call?"

"Sorry to disturb you sir, business I'm afraid. I have reason to believe that my daughter is in trouble. Can you please confirm if there are officers at my address?"

"Let me check and I'll get back to you." There was a pause and Musgrave waited counting the seconds in his head as if they were hours. "No we don't have anyone there. I will send over a patrol car to check things out. Kilo Foxtrot Tango is in the area. Should be there in the next five minutes."

"Thank you sir, I am en route and have an ETA of five minutes. I will meet them there, thank you for your help." He pressed the red receiver button on the steering wheel to end the call and pulled out into the centre of the road to pass the waiting cars.

Musgrave would have preferred to use his own team for something like this as they were highly trained and had firearms, however even with the fastest vehicles that they had it would have taken them at least twenty minutes arrive on scene. He knew that every second counted and being his family he would have liked to have been able to rally every single officer in the Metropolitan Police to respond.

The car was racing down the outside lane now at approximately one-hundred and thirty miles per hour. Despite the cars speed Musgrave would have given anything to be able to get there quicker. He could see cars ahead moving rapidly out of the way. As he approached his junction he began to indicate, checking before he switched lanes and broke hard to deaccelerate the car from its high speed to something more manageable for the next part of his journey.

He pulled off from the dual carriage way onto the slip road. The tyres screeched and the car rolled heavily onto the driver's side. Waters was holding onto the door handle with increasing concern. So much so that her fingers were beginning to turn white. She closed her eyes and bit down onto her lip trying extremely hard not to scream. The only time she had been in a car that was doing these kinds of stunts was when she was doing her driving skills training back before she worked at airports. When she had done this it had been on an empty test track with no other cars around. The reality of knowing that any false move or component of the vehicle choosing to fail at this particular point would cause the journey to end in disaster and possibly not only limited to the occupants of this car.

The slip road went around a banked sloping curve allowing Musgrave to continue to hold the car at a tight angle at speed. It looked as though they were about to go over the bridge but then he stopped suddenly and took a hairpin left into Rowley Lane which resembled something of a country lane. He sensed Waters anxiety and looked over to her side of the car to see how she was doing. He apologised but continued towards his house. Waters relaxed her lips and uttered in the lowest tone she could manage at the time that family came first and she understood. Musgrave knew how brave she was being realising that working at Airport police there would be next to no experience of this sort of driving. He wanted to say something but felt that any compliment would be taken as a belittlement and so decided to just concentrate on getting them both there safely.

He raced down the lane in a blur and pulled onto Barnet Road as the tyres screeched as he took the corner wide with the speed that he was doing. He was using all the momentum that he could to get home to Emily. He could see the silver Hyundai i30 patrol car approaching from the opposite direction with its blue lights flashing on the top of the vehicle. The sirens loud and blasting out a two tone warning. He watched it turning right into Garden Close, he was only about five cars lengths away. Pedestrians who were walking on the pavement turned around to see what all the commotion was.

He turned off the siren to his own car but left the lights flashing as he made his way into the cul-de-sac having to drive around two cars who had tried to be helpful and pulled over to one side of the road. But in fact meant that Musgrave had to overtake them and pull out wider than the really wanted to taking precious time before turning into the road. He scanned the familiar scene of his house looking to see what was out of place. Ahead of him parked across his driveway was a black Ford Transit van. It had a 65 registration plate and looked like it had just been washed. Parked facing the entrance to the cul-du-sac alongside the house and parallel to the black van was a grey coloured Audi S3 with black tinted windows.

Neither of these vehicles were standard police vehicles. It was hard to spot an unmarked police vehicle, like his own, but there were tell-tale marks for an unmarked vehicle such as the grille where the lights would sit and the rear window where the emergency high mounted lights would be located. There were no such accessories applied to these vehicles for him to spot. He slowed the car slightly taking in all that there was to be observed externally, trying to read the situation that lay before him. There was no one outside which was peculiar. If it had been the police there would have been at least one officer outside to deter any onlookers or unwelcome attention.

The front door to his house was wide open but there was no one to be seen. It was suspiciously quiet like the calm before the storm.

He felt the judgemental eyes of the neighbours peeking through the curtains as his car rolled up the road, still with its lights flashing to join the silver patrol car which had now come to a stop just behind the black Transit van purposely blocking it in. The two officers cautiously got out of the car and put on their flat caps while looking over the house.

There was a moment of tensioned calm stillness. Suddenly the tranquillity was interrupted as the doors to the back of the Transit van flew wide open. Three men sprang out of the back of the van wearing black combat type trousers, high visibility bomber jackets and black balaclavas masking their identity. Each one was carrying a weapon of varying calibre.

The officer who had been driving the patrol car quickly pulled open the door of the i30 and ducked down attempting to use the door leaf as a shield. The car was sprayed with a hail of shots. The lead figure was firing an AK-47 Kalashnikov automatic rifle almost uncontrollably while the other two had German made Heckler & Koch G3 selective fire assault rifles. The second officer who had not been able to react fast enough was visibly struck several times before he fell back on his haunches and slowly rolled over onto his side. A couple of ricocheting bullets made contact with the body work of Musgrave's BMW 5 series. Sarah was holding the seatbelt and was preparing for the worst. There were three loud dull thuds as they hit home.

"Try not to worry," Musgrave attempted to reassure her "This car is ballistic rated –we should be alright so long as we stay mobile."

He knew that he needed to make a snap decision, he hated being forced to react without careful consideration but there was no time to fully consider the situation but given the actions of the three assailants. His only option as he could see it was to use lethal force and end this quickly to prevent further loss of life.

The officer who was taking refuge behind the door of his patrol was now trying to climb into the car in an attempt to make an escape. It was too late as the engine was shot to pieces as a result of the spray of gunfire. As he pulled his body into the car right shoulder just became visible through what was left of the smashed windscreen. All three focused their attention on the spot and he disappeared below the dashboard into the foot well of the vehicle.

Musgrave quickly made the decision and calculated the risks before committing to the action. The three gunmen had emerged from the back of the van. Now he could clearly see that there was no one else in the van where the loading bay was part of the internal cabin where the front seats were. He could not make out any figures in the front seats nor in the van so it was improbable that Emily was being held in the van. In any case if she was going to be held hostage the logical place to keep her would be in the back of the van out of sight rather than in the front of the vehicle. There was an extremely small chance that he was wrong but with his years of experience it was a chance worth taking.

He almost forgot about the grey Audi had now been started by someone who must have been in the car already. Its front day running lights came on and the car began to speed forward. Grey smoke came from the tyres and a horrendous screeching noise filled the cul-du-sac. He tried to see if he could make out the face of the driver but it was just too far. All he could take in at this time was that there was more than one figure in the car. The other seemed to be moving quite frantically. Either they were trying to distract the driver or they had been hit by one of the stray rounds.

Another volley of gunfire made thudding sounds as they stuck into the bonnet, this time purposefully directed at his vehicle. "Waters, hold on to something."

He jammed his foot hard on the brakes and the car leached as the computers took over and applied the anti-lock braking system. Before the car came to a stop he stamped his foot down hard on the accelerator making the front of the car rise up as if it was caught on a riding wave. To their great surprise the car charged directly towards the three armed men. All three tried to focus their gunfire at the windscreen towards the driver's side position. They could not understand why any of their shots were not ending the vehicles charge towards them. The beast was approaching at full speed now and they were out of options.

Like rabbits caught in the headlights the three gunmen remained planted in their positions firing wildly at the car approaching them at speed and not able to reason why it was not coming to an abrupt stop or swerving to avoid the hail of bullets. He mounted the curb slightly and clipped his the nearside wing mirror on the corner of the stationary patrol car. He jolted the steering wheel to the right and as the car leaned to one side quickly reversed the steering wheel which now felt much lighter as the car swayed across to the other side. He pulled up the handbrake and heard the screeching of the tyres as the car glided across the driveway swinging the tail out towards the gunmen. There were three successive hits on against the side of the car as it made contact with each of the assailants, who were sent flying through the air.

The car came to a rest but there was no time to stop now, even with Sarah's profanity outburst. He pushed down hard on the accelerator to get after the grey Audi which was slipping away. "What, what are you doing?!" She shouted unable to control the fear in her voice.

He could feel the adrenaline in his system and he knew how to deal with it from his extensive training. He had a flashback to his first lesson on the skid pan during his advanced driver training. It was a day not too dissimilar to today. It was in the summer and despite the heat it was still a requirement for everyone to appear in full uniform. Sprinklers were gently spraying the surface of the concrete that they were about to be sliding on. The car that they were learning on was a Police Rover 827 V6 litre engine which had been stripped out specifically as a tuition car making it lighter than a fully kitted out version and therefore much faster. It was a sublime sophisticated car when compared to the Mark II Rover Metro 100 that the students there would be more familiar with as their everyday patrol car. The instructor gave an impressive demonstration of what the car was capable of achieving with strategic J-turns, road craft, analysing treat and risks, hazard observation, anti-ambush, hi-jack drills and defensive driving.

As soon as he was behind the steering wheel the instructor disappeared along with all the others in the car. It was him and the road ahead. He knew what the circuit was and what he had to do but he had to respect the car and feel everything about it to be able to master the skills of positioning the vehicle exactly where and how he wanted it. Nothing could take away that fear and excitement even with all of the years of experience that he had he was still surprised at how powerful the adrenaline rush was. He needed to remember how to channel and control it for the sake of his family. He calmly turned towards Waters and said, "Just some tactical contact, nothing more," as he said, tightening his grip on the steering wheel.

His car was just behind the Audi now he swung out as if to overtake and accelerated as he nudged the hind quarter of the grey bumper. As the two cars made contact there was a dull crumpling sound of mangled plastic. He slowed down seeing that the contact had made the Audi snake in its line of travel. The driver of the Audi over compensated to correct the car and it span out making the car come to a quick and safe stop.

Musgrave stopped his charge and both car were now facing one another. All routes were now blocked and there was nowhere else to escape to. Musgrave knew that he had already won but he could not get overly confident now as it was that moment of respite that things usually went wrong. He quickly got out of the car leaving Waters holding onto the door handle, hyperventilating and shaking. He drew his weapon, a Glock 34 with GTL 22 attachment light and laser pointer, from its concealed holster in a single action training it on the driver of the other car. At this point he knew he did not need to shout

out any instructions as he could see the palms of the driver clearly surrendering behind the steering wheel.

There was a clicking noise as the rear passenger door began to open slowly and a recognisable head of hair appeared just above the door sill. Followed by a short shriek, "Dad!" It was Emily getting out of the car first, but he could see that she was being held by a controlling hand which was on her arm guiding her direction and making sure that she could not get away.

Despite her efforts Sarah could not move. She was frozen to her seat watching the story unfold in front of her. She had slightly recovered now and was breathing more normally, but she could feel her heart beating a mile a minute. A tall man followed Emily out of the car, he was armed with a Beretta 92 Brigadier Inox which he now had trained at Emily's temple.

"Put your weapon down," Musgrave called across "Armed officers will be here any moment. You have no option but to surrender, now!"

There was an uneasy pause while the hostage-taker thought. Musgrave felt a bead of sweat trickle down his temple. He was expecting some sort of list of demands or at least some sort of rebuff remark but to his surprise the man let the gun fall in his hand so that it was no longer pointing at Emily. He kept his grip on Emily fearing that if he let her go now that Musgrave would simply shoot him. He carefully put the gun on the ground and kicked it across the tarmac towards Musgrave.

Emily broke free of the man's hold and ran across to her father standing behind him so that he could keep his gun trained on the suspect. She wanted to through her arms around her dad but realised this was not the time. There would be time for that later. Sarah got out of the car having composed herself. She asked Musgrave to cover her as she approached the man pulling out her handcuffs to arrest him. Surprisingly he did not put up any fuss at all as he was read his rights and was placed in the back of Musgraves car until a police van turned up to take him into custody.

When Elizabeth Musgrave arrived home from shopping the street had been cordoned off and there were several forensic officers studying the front of their house and the street. She looked horrified as she quickly looked around trying to ascertain what had happened. Suddenly she felt a warm embrace squeezing her ever so tightly. "Mum thank goodness you're home!" It had been some time since Emily had embraced her mother seeking such comfort. Elizabeth always the attentive parent kissed her on the forehead, cupping her face in her hands and telling her everything was going to be alright.

"I think it would be for the best if you two stay at your mother's tonight," Musgrave said to his wife placing a caring hand on her shoulder smiling.

"I need to find out who was behind this and I need to know that you are safe. I am assigning two officers Kevin and Megan who you already know from the christening last month to escort and keep watch for the next forty-eight hours. By then we will have those responsible in custody," he said reassuringly but not really believing it. Elizabeth agreed they packed some clothes into an overnight bag.

Emily gave him a big hug before she got in the car, "Thanks Dad for coming to save me." His heart froze as he was only really now beginning to realise how close he came to losing her. Before he could dwell on that Elizabeth kissed him goodbye and looked him in the eye. She had a way of communicating with him without speaking. Telling him to go do what he needed to do to make them safe but to remember he was Emily's dad and her husband and to make sure he came home too. "I love you," she finally said.

"Call me to let me know that you arrive there safely," Musgrave said holding the embrace for a few moments longer.

"You will probably hear from you own team before you hear it from me!" she chuckled.

"Ha, that is probably true, but I'd still rather hear it from you," he smiled knowing how to charm her.

As his family drove away Sarah approached Musgrave and questioned what was going to happen with their murder investigation from the airport. He thought for a moment and then proceeded to explain that he believed that they may be connected. He could not think why else anyone would take such bold action at this particular time unless someone wanted him to drop the case. This was not his style at all and would only strengthen his resolve.

His team were to set up shop in Barnet police station where the suspected kidnapper was being held. As Waters and Musgrave made their way to the station it seemed oddly quiet compared to the airport office that Waters was used to and the station that Musgrave was more familiar with. They entered the police station through the custody suite. Again this was rather quiet from what they were used to. There did not seem to be anyone there, Waters looked over the top of the raised desk and saw that there was a cup of tea resting on the table with some steam emanating from the milky surface indicating that it was still hot. There was a noise and some light footsteps. A large figure stood in the doorway from the custody suite to the office behind.

"Who are you and why should I care?" The delivery was said with some authority and old policing style from the 1970s. He was verging on overweight and wore a jumper that was slightly too tight. He had a three-striped pin on each epaulette indicating that he was one of the custody sergeants, and he held a file under one arm. His thin rectangular frameless glasses which were comparatively small against his other features. He was balding and what was left of his hair was a short whitening stubble around the back of his head. His face was drawn without expression, he was definitely due for retirement, and he had lost all respect for authority but considered the custody suite to be his domain which he ruled diligently.

"This is Inspector Sarah Waters and I am Detective Chief Inspector Hamilton Musgrave. You have a suspect here being held here under the Anti-terrorism Act which we would like to interview at your earliest convenience please." It was said more as a statement than a request. Musgrave wanted to fold his arms across this chest but thought it would send the message of a standoff.

The sergeant waded over towards to the desk which was just enough to protect himself against anyone who was not cooperating with them when being processed in custody. He fiddled around with something things on the desk outside of their vision and picked up the cup of tea and took a slurp while typing into the keyboard with his free hand. It seemed to take an age as one finger typing broke the silence of the custody room. There was a slight pause in the typing before he sucked his teeth making a 'tsk' noise. "If you want to speak to him it certainly won't be 'ere. You'll have to go somewhere else." He sat back down in his chair and looked off into the middle distance trying to avoid eye contact with either of them.

"What do you mean somewhere else?" Waters almost shouted at him as she leaned across the sergeant's desk trying to get him to engage or at least wake his ideas up. He leaned forward studying her with a blank look in his eyes, not saying a word and produced a biro pen from his desk and pointed the end of the lid towards Waters' elbow, which was resting on the counter, and quickly flicked it upwards as an indication for her to not lean on the counter. He knew that she was a senior officer but as the custody sergeant this was his domain with admin, paperwork and pencil pushing. She was enraged and wanted to drag the guy over the desk by the scruff of his neck and make him realise this was the twenty-first century and he would just have to live with female authority. She took a breath and consoled herself that any resistance to this philistine would only be met with a wall of unashamed insolence and obstructiveness. She lifted her elbow and stood back. He leaned back in his chair before explaining that "The prisoner was transferred to someone else's custody."

Musgrave tried to resist the urge but found that he had already put his hands on his hips and was about to bark orders at this snivelling low life. "On whose bloody authority was the transfer made? I'm leading this investigation. Think carefully before you answer."

The sergeant took this to be a questioning of his abilities. "All the correct paperwork is there. Signed, sealed and delivered."

"Let's see," he leaned forward in his seat looking down his nose at the screen in front of him.

"There it is, certainly unusual, released into the custody of Arthur Williams under the Armed Forces Act 2006. It would seem that your prisoner is tied into the military and is now with the Regimental Provost." He sat back in his chair and folded his arms as if to supress any further conversation.

"Do you have any further details, how can we contact this Arthur Williams?" Waters pressed patiently.

"Not within my remit. You're the inspector, I'd suggest you go and investigate. All of the paperwork is as it should be," he said as he took another slurp from his tea.

Musgrave placed his thumb and index finger on Waters' elbow in a claw-like fashion gently squeezing it to get her attention. "We've got enough" he whispered into her ear before heading towards the door. Waters in pursuit choosing to offer no leave to the desk sergeant.

"Is that it, you're just going to let this be taken over by some military outfit?" Waters called after Musgrave as she pushed open the door in temper.

Musgrave span on his heels and in a venomous tone, through gritted teeth replied "Are you insane? That bastard tried to take my daughter at gunpoint to get to me. I want him hung, drawn and quartered."

Taking a deep breath and composing himself he relaxed before continuing in a more professional manner. "First we need to find out who this Arthur Williams is and there is only one person who can answer that question."

"Who would that be" Waters asked.

"The head of Military Strategic Intelligence more commonly known as the Secret Intelligence Service or MI6. Major-General Lucinda Greening."

Chapter Six

Clifton could see the faces looking up at him followed by calls questioning who was up there. From this angle it was possible for him to see them, but for them only to just make out a figure through the grating where the torch had fallen from.

He was about to call out an apology before he noticed some movement of two of the five people below breaking away from the group and heading towards the cat ladders which lead up to this mezzanine level. He got up from his crouched position and walked briskly rather than running, considering that if he was caught then if he was running it would definitely look suspicious, but if he walked away he could always argue that he did not hear the calls from below with all of the noise from the background machinery. The room was a typical plant room. It was very warm and had a chemical smell that wafted in the air. It was one of those that you could not immediately identify but lingered at the back of the throat even after one had left the room.

The room was filled with brightly coloured pipes of varying sizes. It resembled something which could only be described as a cross between a scaled down amusement water park with all the multi-coloured pipe rides, and an engineering room on an aircraft carrier filled with various vessels. Large blue circular steering wheels like values were fixed to the side of the pipes. The pipes were not quite large enough to fit a person in but they were not far from that range. The dull rumble of the green painted water pumps hummed away in the background, constantly adjusting to the requirements of the building. The room was alive with noise and the sound of moving pressures.

The warm water that was returning to the plant area was fed through a large heat exchanger container. This was a device that would transfer the heat from the returning hot water to the cooler domestic hot water. The exchange of the heat meant that the cooling process of the returning hot water was less wasteful as the heat from that returning water was used to heat the domestic hot water for the campus. The waters were separated and ran in twin tubes which increased the exposure of the surface area of the exchange plates making it highly efficient. Because the liquids remained separated and were never in direct contact there was no further water treatment required to the domestic hot water which could then be used throughout the wider campus site.

The system worked very much like a car engine with the circulating engine coolant flowing though the cars radiator coils and the surrounding cooler air flowing over the coils, cooling the coolant while also using the waste heat to warm the incoming air during the cooler months of the year.

Clifton could see someone who had just made it up to the mezzanine level as he ducked in between the small gap between a blue and red pipe. There was a small niche there with the tank for the water dosing behind him. It was green in colour and was held together with several silver rivets. He pressed himself up between the pipe and the tank. It was necessary to turn his head slightly to the left as the peak of his hard hat was just too long to fit in the space. His hands rested on the pipe and he could feel the energy of the water vibrating within the pipe. It must have been under intense pressure. If there was a single weakness in the system, one joint that was not quite sealed, water would always find its way through and the compartment would be flooded. When it was requested in the initial design for the room to be tanked to a height of one and a half metres Clifton could not believe that much water could be lost before someone realised it.

It was extremely hard to hear, especially in his hiding place which seemed to magnify the noise from all directions. He wanted to peek around the corner of the pipe to see if the people who were investigating the dropped torch would have gone yet. He could not be sure and it was too risky for him to stick his head around the corner now. He considered his options. In reality he was not that far from another access ladder which would drop him in the corner of the water treatment room. He could use the various tanks, panels and pipework to duck behind. The only problem was how to get out of his current hiding place without anyone noticing.

The gap between the tank and the pipe where he was currently hiding was very tight but if he stood up straight, took off his hard hat and twisted himself as much as he could he was able to force himself between the narrow space. He had seen people doing something similar with caving, a pastime where people would move through naturally occurring caves and crevices to an organised waypoint or destination and then retrace their footsteps back through. It was quite a dangerous hobby to the untrained person who had not prepared correctly or lacked the necessary experience. Clifton then started to go into a panic thinking about small spaces and becoming crushed between the two great masses. He could feel his heart rate suddenly begin to race and he started to become a bit less careful dragging himself through catching his watch face on the pipe. He bought up his trailing leg too quickly and caught his knee cap hard on a protruding seam of the water tank. The pain shot up his thigh instantly. He bit his lip and closed his eyes. Trying to calm himself down. He began to think about the claustrophobic train carriage again with the people pushing and shoving to get on. A calming voice spoke to him from inside. 'C'mon Clifton stop being so silly. You've been in worse places than this. Think of the coast. Think of a beach. You are standing on that beach, looking out at the horizon. It is a warm day and you can see the sun and a gentle breeze picking up the tops of the waves. You are safe here. You are safe.'

As if someone had flicked on a light switch, Clifton was feeling much better. He was able to press on and fought his way towards the cat ladder without further incident. Placing his feet each side of the ladder and cupping his hands on the side rails he slid quietly to the bottom unnoticed by anyone on the mezzanine.

It was a way of descending fixed ladders very quickly which was strictly against any health and safety guidance. He had come by the technique from seeing it in films and replicated it many times from when he used to work behind the scenes during school productions.

He was never one of the students to be selected for any of the main roles especially with his lack of self-confidence and remembering lines. He certainly was no actor, but he did used to really enjoy the being part of the wider production and working behind the scenes. He was in his element. Behind the scenes was quite literally another world of architectural trickery and magic of stage design with folding sets, trap doors and catwalks across the main stage.

He used to view everything from his vantage point in the control booth set above the left wing. From there he could see all that was taking place on and off the stage, as well as having a fine mesh screen porthole which allowed him to look out into the audience and see their reactions to the show. It was another world backstage, far more dramatic than what was being played out on the actual stage below. It was often the case that something would go wrong. Being a practical sort of person the responsibility for dealing with it quickly, so that 'the show could go on', rested with him.

Before long he was in the electrical room where all of the uninterruptible power source, or UPS for short, was housed. The UPS system was setup to protect computer equipment from a sudden loss of power and sudden shut down during a power outage or loss. Like all financial institution data centres, MyLife created data centres had had to be completely reliable. It would be unacceptable to have a system that went down and half the world not be able to access their banking details, as such all data centres have built in reliance with redundancy power protection. Depending on what they considered the risk allocation was assigned to the facility would determine what N+ (number plus) would be required. In this instance MyLife went for N2 which meant in the case of a mains power failure or loss there were at least two additional back-up systems meaning that the risk of non-operation through any critical event was highly unlikely.

The two systems relied on a bank of batteries known as a static UPS system which were constantly on standby should the worst happen. The single batteries, which were a similar size to that of a car battery, were set into shelving racking five tiers high which was just enough to be accessible for change over when the batteries needed to be switched out. These batteries would kick in immediately if there was any electrical fluctuation in the mains power. Even with a room full of batteries the stopwatch was ticking to restore power as the battery system was only a band aid to support the system for a short time giving time for the generators to fire up and get up to speed to power the data centre off grid. In an idea scenario it would take less than two minutes but the reality is that in an emergency situation nothing takes the time that it is supposed to, so the UPS system was set to allow full battery support for up to fifteen minutes. This would allow an engineer to go and manually start the generator should it have failed to start automatically.

This room was alive with the buzzing of electrical panels, switchgear and batteries. The nature of DC power was quite dangerous and there were warning signs posted around the room cautioning of arc flashes. Thankfully they were not that common but it was not unheard of and if someone were to be standing in front of a panel which was about to flash then the likelihood would be that they would not survive it with temperatures being able to reach 19,000 degrees centigrade at the arc terminals. The huge amount of energy released during the fault vaporises metal and other material, a blinding light and makes a deafening noise and sends blast wave in all directions sending hot shrapnel firing in all directions.

In the next compartment sat the engine coupled UPS system which, like the static UPS system, provided short term power but with the addition of a generator attached would allow for longer running periods. This system was their redundancy should the static UPS system fail to work for any reason. These 'rotary' systems as they are known by from the flywheel energy storage. Typically this type of system is not really known outside of the United States however being an American founded company MyLife had insisted on the technology which make up only 4% of the use of rotary backup systems in the data centre industry. The only real benefit of the rotary system was the space it could be installed in verses the rows and rows of static batteries it takes to store the same amount of power. Most clients were put off by the ongoing down time for maintenance of the rotary systems such as changing out a ball bearing. However a rotary system, if properly maintained, was able to sustain a life cycle of thirty plus years, unlike a battery which has a much shorter life cycle before needing to be replaced.

Clifton made his way out of the live rooms and found himself once again in a corridor space but he could now see the point of presence room that he had been heading towards. It almost looked as though there was a glow around the door frame. He could see someone approaching the door dressed in the MyLife technician's overalls. As the technician held his card up to the card reader Clifton stood next to him and wished him a good morning with a nod of his head maintaining eye contact.

He was hoping that his old trick from his university days would still work. His class had been told that if there was anywhere that they wanted to go all they had to do was look the part. As long as you had a white hat, clipboard, high visibility vest and had the confidence to pull it off it would be seldom that anyone would question why you were there. Ironically they would probably be more concerned about looking like they were doing something important in your presence.

The old trick paid off and the technician held the door open for him and he entered the Point of Presence Colocation room where he would need to complete his task and plant the device he had been entrusted with this far.

Once in the room the technician waited to see where Clifton went. Clifton stood there admiring the array of flashing lights and put his arms behind his back and turned to look at the technician. It was now a waiting game to see who would lose their nerve first and blink. Fortunately for Clifton, the technician folded rather quickly wishing him well and if there was anything he needed to just come and find him.

Clifton did a perimeter sweep of the room and could see that technicians were working in each row. He looked around the room as saw a vacant cable ladder leading up to the ceiling. A lot of future infrastructure had been installed already to make imminent installations easier. He looked around and no one was paying any attention to him, too busy with their patch panels. He climbed up the ladder and into the hot air plenum above the ceiling. This would allow him to drop down to a rack from above and hopefully unseen.

He crawled across the ceiling grid framework which he knew was capable of supporting up to one hundred and fifty kilograms per square metre although that was just the grid. The ceiling tiles around him were not structural and would be able to be pushed out with one false move.

Clifton eased himself down from the return air plenum ductwork and into the hot aisle containment. He managed to swing one foot towards the server cabinet and managed to get a footing there. He drew up his other foot towards the server cabinet with it flashing lights and succeeded to make the same connection. His fingertips were beginning to cut into the metal frame work of the suspended ceiling. The site gloves that he was wearing offered limited protection with his weight pulling on the edge of the metal framing.

He felt a bead of sweat run down from the plastic strap of his hard hat down the side of his temple. The towelling head band inside the hat was saturated but keeping the sweat out from his eyes. Dropping out of the ductwork had not made it any cooler and he was still being heated up by a constant twenty-six degree wind. Back inside the room he noticed that his safety glasses were beginning to get foggy with the condensation forming. He pushed them slightly further away from his face so that some of the air passing would clear his vision. He let go of the grid with one hand and in a single movement swung himself onto the top of the cabinet against the side of the panel which divided the cold and hot aisle. He felt the warmth of the metallic finish through his clothing. It was not as hot as the metal of the ductwork had been but it was still uncomfortable. He lay still on top of the row of cabinets taking in shallow breaths.

Listening and waiting for the presence of any footsteps or movement from below. There was some distant rustling which he was not sure of. He decided that it was the echo of the indirect air cooler above him whirling around creating the whirlwind in the room. He slowly and cautiously brought his sleeve up to his eye level and detached the USB connector from the cufflink. Turning slowly onto his left side he reached down the face of the server cabinet exploring the ports with is fingers. Each seemed to be uniform in size and too large for a USB connection.

He wanted to look over the edge so that he was not feeling for the right connection. As he looked over the edge he felt the tightness of the plastic band of his hat begin to slide across his wet hair. He could not grab his hat as to do so he would have dropped the device and his left arm was pinned beneath him. Flicking his head backwards the hat rolled off onto the top of the cabinet spinning slightly round showing the mark on the front where he had hit his head inside the duct. It has left a black mark on the hat and scratched it pretty deeply.

He concentrated on his breathing again, concentrating on the task at hand; he couldn't afford any more distractions. He continued to scout the face of the server amongst the array of ports and cables below him. Carefully holding back a purple cable he found a USB port and quickly placed the blue gem inside letting the purple cables fall naturally back into place concealing the device. He turned back over so that he was again lying on his back and staring at the suspended ceiling.

He waited for a few moments to allow his heart to stop racing. It felt as though the cabinet below him was joining in with the rhythm that was thumping in his ears. He sat up and dangled his legs over the side of the cabinet deciding whether to use the servers as a makeshift ladder or risk jumping the two-point-seven metre drop. As he replaced the hard hat on his head the dampness of the band pressing against his forehead. He adjusted the strap at the back to tighten it as he decided to jump. He thought back to the days of jumping over his family houses' back gate during the summer months as a short cut back to the old house which was only six foot high when he was sixteen. He remembered that landing and bending his knees would soften the impact. If he did not soften the impact not only would he certainly injure himself but landing heavily, especially with steel toe capped site boots, would surely alert any technicians working in the room or worse crash through the raised floor plate.

He took a deep breath and held it as he made his leap. As he fell through the air he lifted his arms in an attempt to slow down his decent. He kept focus on the floor anticipating the moment of impact as he controlled his exhaling breath. His toes made contact with the floor first as the rolled his foot so that his heel was now parallel to the floor tile. He bent his knees and swooped his arms in as if to give lift. He remained in a crouched position for a short time listening out for any noise of approaching footsteps. His landing was faultless as the impact has been muted to such a high degree.

He stood up quickly sliding across the floor tile so that his back was up against the nearest server cabinet. He remained still, listened and heard the approach of footsteps on the laminated floor tiles coming from the row of cabinets opposite him. He had forgotten to breathe in with the stress and was beginning to get light headed and seeing stars. He took in three short sharp breaths to return his vision and awareness.

He looked frantically around for an escape route. He was not able to climb through one of the incomplete server racks as the cables and lights flickered from the active server blades. Each end of the hot aisle had a door which was masked with opaque glazing allowing a shadow of light through but would not disclose the location of the approaching footsteps. It would have been a fifty-fifty chance using the doors as an exit route.

He was running out of time and needed to make a decision fast. Like a train approaching the station the footsteps were becoming louder and nearer.

He looked up at the opening in the ceiling to the return plenum his heart racing. He knew that he would not be able to scramble back up there in time and in silence before the person was there. He looked down at his feet and at the square tiles which made up the raised access flooring below him. He got down on his knees and started to pull on the corner of one of the tiles. He managed to prise the edge up just enough to get some form of leverage. He knew he could not hold it on its own as the noise of the cold air below began to make the de-pressurising sound resonating in the hot aisle. He put one hand into the pocket of his high visibility vest and pulled out his steel pen and rested it across below the corner of the tile at forty-five degrees. He quickly went to work on the opposite corner and managed to pull it up from the supporting pedestals. Opening the tile up so that it created a square window into the darkness of the cold void he saw the handle of the door at the end of the row begin to turn as he jumped into the void, pulling the tile across the floor and aligning it to its previous position.

There was a sudden jerk and click as the tile was sucked back into position with the differences in pressure. He was alone now and in complete darkness. He could feel the difference in temperature here. Inside the hot aisle it had been about twenty-six degrees but in this void it was approaching ten degrees. The noise of the indirect cooling equipment was deafening, all that could be heard was the constant cold wind being sucked through the floor cavity.

He was pleased that he had covered his escape so well. He looked around to see if there was any way of orientating himself in the darkness. Reaching out he felt a pedestal which was supporting the tile above. They were set out in rows six hundred by twelve hundred millimetres forming a metal array of posts below the floor. He could work out his north from south by stretching to the next pedestal, if it was twelve hundred he knew that he was facing east or west. He felt the vibration of the footsteps in the tile above. There was a brief pause which lasted about thirty seconds but felt like a lifetime to Clifton.

He dared not move for fear that any movement would create a detectable sound within the void. He made himself into a ball inside the darkness in anticipation for the footsteps to continue onwards. The droplets of sweat which had been running down his spine were now cooling in the cold place. The towelling inside his hard hat felt cold and wet. He was rapidly becoming cold.

He thought that he could hear footsteps but could not tell if they were real or not. He studied the sound in the darkness and closed his eyes in concentration, any noise was far too quiet to detect which direction they were coming from or going to, or even if it was footsteps that he thought that he could hear.

He could not take the risk of being caught in the room so he began lurching through the darkness beneath the floor void. The coldness of the space was beginning to take its toll within a few minutes as Clifton scrambled between the pedestals. It was difficult to manoeuvre in such a small space. From the floor above him to the concrete slab below him was a mere metre. What made it all the more difficult was the constant blasting of cold air which against his warm skin felt like ice. He crouched down so that his knees were tucked up against his chest and he reached out with his hands grabbing the pedestals to steady himself and to navigate through the maze in the darkness. To move he shuffled his feet and made slow progress towards the edge of the maze of pedestals. Out of his peripheral vision he could see some form of light from the floor above. He saw the shadow of movement gliding up the line of supply grilles to the cold aisles above.

This must be a technician working in the room, he thought to himself. Although he could see the dancing of the shadow above he could not hear the accompanying footfalls above the din of the background fans whirling away. He had reached the end wall as he felt the solid concrete retaining wall in front of him. If the room had been installed to the drawings that were in his head he should be positioned just below the end of the cold aisle near to the exit door into the corridor. He knew that he could not rely on his ears nor could he truly rely on the dancing shadows from the grilles as they only would show movement if someone was walking directly over them. He knew that it would be game over if he was discovered here by anyone, it was more critical now than ever that he was not detected. How could he know what was going on top side when he was blind and deaf below the floor?

He shivered as his core temperature began to drop. Clifton knew that he had to escape this prison within the void and soon, before hypothermia set in and he would be trapped there unable to move.

He placed his fingers carefully on the tiles above him, studying the panel until he could trace the joint line of the tile edge with his fingertips. Placing his hands in the opposite corners of the six hundred millimetre square. He could feel vibrations like he had before in the pedestals of footfalls in a rhythm. There was a pause like before for around thirty seconds and then the vibrations seemed to carry on. Clifton was unsure whether to attempt moving or not. Staring at the tile in the darkness he waited a few seconds more and then tried to listen for any sound by pushing his ear up again the tile joint. He could not hear anything and returned to his crouching position with his hands raised on the corners of the tile.

"It is now or never," he thought to himself as he pushed on the corners of the tile. His arms shook with the strain but the tile only moved a few millimetres. The pressure difference seemed to be too great. He took a few deep breaths beginning to feel exhausted. He was used to running in the mornings covering about four miles every other day and going for a prolonged six mile run on a Sunday. Every time he went for a run he was competing with himself and tried harder every time to improve. Sometimes on the longer runs he would get to a point of feeling exhausted and would want to stop and take a break but found that he had a hidden reserve which he could call upon to complete the circuit.

He was now relying on that same reserve to save his life. He positioned himself so that the nape of his neck was hard up against the back of the tile. He raised his back and balanced his knees and began to try and stand up against the tile. He took in a deep breath as his body prepared itself. Then he gave the push and the tile started to lift as it came up he let his breath go through his clenched teeth in a shushing noise. He pushed the tile aside as the noise of the void began to fill the cold aisle. He placed his hands either side of him and heaved his body out of the void. The heat of the room hit him like a solid wall.

Every part of his body was aching and crying out for rest but he knew that he had to act quickly. He slid the tile back into position and there was a muffled click noise as the tile was sucked back into place.

Clifton noticed the distant silence of this room compared to the roar of air inside the void. He hurriedly checked himself and looked for the door which was just to his left as he had remembered from the drawings.

He rose to his feet and started to see stars and his ears began to thump. He took in three deep breaths to clear away the light-headedness before leaning forward forcing his body to put one foot in front of the other towards escape. He checked the push bar which was active. If he used it now to operate the door the security contacts would detect that the door had been opened without authorisation. Clifton could hear the sound of approaching footsteps and could make out the purple uniform of the technician through the flashes of movement through the gaps of the server racks ahead of him. He had to act fast.

He fiddled with the zip on his jacket trying to break the finger pull away but it was secured well. He then scrambled in his pockets feeling for anything metallic that he might be able to use, and then he found a paper clip in the pocket of this site high visibility vest. He bent the clip into an S shape before bending it further to create a flat folded edge and an angle to hold it in place on the edge of the door leaf. He placed it carefully in the gap between the door leaf and the door frame sliding it back gently until he found where the door contact device had been positioned. He could feel the slightly bevelled edges of the device and secured the clip in between the door leaf and the frame, hoping that there would be enough metal in the folded section to fool the contact that there was still a magnetic connection and make the contact believe that the door was still closed.

He gently pushed on the door bar closing his eyes and saying a silent prayer. He felt the latch retract into the door leaf. He twisted and turned as he went through the door holding the lever handle down on the outside of the door afraid that the door would latch back with a indicative click alerting the technician to the recent departure. He made sure that he eased the door closed silently as the door rested back on the seals around the frame cushioning the sound. Gradually he released the lever handle until he felt the metallic connection of the lock latching into the strike plate.

A sense of relief swept over him as he rested his head against the door. "You can't go in t'here, it's been handed over!" A voice sounded down the corridor. Clifton froze unsure what to do next. Should he try to run or bluff his way out. His heart was pounding in his chest and his ears were thumping. His muscles ached and he knew that he could be easily identified here, so running was out of the question, subsequently he chose to bluff. Looking in the direction of the voice he put on his showman smile and said that he was just checking that there was no play in the handle and that all of the doors were being checked for the same reason. As the architect this was his job to do. It had been pointed out on a previous site visit by the client's representative that that a couple of the doors had faulty handles which meant that all of them needed to be checked for quality assurance prior to hand over.

The authoritative figure drew nearer and Clifton made out the security writing on his high visibility jacket. "Just checkin'," the security guard said, "we've been told t' be extra diligent now that the early release rooms have been handed over. We can't jus' have anyone walkin' around ya know!"

"Of course," Clifton replied he purposefully started to feel around the frame, appearing to be inspecting the edges of the architrave against the flushness of the wall. The security guard left and he breathed a sigh of relief knowing that his task was complete. He had done what had been asked of him and he was out of the playing field. He continued slowly down the corridor taking photographs of incomplete fire stopping around the cable tray, penetrations in the walls and incomplete trolley wall protection on his mobile phone camera which he would typically do on such site visits.

After all this exertion he decided that it was time to have something to eat. He had not eaten anything since the early hours of this morning. He would not normally have a big breakfast before flying for fear of a turbulent flight. Normally when he arrived on site in the morning the smell of fresh bacon being cooked in the canteen was enough to tempt him to have a cooked breakfast around ten o'clock. This was usually a very filling full Irish breakfast; two rashers of succulent bacon, scrambled egg, toasty hash browns, delicious pork and herb sausages, plump mushrooms, rich baked beans, black pudding and white pudding, which made it an Irish breakfast. As much as he had wanted to indulge in this appetising milestone, today he needed to remain focused. Today he needed all his wits about him. He could not afford the tiredness that a filling meal brought to distract him this morning.

His mouth began to water thinking about what he might have for lunch today. On his last visit they had ham hock which had been cooked most delicately with a light mashed potatoes, thick comforting gravy, mini-carrots and peas. He made his way out of the building towards the external plant area which wrapped itself around the perimeter of the building. The cladding around this area acted to screen the plant equipment from the neighbouring town but it also acted as an anti-climb fence. The small openings in the expanded mesh would allow air to permeate through but anything else would struggle. The material started its life as a single sheet of aluminium and would have slits cut into the surface forming a regularised pattern. The sheet would then be fed into a machine that would effectively stamp the profile into the metal sheet turning a flat two dimensional material into a ridged three dimensional screening material. The longer opening was approximately fifty millimetres long and 10 millimetres wide. The shape formed an angle which encouraged rain to drip off. What made this material anti-climb thought was the razor sharp edges that the forming process left behind. Beautiful to look at as it reflected its silver high-tech face towards the sun but cruelly vindictive if mis-treated.

He soon found his way to the safe route back to the site hut which had been designated with red and white barriers. At the gate he swiped his pass card and the light went green while the sounder buzzed. The gate rotated allowing him through its spokes. The smell from the canteen grew stronger with every step as Clifton began removing his Personal Protection Equipment in anticipation. First went the gloves into his pocket, he let his glasses dangle on their tethering strap and removed his hat holding it beneath his left armpit resting his fingers on the brim of the hat. The canteen was packed out as usual and the noise of numerous conversations happening simultaneously brought the room to life. All different hard hats were seen there and it was the easiest way of identifying the various trades. Clifton got into the queue and squinted as he tried to read the menu at a distance. The options today were pretty good, in fact by most site canteen standards the food here was excellent.

He picked up a tray from the rack. Wiping his hand on his vest he mumbled to himself, "One day someone will invent something that will actually dry trays before they are stacked and they'll be a millionaire!" The electrician behind him in the queue gave a hearty chuckle as he too selected a tray and shook off the water droplets. Clifton looked at the plates laid out in front of him and went for the mincemeat, mashed potato, broccoli and carrots with gravy. The plate was rather hot in his hands and he quickly placed in on the tray taking care not to spill any of the precious gravy. The electrician behind him went for the same but seemed to have no problems with the heat of the plate. Clifton raised an eyebrow unconsciously.

"Sure ma' hands be made of asbestos!" followed by more hearty laughter. His accent seemed slightly different to Clifton and he was having trouble trying to place which part of Ireland he was from before he realised that it was actually a board Scottish accent. He laughed along as well in his humorous chuckle. As they shuffled down the servery taking something for dessert and finally a drink from the last counter they talked about the weather and how uncharacteristically dry it had been. This summer it had been particularly dry in Ireland, so much so that on site to keep the dust down from the surrounding neighbours a tanker truck which was typically used to carry petroleum rather than water was sent around three times a day in order to spray clean water over the site roads to prevent passing vehicles throwing the dried mud which was now dust into the air.

Chapter Seven

Musgrave pulled up into the parking bay and they both got out of the car into the dimly lit underground carpark. With a flash of the indicators the car was locked and the wing mirrors began to fold closed. The arrangement of cars and equipment was generous given the low ceiling height, which made the space seem somehow smaller and more confined than it really was. It was very warm in there despite the galvanised metal rectangular ducts whispering cooler air into the space, and seemed to retain some dampness, despite the ventilation, which you would associate with any subterranean environment.

To the corner of the garage there was a secure area made from black cages which housed two banks of black metal lockers, which were further secured with a combination locks. Waters wondered if these contained a small arsenal of weaponry. Chipboard shelving racking made up the rest of the space. There were metal warning signs propped up against the cage walls and some traffic cones stacked in the corner. The shelves were adorned with a series of black canvass holdall bags and other kinds of containers. They only identifiable markings were made on the facing frame of the shelves which showed an MP code printed in black writing on a white sticky back label which would identify to those only with the knowledge what each receptacle contained.

There were two white transit vans parked there which looked as though they had seen better days but on closer inspection the new tyres with ample tread showed that these were actually very well maintained vehicles. The garage was a mixture of some rather unremarkable cars; a navy Volvo V60 with a 2014 plate, a grey Ford Mondeo with a 66 plate and a black LTI London taxi and other more notable such as the silver Mercedes CLS Coupé and Porsche S which was capable of achieving zero to sixty-two miles per hour within four-point-three seconds. There was also a collection of motorcycles which included a deep blue and black BMW F800 GT.

Someone had been very specific in the selection of the motorcycles, very possibly someone who had an affinity with them as it was clear to see the artistry that had gone into crafting the designs of the machines, it was not just purely about an engine and two wheels. Waters could see that all of the vehicles had been purposefully selected to get around London either extremely quickly or as secretly as possible without drawing any unwanted attention.

Waters called out to Musgrave who was just ahead of her searching for the exit, "You have quite an impressive garage here. It rather puts ours to shame. All I have available to me is three outdated cars, two of which are ex-highway Volvo V70 estates which have seen better days. You must get the very best of the best with your budget!" Musgrave looked over his shoulder and smiled politely without confirming or denying.

The underground carpark on Bury Street was accessed through a discreet bronze-coloured metal door which was panelised into solid sections for security purposes. The array of panels made the door far more secure than a single piece alone. It was crash rated should anyone attempt to break into the garage by ram raiding the doors.

The door was positioned between two opulent office buildings. Neither of which could lay claim to it although it blended in seamlessly with the streetscape. To the untrained eye the door appeared to be some sort of delivery or service door to one of those adjacent buildings. The doors were permanently closed and would only be activated with the approach of one of the cars which had transmitters to signal to the door to open. From the outside it was almost invisible, camouflaged in plain sight.

There was an alternative entrance to the building on Jermyn Street which was accessed from a sunken staircase to a basement passageway. At ground level there was a retail unit which for the past seven years had been a rather fine sculpture gallery showcasing the best of British sculpture. Musgrave decided to take Waters around to ever so slightly grander main entrance on Piccadilly.

They passed a street cleaner who was busily picking up discarded cups and paper plates that lay around with a pair of litter pickers. His cart was stopped at an angle just outside Patisserie Valerie with all the cakes and pastries displayed on several tiered shelves, tempting passers-by into the shop to sample the delights.

It was turning into a warm day and Waters could feel the heat of the sun on her shoulders. The noise of everything around her was exciting. The traffic slowly laboured by, there was a mix of black taxis, silver private hire cars and buses. Waters observed that all of the buses were the new bright red Routemaster buses which had replaced many of the Enviro400 buses. The new bus had the stylistic curved backs which followed the curled staircase that hugged the bus designed by Heatherwick Studio with Wrightbus and Transport of London.

As they passed Pret A Manger people were seated outside at small coffee tables huddled over their mobile phones while their coffees and food laid unattended on the table. What was it with everyone not being able to leave their phone alone for ten minutes? She thought to herself

Waters brush her hair away from her face and commented. "You don't see many bins in London do you?"

"Sorry?" Musgrave looked puzzled.

"I mean anywhere else you would have bins on the street but in London people just discard rubbish onto the street for someone else to pick up. It's not right."

"Most of the public bins were removed in London in the early 90s following the Bishopsgate bombing. It was thought that post boxes and bins would be ideal targets for detonating an improvised device as the casings would add to the shrapnel. Besides when you look down this street what do you see?"

"People," Water muttered.

"Exactly, now imagine if there were bins every couple of hundred yards. Litter would pile up quicker than it could be emptied."

Guy was standing outside the entrance with a mobile phone in one hand and a cigarette in the other. He was looking vacantly out towards the passing traffic. "Good afternoon, Guy."

"Hello sir." Quickly dropping the cigarette and grinding it beneath his loafers into the pavement below.

"Do you remember the email about where staff are allowed to smoke?"

"Yes sir, sorry sir, I was on my way back from taking a statement on the Rogers case and well I thought I would have finished it before I got to the office."

"Well I'd rather you did not loiter around the entrance. The smoke gets sucked up into the ventilation system and stinks the whole place out, not to mention you could set off the smoke detectors and have the whole building evacuated because of your inconsiderate habit!"

"It won't happen again."

"See to it that it doesn't. Now tell me more about this statement that you were taking on the Rogers case…" They disappeared into the lobby. The entrance was modest against its backdrop. When studied independently the reinforced doors would have stopped all but Attila the Hun. The solid looking ballistic rated glazing above the door frame displayed the address in vinyl print applied to the glazing. Inside the lobby were another set of doors which required a palm print to open. The lobby was monitored by the watchful eye of Craig the building's concierge.

Musgrave walked over to Craig manoeuvring himself so that Waters followed. "I have a guest that I would like to sign in please."

"Certainly sir. If I could just ask Madam to fill out this form and sign?" He handed an iPad through the pass-through tray for Waters to complete.

He was very traditional in his attire choosing to wear a morning suit with a duck egg blue tie fashioned into the most impressive St. Andrew knot with a matching waistcoat. His jacket had the traditional golden crossed keys on its lapels with a small rectangular golden name tag which read Craig Andrews Foxglove Estates.

Not much was really known about Mr Andrews' background. Musgrave had suspected that he had served in the forces. As he had a certain discipline which most military personnel carry throughout their lives. He could not think of a time that he had not seen Andrews manning the desk. It was almost as if he was a Porter like the sort that you would find at the Colleges at Oxford and Cambridge, living in their Porters' Lodge. Or in this case Foxglove House. He was someone that you felt that you could go to when you needed a council and for it to remain strictly confidential.

His skill was in anticipating and preventing problems. Musgrave had realised long ago that there were never any issues or problems brought to him from Andrews. This was the only office that he had worked in where there had not been some sort of problem, protest or incident whereby he was called upon to assemble officers to assist at the reception. He believed very much in the old philosophy that if someone does their job well, you would not even notice it was being done and that very much summed up Andrews.

Musgrave and Waters along with their senior team leads were collected around one of the standing break out spaces in the open plan office. The décor that surrounded them evoked an abstinent atmosphere. The offices had state of the art equipment and had only been refurbished within the last two years but in an attempt modernise the offices it in fact made it a very cold space with loss of character. The walls were plain matte white, glazed office partitions flanked the left-hand side of the space. The frosted glass bands made these rooms private for meetings, interviews and formal discussions but did allowed some natural light from outside to filter through into the main space which was a semi-atrium space being two storey with a flying bridge crossing on the mezzanine level which was home to the senior officers. Rows of white laminate desks with multiple monitors were set out in rows no longer than four to an island. This was a modern concept as it was said that the long rows that were used before were not conducive to an efficient environment. At the end of each island of desks there was a break out space where colleagues could have impromptu meetings using the digital displays fixed to flexible arms which came out of the desks.

What made the space more restrained was the dark grey carpet which was selected as it helped to disguise the highly trafficked areas and spilt coffee. The central aisle which was delineated with a black corridor with two royal blue thin parallel lines, ironically nicknamed the thin blue lines. Anyone who was foolish enough to trespass beyond the blue lines with their files, bags or boxes were treated as antisocial miscreants. The volume of the space was accentuated by the exposed shiny metal deck soffit which reflected some of the light from the lighting array which hung at least a meter and a half below the ceiling.

The concept design of the open plan office was that it would be fully adaptable to be able to serve as and when cases came along which would require larger or smaller teams. The space could be re-modulated in several options to suit their requirements. As a two height space the major problem was the acoustics of the space.

It was difficult to talk on a phone call without being able to hear local conversation being picked up in the background. In other places this was dealt with by partitioning the workstations however there had been feedback that these spaces felt too enclosed for the sharing of ideas and that it played a negative role in preventing successful team bonding.

As a result there were no fixed screens between the desks here except for low dividers which allowed the dual monitor screen arms to be fixed to. This meant that the acoustics had to be treated in a different way to prevent reverberation and crosstalk.

Soft room dividers were the answer which, as with the rest of the space, were fully adaptable. The modular pyramids dividers which formed the total screen was suspended on an overhead track system and could be moved around to suit any new configuration of the open plan space. Its main purpose was to deal with sound diffusion so that sound was disturbed enough to avoid echoes.

Unfortunately some officers took to using the acoustic screens as pin boards covering them in case notes and photos. Not only did this make the space look slightly messy but it also prevented the screens from performing as an acoustic panel.

Musgrave asked Thomas, a new detective constable recently transferred from Scotland Yard to lead the briefing. He was very pleased to be given such a responsibility, especially so, since being one of the youngest member of the wider team. He was fresh and enthusiast which reminded Musgrave of himself when he was younger and working in the City. Thomas sipped his cup of coffee quickly before he began his narrative.

"Sir, ma'am, we have been able to confirm the identity of the three persons of interest which were recorded as being at Stansted airport this morning around the time of the murder. The first you will already know as Gialietta De Luca"

The detective constable pulled up a fixed image and place it in the centre of the screen they were gathering around.

"She was using the alias Juila Milani to get into the airport. Both names are known it Interpol although we believe that she has at least two others.

"We have very little background information on her, only that she is wanted in Madrid for questioning in relation to the assignation of three agents of Centro Nacional de Inteligencia at a safe house, a solicitors office, in September 2016.

"Reading the case notes a passer-by reported the smell of burning emanating from an office building and suspected that a fire had broken out. Fire brigade attended, however the police were the first on scene and when they arrived they discovered the three bodies, each with their throat cut. It was believed that the fire was meant to engulf the building to destroy the bodies and disguise the three murders. Fortunately the bodies were able to be identified by the authorities. By the time that the fire brigade arrived the offices were fully ablaze and there was very little forensic evidence to go on so the trail went cold.

"In Berlin officials wish to speak to her about the disappearance of a software engineer called Marcus Schulz. He is believed to be behind some of the more successful hacking schemes in recent years. He was arrested in 2006 after attempting to hack into NASA's internal email network but the charges were dropped before it went to court.

"His neighbours reported their concerns that he had not been seen or heard from for several weeks without any clue as to where he had gone. The police broke into his apartment to discover the apartment completely empty but his computer still switched on and half a written sentence of incomprehensible jargon left open. Investigators have attempted to understand if it was some sort of code detailing where he had gone. Even some computer nerds were brought in to see if it meant anything in coding but it still remains unknown.

"No one has heard from him or of him in the last six months although there has been some rumours circulating on the dark web that he is still alive. Fellow hackers are concerned that he may have been attempting to hack into MyLife profiles to steal personal information before his disappearance.

"Forensic officers studying the apartment, according to the case file, found what they believe to be the finger prints of Gialietta on the keyboard. They also found a hair trodden into the carpet pile that they were able to take for DNA sampling. This helped to identify Gialietta."

He returned his attention back to the screen and enlarged the images so that everyone could get a good look at the faces.

"The male, seen here wearing the baseball cap, is Lutz Jäger. Quite an infamous character, usually where he goes people tend to disappear. He was accompanied by this blonde female who we believe to be his sister and accomplice, Gisela Jäger."

He flicked up another image of a male and a female drawing specific attention to their features from different angles. The constable continued his briefing.

"I have to make you aware that I can only say that we *believe* this to be her because there are no corroborated images of her on file. All we have are these images here which are grainy at best. They were captured by a surveillance officer who was on assignment to follow a known Lieutenant of the Vårvädersligan Swedish Drug Cartel. These images came from a camera phone from 2008, the technology was still evolving back then so they are not the clearest of images.

"As you can see in the pictures they are having some sort of meeting on what appears to be a commuter train carriage. We have narrowed down the location the Copenhagen Metro system based on the internal signage of the carriage and the advertisements. It was very brief meeting only lasting for one stop according to the report. Not long after this sighting there was a shooting in the Biskopsgården neighbourhood of Gothenburg.

"The official reports say that two armed persons walked into a bar and without any provocation just started indiscriminatingly shooting. The bar was known to be owned and run by a rival gang to the local Vårvädersligan.

"What links this to the Jägers?

"Well, after the shootings the few who had survived the original onslaught were tortured to death by burning them with sulphuric acid which is a method that we know is employed by the Jägers.

"Our intelligence suggests the brother and sister team use the Netherlands as a base of operations. It is quite easy to move between boarders in the Noric Countries unchallenged.

"Gisela Jäger got her two-one degree here in London studying applied medical sciences. She had a few job offers that were made to her from various organisations but she chose to return home to Germany. Her tutors praised her greatly insisting that she was incredibly gifted academically. There were concerns that she was a communist sympathiser and some high level checks were made although it was not confirmed if she was a member of the Communist Party. We know however that she had friends who were card carrying members of the Party and were known to the authorities for their communist militant actions."

Musgrave studied the faces on the screen in front of him carefully. "The Hunters, yes I knew I recognised those faces from somewhere." Musgrave said under his breathe aloud without realising. Waters looked at him in a quizzical way before Musgrave explained.

"We nicknamed them the Hunters after the German 'Jäger'. They are a brother and sister pair, mercenaries for hire.

"They were trained in the former Eastern bloc of Germany by the Stasi and were known for their cruelty and particularly nasty specialism in extracting information through brutal torture. Most of the European police forces would want to make this duo simply disappear. They have been linked to several high profile missing persons. Usually defectors or former intelligence officers. So far they have been unable to trace, as Thomas has said, it is believed that they operate out of Northern Europe. They have worked for the Russians, the Islamic Movement of Uzbekistan, Hamas, ETA, Hezbollah and even the CIA at one stage.

They are not fundamentalists and have no loyalty to any flag but they are extremely dangerous and have no allegiance to anyone or anything except themselves. Remember they will always be thinking about the next job and in their trade, the mercenary industry, you are only as good as your last job."

The constable whose desk everyone was crowded around nodded recognition and began his explanation of his findings. Thomas continued "We have Juila Milani captured here on CCTV from the airport which we have received this morning. She was boarding the Ryanair flight FR1518 to Hamburg at 7:50am."

He drew up the image showing a line of people with a woman standing at the head of the priority queue. With the option of two queues and most people liking the thought of being in some sort of *priority* line meant that in actual fact the speed of processing the priority passengers was not dissimilar to the standard queue. The only real difference these days was the fact that with a priority ticket you were guaranteed space in one of the overhead compartments for baggage. She glanced up towards the camera with a scarf about her before putting her head down and appearing to rummage in a bag for her passport as she approached the front of the queue. He froze the image like capturing a moment in time.

"We have alerted the German Federal Intelligence Service and flagged her whereabouts to the Interpol. It is quite a short flight however we are hopeful that we have been able to alert them in time for them to pick her up for questioning.

"Using the handy Ryanair app I have been able to see that her flight has landed only ten minutes ago. Everyone should have departed by now and be making their way towards passport control. She may attempt to use another false passport but I have circulated the images from Stansted's CCTV so they know who to look out for."

"That is good thinking Constable," Waters spoke up. "That is assuming that she has not changed her clothing on the flight. Sometimes circulating specific information like that can actually work against us as it blinkers the mind from thinking laterally. The authorities there may well be looking for this exact image and filter out anyone else who does not fit allowing her to breeze past the checks. But you cannot anticipate that sort of thing so you made the right call."

Taking a natural pause for this to sink in he took a sip from his mug of coffee and licked his top lip before he continued.

"The Jägers' have headed out towards Dublin on the Ryanair flight FR205. We believe that they were following someone.

"From the CCTV that we have reviewed from the airport they were spotted standing around for a time at the hub point just past the security area almost as if waiting for someone. They seem to be taking an interest in who is going through. That is of course until this man clears security."

He enlarged the grainy image on his computer screen and clicked again as a wave went down the image improving its quality.

"It looks like they have forgotten something there, look they are both walking back from where they have just been," Waters said as she watched the images running.

"It could be that, but is suspect they are purposefully retracing their steps to ensure that no one is following them. If they were being followed it would be hard to keep up with that erratic movement and not get yourself noticed," Musgrave said.

The constable continued pulling up another image from the CCTV. "This is someone of interest as he was in the shop around the estimated time of death. We don't know how or if he is connected with the others but we should be looking to make contact with him." Focusing on the face of the figure captured in the image he resumed.

"Meet Alex Clifton. He has not shown up on anyone's radar before. As far as we can tell he is a civilian. He has no criminal record, nothing on Crimint. He does not appear on any MI5 watch lists and nada from the National Crime Agency. Put simply he has kept to the right side of the law. In fact the only way we have been able to identify him is using the face recognition software linked to the internet which has picked up his face from his MyLife and his professional CoNet page.

"He's in his late thirties based on the years that he started university. He is a qualified architect and runs his own business. His CoNet page says that he can speak four languages and he is also an avid supporter of the arts."

Waters studied the face intently trying to see if there was anything that, like a poker players tell, would articulate something to her about him. She pointed to the moving image to freeze it still. "I can see possibly two angles here. Either he is completely clueless and has got involved in something unwittingly, like a drug mule or he could be a major piece of the puzzle that we have yet to have come into contact with. He doesn't look like a contender for the latter but maybe that's the whole point and how he has managed to stay below the radar for so long. Looks alone can be deceiving and the question I have to ask myself is that the face of someone capable of the cold-blooded murder of a young shop assistant and what possible motive could there be?"

There was a pause around the room while everyone considered Waters reflective thoughts.

Waters then asked if there was any further CCTV footage available to the constable who seemed to be leading the presentation.

"We were unable to recover anything from the Hugo Boss Stores' CCTV however we have managed to gain access to the CCTV footage from the chemist outlet which is situated on the opposite side of the concourse. They have a camera which is pointed in the general direction of the Boss Store which is to cover only their front entrance.

"Here you can see that an IC1 female walks past the shop at five-thirty-two in the morning and glances into the shop from the outside, here." He types quickly and within a few seconds the image of a women walking is playing out on the screen and it freezes.

"A minute later she walks back and goes into the store." The frozen image is re-animated but speeded up slightly. The female figure seems to loiter for a short time outside the shop changing her weight from one foot to the other before turning towards the seating area and breaking out into a fast pace walk. A few seconds goes by with people zooming past in and around the store, no one else seems to enter the Hugo Boss shop. The lone female figure then is seen returning along the same path and enters directly into the shop. The camera is not focused on the other shop. Once the figure has entered the shop the internal is a blur.

"We don't seem to see her leave. The store remains quiet with many people looking through the storefront but not going in.

At a quarter to six an IC1 male walks directly into the shop." He froze the screen again holding the image of the male entering the shop. It is hard to see any features at this angle however it is an unmistakable likeness to the earlier images of Clifton that were shown to the team.

"This is slightly strange in that everyone else has slowed and looked in from outside before entering whereas he has walked in there without pausing at all. Which I suspect shows us that he was going there with some sort of intent, see he is walking decisively without a hint of hesitation. Maybe for some sort of planned rendezvous?

"There is about a ten minute period before the IC1 male emerges from the store. As you can see it is our Mr. Clifton." The image is fast forwarded once more before returning to normal speed. "Who is shortly followed by this female wearing glasses and the scarf, who we have confidence in being Juila Milani.

"It was very difficult for the face recognition software to pick her up, she has done extremely well to disguise her features and cover her face. It was merely the fact that we have such a heavy presence of cameras at the airport that we were able to piece together a whole face from several captured images and to build up a full picture from several angles."

A smartly dressed female officer approached the team clustered around the desk. There was no specific uniform policy in the office as it depended a lot on what the teams were working on. Some wore more formal office attire than others more suited to blending in around crowds. "Sir, I am sorry to interrupt however I have Military Strategic Intelligence in the reception area waiting for you."

"Very good Liz. Can you please show them into Gold Command room and get them any teas and coffees they need. Can you tell them that we will be joining them shortly, thank you." Musgrave rubbed the back of his head as he spoke. Things were about to get a lot more complicated.

"Right everyone let's make our way there. Thomas, this would be a good opportunity for me to introduce you to Lucinda and her team."

They sat around a large walnut table in a quiet room with a large screen at one end. The central pendent light offered just about enough light to make notes on the pads which were already assembled on the table. The rest of the room was quite dark with the attention focused on the screens. The room was one of several named Gold, Silver and Bronze which indicated the hierarchy of the operations structure. This was the briefing room which adjoined the Gold Command control room. The briefing room was where the team leads would formulate strategies for dealing with major incidents. The room was able to communicate with any other agencies or organisations by secured video conferencing.

Musgrave chaired the meeting taking things through a timeline of the events that had transpired that morning, starting with the murder of Sophie Lane, the three pings registered at the airport, the attempted abduction of his daughter and the mysterious disappearance of their arrested suspect.

Musgrave leaned forward in his chair addressing the whole room. "Thank you for coming at such short notice Lucinda. As you can see this is a rapidly moving case. We suspect that this is part of something much bigger but what we need at the moment above all else is some intelligence. It feels as though we are one step behind and playing catch-up. We need to get ahead of the game and at least find out who is behind this.

"All of this morning's events have to be more than just a coincidence, I believe that they are all in some way connected to one another. To get three pings at the airport, a murder and the attempted abduction of my daughter all within one day is by no means an accident."

Lucinda was a very guarded figure, she knew how to control her facial features so not to show any reaction and disguise her immediate response. She had carefully digested everything that Musgrave had briefed her on before making a considered response.

"I have an operative currently in the area at the moment who I can ask to make some enquiries and make contact with this Alex Clifton, get close to him and find out more about him. He seems to be our best lead, in fact our only lead presently."

Waters took the forum "From what we know about Mr Clifton he is thirty-five, lives in St Albans in Hertfordshire, works as an architect, drives a Jaguar E type classic car, no previous record, is single and has been for some time. He was living with a woman by the name of Chloe Summers for a time but that seems to have ended five years ago. I suspect that he will be more responsive to a female for debriefing."

"The operative I have in mind is a female which, if you are right, will allow her to get close to him. What is your view on what is coming next?"

"We cannot be certain of course but my gut tells me that it is going to be big. I would like to be able to give you some something more solid that that but I simply cannot only that in all my years in the job it has given me a certain instinct and that instinct is telling me now that a storm is brewing, bigger than we can imagine."

"As you will already know we cannot actively go stomping around in someone else's playground without requesting their permission first, especially in Ireland of all places, unless of course, there is an imminent threat to this country. If you can tell me that this is what we have then I have the authority to get the SAS involved. But I cannot stress that this is an end only option after we have exhausted every other avenue and opportunity."

"Thank you and I appreciate what you are doing. Are you able to explain the disappearance of the suspect that we arrested for the attempted abduction of my daughter?"

"We have been searching through the Regimental Provosts and there is no Arthur Williams currently serving in the Military Provost Guard Service. That being said, we did have a Lieutenant Arthur Williams who was missing in action, presumed dead following a routine patrol of Camp Shorabak, formally Camp Bastion, in Afghanistan. There was an attack lead by the Taliban in September 2012 which saw United States Marine Corps service personnel killed. Several of the attacking Taliban forces were killed and one was captured for further interrogation. Lieutenant Williams was part of a three man patrol.

"The bodies of his colleagues were accounted for however his was not amongst the dead. It is possible that he was wounded and taken prisoner in hope of some form of future exchange but there was no evidence which would lead us to believe that was the case.

"It is not completely uncommon for former service persons to go native or rouge especially if they have been playing the game for some time. But usually they would take up an alias rather than use their actual name. Maybe vanity or possibly not too bright it is hard to say. These sorts often fall into mercenary circles as a hired gun, they have great training but lack discipline and hate taking orders from others which makes them reckless. Our game is our game so they say. Sometimes paranoia can set in with the constant watching over your shoulder or sometimes it is simply an opportunity to get out with enough money to last the rest of your life and not have to turn back.

"We have the vehicle on CCTV leaving the police station and have also picked up said vehicle, which was dumped at Stratford station. The vehicle is registered to a Barry Clark who reported the car missing earlier this morning.

"We now know that they took a black cab instead all the way from Stratford to London City Airport, where they then caught a flight directly to Dublin."

"But why would they want go to all that trouble and expense to make you think that they had used public transport?" asked the young officer at the table.

Musgrave "If you will allow me to answer that, ma'am?" Major-General Greening nodded in acknowledgement.

"Since the car was stolen and would have been picked up on the ANPR camera on the approaches to the airport and would have automatically alerted the airport police." Waters nodded but others looked a little lost.

"ANPR, Automatic Number Plate Recognition cameras cover every area of special interest. Say as an example Piccadilly Circus, the Mall, roads in and out of the city, major ports, airports and trains stations. They all have ANPR technology to automatically read vehicle number plates which we can then use to tackle crime and terrorist groups by monitoring specific vehicle movements.

"We have instant real time access connection to the data that is captured by these cameras from the National ANPR Data Centre. Theoretically we can track any vehicle in the country so if they had driven the car directly to the airport then they would have been stopped long before they ever made it near to the airport as it would have been considered a threat to the airport.

"By using a black cab there would be no trace of their movements apart from the driver knowing where he picked them up from and where he dropped them off. They will have paid in cash so there would be no way of tracking payments or cards. There is no CCTV in the cab either. London Underground trains keep their CCTV for 72 hours after it is originally captured, stations 14 days and buses 30 days. By making us think that they used public transport they make us waste our time and resources searching through hours upon hours of CCTV without any result rather than focusing on other leads." Everyone around the table nodded in response.

The General continued "This was an extremely well-coordinated attack. Which tells us that there has to be someone involved in the operation controlling from the team on the ground. I also would go as far to say that the intention was that your daughter was to be on that flight. The seats were booked a week ago and paid for by cash from the airport. We have been through the CCTV there at the time of the transaction and it has not shown us anything useful. We do know that the number of seats booked totalled nine, all on passports numbers which seem to exist. I would hazard a guess including the team that you intercepted," indicating towards Musgrave, "plus one more."

"It all seems quite circumstantial," Waters jumped in.

The General turned to address Waters directly as she continued "Sometimes in these early hours of an event 'circumstantial' is all we have to go on until the facts and truth start to emerge."

Chapter Eight

Derek's black Skoda Octavian drifted over the tarmac drive towards the grand entrance of the K Club. Clifton sat up in his seat and took a deep breath. He admired this building. Like most inspirational architecture, each time he saw it he took in its magnificence, he discovered something new about it.

The car swept across the gravel driveway making a crisp crunching noise as it slowed down past the series of white colonnades. From the front it resembled American grandeur with the addition of soft French stylings. The hotel building originated from Straffan House which was built in 1832 by wine baron Hugh Barton who was made famous for Barton & Guestier Wines.

The history of the hotel was as rich as its surroundings. The family run business was founded by Thomas Barton who had left Ireland in 1722 and had established his business in the Bordeaux region of France. Over the years of refining and growing the business thrived and his grandson, Hugh Barton carried on the family's legacy and wine production. During la Terreur in seventeen ninety-three, Hugh managed to escape the clutches of the French Revolution and fled to Ireland leaving the business under the custody of his business partner Guestier.

Clifton had read the history of the hotel in the bar one evening and discovered that the house was loosely based on Château Louveciennes, near to Versailles. The striking interior retained may of the original architectural features, antique furnishings and a broad art collection from the original built era with its finery and elegance with the facilities expected of the present day. The celebrated Irish Expressionist painter, J. B Yeats even had a room dedicated to his artwork.

The Staffan House had been converted into a hotel in the early 1990s after the estate had changed hands and Ireland was entering into what was known as the Celtic Tiger period. The Celtic Tiger or 'An Tiogar Ceilteach' in Gaeilge was a term used to describe the period of rapid economic growth driven by foreign investment in the Republic of Ireland from the 1990s to the late 2000s.

The recession of 2008 saw a sudden cliff edge drop in the economy heralding an abrupt end to the economic growth. This was compounded with various banking scandals which drove prices spiralling down. Large housing estates that had been started were abandoned and shells of homes remained for many years until reinvestment could be sought to deal with the housing shortage. It was not until a bailout deal agreed in 2013 that saw things begin to turn around.

Clifton had often wondered where the origins of this phrase 'Celtic Tiger' had come from and what connection there was between Ireland and Tigers. One day as he was in the queue to pay for his lunch in the site canteen and he had gotten into deep conversation with one of the others standing in line. Andrew was one of the vast army of security guards on site. They had befriended one another and often spoke to on a regular basis during Clifton's visits to the site. Andrew was a fountain of knowledge and could talk to you about anything and to anyone. He used to wear all black as part of his site uniform and had a beard of a wise man with greying features. He certainly had a storyteller's ways with a certain charisma and also seemed to be on first-name terms with almost everyone on the site. It was hard to believe that one person could retain all that knowledge and on occasion Clifton would tease him insisting that he was exaggerating but whether the stories were true or not they were still great anecdotes.

It was sometimes difficult to have a conversation in an open place as he was often being interrupted mid-narrative with friendly greetings from passers-by. On this occasion Clifton and Andrew dinned together in the canteen and Clifton asked him where the phrase originated from.

"It came from Asia you see, the East Asia Tigers bein' Singapore, Taiwan, Hong Kong and South Korea who all experienced rapid growth between the 1960s, long before I was even born you know, and 1990s. You'll remember as a kid looking and products and finding somewhere printed on it 'Made in Taiwan' or 'Hong Kong'. If you ever had a happy meal at McDonald's you'll remember the toys having 'Made in Taiwan' in tiny writing on them. With the parallels between t'em and us we were the Irish version of their success story, so it became known as the Celtic Tiger."

The rear of the house overlooked the banks of the River Liffey, which was framed between alder trees. The river at this part was narrow compared to when it flowed into the heart of Dublin. Here the movement of the water was slow and calm, only comparable with the River Cam in Cambridge which gently flowed through the city.

When there was a nice warm dry summer evening Clifton would sit out on the Kilkenny flagstone terrace, read one of his latest purchases from the airport bookshop and watch the sun set behind the silhouetted trees until it was too dark to continue reading. Being further west it seemed to stay lighter much longer there than it did back at home which he used to his full advantage. Once the sun had gone down but before the chill of the night air lingered onto the grounds he would take the opportunity to retreat to frequent one of the bars and meet new people. He would enjoy finding out about them, doing a little bit of networking and hearing their stories before retiring to bed for the evening.

The car slowed to a gently stop outside the main entrance as Derek and Clifton both got out from the car. Derek opened the lid of the boot and retrieved Clifton's dispatch bag and cabin bag. "Do you even have anyt'ing in this? It's so light!" Bouncing the cabin bag up and down showing his strength as he handed it to Clifton.

"Just clothes for tomorrow and tonight, I like to travel light." Clifton smiled briefly while rubbing his eyes.

"Right t'en… Is t'ere anyt'ing else you be needing?"

"No not tonight I think, I'm going to stay here and get an early night."

"Too right, your liver couldn't handle a proper night out in Dublin!" Derek chuckled. "What time do you want me to be here in the mornin'?"

"Would half seven be alright? I want to make sure that I get a proper breakfast tomorrow"

"Ah, of course. Gotta' make sure you get your Weetabix in the mornin'! See ya tomorrow t'en, God Bless," Derek said making his way back towards the driver's door.

"Have a good night, see you in the morning" Clifton said turning and waved with the back of his hand as he approached the steps up to the reception area bumping the cabin bag up each one. He heard the car start up and the shingle beneath the tyres crunch as it rolled away.

Clifton stood in the entrance archway and took in the reception area in all its splendour before he was quickly greeted by a smiling receptionist who was standing behind the main desk.

"Good evening sir, how might I help you?" said the receptionist in a smooth Kildare accent.

"Hello. I'm here to check in, Alex Clifton, the company should have sorted out all of the payments in advance?" he said as he strolled over causally towards the desk.

She typed away into the computer, its screen was obscured by the granite work surface which also had an arrangement of orchids. They looked so elegant Clifton question if they were really genuine orchids or a very clever imitation. He gently caressed the plant's leaf between his thumb and forefinger to discover that it was indeed authentic.

The receptionist had golden blonde hair which looked as though it had been dyed awhile ago as her chocolate brown hair was starting to show through at the roots and hung loosely around her shoulders. It was possible to see that she had been repeatedly trying to push her hair behind her ear to the right side although every time she leaned forward to read the monitor screen her hair would escape. Her skin was pale and without blemish. She had large soft light blue eyes which darted left and right looking at the computer monitor. If Clifton were asked to describe her in a single word it would simply be 'charming'.

"Clifton... Clifton, ah yes here we have it. Double bedroom single occupancy. Is this right, you are you only staying with us for only one night?"

"Yes, I'm flying back tomorrow afternoon all being well." Clifton replied in a slightly impatient way, wanting to just rid himself of the baggage and his jacket after the long day.

"Hmm It's is a shame that you cannot stay longer. We are due some very fine weather this week. I can see here that you've have been staying with us a lot recently. I will see if I can upgrade your room to the bridal suite for tonight."

"Oh no please don't do that. I'm quite happy with whatever room you have... Besides I'm not a bride and it would just be a bit weird."

She giggled and typed into the computer and charged the room card. "It's no bother. Would you be wanting a wakeup call?"

"No, thank you. I try to avoid mornings if at all possible when I'm staying over!" He smiled at his own joke.

She gave a courtesy half smiled. "The breakfast here is pretty good. It is served from seven until eleven-thirty in the River Room. I hope you have a pleasant stay," she said handing over the room key. "If you need anything please let me know, you can reach me at the desk by dialling zero on the room telephone. My name is Colleen."

He took the key card from the desk which was inside a flyleaf with the room number she had written on the inside leaf and stuffed it into his trouser pocket.

"Well it's been very nice to meet you Coleen. Thank you."

He could feel his right eye starting to twitch. Which was an indication that that he was indeed very tired and stressed. It was not something that was visible to anyone looking at him, but to

Clifton it felt as though it caused some sort of distortion to his face. He quickly turned towards the staircase to make his escape.

He made his way to his room taking his time not to rush through the hallways, savouring his surroundings. Another feature that he appreciated about this hotel was that not only was the accommodation luxurious but each room was individually designed and decorated. No two rooms were alike and each with original paintings complementing the décor of the room which he would take time to study. He was sure that not every guest took the time to properly appreciate the works of art in their rooms but he felt a duty to do so. Every time he stayed in the hotel it was like staying somewhere completely different with a whole new experience.

He put the key card in the lock and the light went green. He pushed the handle down with his elbow and push the door open so that he could explored this new room.

On this visit his room was traditionally decorated. The walls were adorned with a soft light lime green and cream flower swirl pattern similar to the great William Morris patterns. There was a king-sized bed to the right-hand side of the room with an oiled oak bedhead which contrasted grandly with the walls.

The room appeared larger than it really was thanks to the high ceilings which had intricate detailed decorative coving to the junction between the walls and ceiling. A single chandelier hung in the centre of the room shining through cut crystal glass casting miniature rainbows as the light caught the edges of the crystal.

The bed had soft golden cushions and a duck egg blue throw which stretched all the way across the bed. At the foot of the bed there was a low level wooden bench that matched the oak bedhead which had a tower of sequentially smaller towels carefully arranged and placed on the top.

There was a small wooden circular coffee table to the corner of the room with two lounge chairs which were upholstered in a burgundy red and golden stripe. The pelmet at the head of the windows was a complementary pattern to the walls reflecting the design and edged in a green to match the walls. The pelmet and curtains created a three-sided frame to the sash windows which overlooked the grounds. Generally the soft furnishings were cream and gold adding to the allure of the room.

He sat on the bed and kicked off his shoes which were beginning to cut into his heels. He looked out of the window towards the trees that bordered the river and the profile of the mounds of the golf course beyond. It was seven o'clock and the sun was just starting to cast a shadow through the trees and onto the warm indulgent curves of the grass course.

He fell back onto the bed with his arms stretched out moaning as he worked his body into the depths of the thick duvet. He closed his eyes and took a deep breath in and held it for a moment before releasing it slowly letting go of the tensions that he was carrying around. His muscles still ached from the day's energetic adventure and he was feeling tired but it seemed wrong with all this beauty around him to simply go to sleep. He felt as though his limbs were incredibly heavy and sinking into the bed.

Despite his body fatigue his mind was racing considering all his options for the evening ahead now that his task was completed. He decided that the first stop would have to be the bar for some well-deserved refreshment. Then, if there was time, onto the spa area for some relaxation of both the body and mind before a late dinner in the enchanting Byerley Turk dining room.

He laid there for a few minutes willing his body to move before he tore himself from the comfort of the bed. He put his cabin bag up on the bed an unzipped around the edge. He put his toiletries on the countertop in the bathroom, laid out his clothes for tomorrow and unpacked his swimming shorts. He looked around the room checking that he had everything that he needed before ensuring that he picked up a towel from the foot of the bed before he headed out of the room.

He made his way downstairs and to the Vintage Crop cocktail bar in all its splendour. The room was as carefully considered as all of the latter ones. The walls were half papered in a teal colour with a slight pattern that was only readable with closer inspection and gave a certain character to the space. Below the paper was a band of golden dado rail which sat above white wooden panelling which resembled something from an old club. Equestrian paintings hung on the surrounding walls in thickly decorated golden frames reminiscent of the long tradition of Irish trainers and thoroughbred horse racing.

The room was filled with small circular tables surrounded with a golden bar which kept glasses firmly on the table. Clifton had only seen such bars fitted to tables and shelves on large old fashioned luxury cruise ships to prevent items sliding off and falling in less mild seas. Each table was like an island with at least four chairs surrounding them, a short table lamp adorned each table at its centre. Some tables had snack bowls filled with savoury treats and the ocean blue menu with the hotels icon in gold print stood proudly on each table with a golden tassel piece at the spine of the menu.

The bar was nicely full with conversations happening all around within small groups of people. Every now and then a table would burst with laughter; it was a happy atmosphere.

Clifton walked up to the bar and deliberated over his options as he reviewed the menu. He saw that they had a vodka martini in the cocktail menu but he thought better of it an ordered a glass of Kir Imperiale instead.

"You have quite a fine collection there," Clifton said to the bar man returning the menu to its standing position atop the bar counter.

"We do aim to please" said the barman who was cleaning a wine glass and holding it towards the light to spot any imperfections. Clifton wondered why it was that when bartenders were seemly not otherwise detained they would be characteristically polishing glasses with tea towels, as if it were going to be on some sort of display for critical review later on.

He watched as the bartender mixed the Crème de Framboises with the Laurent Pierrier Champagne and placed it caringly onto a napkin. The bartender looked to be in his early twenties and seemed rather passionate about his role, taking great pride in memorising all of the menu and cocktail entertainment trickery. Clifton felt somewhat guilty for ordering something so plain and denying the barman an opportunity to show off one of his various entertaining spectacles which he had been practicing. The bar staff all wore the same navy waistcoats with a thin golden vertical stripe pattern over white shirts. They all wore black ties which were always done up to the top button looking extremely smart and refined.

"And how would you like to pay for that, sir?"

"Can I stick it on the room please?" Clifton said holding up the flyleaf with the room card tucked inside which had the room number written on the outside.

"Certainly sir, I will just need you to sign this for me," the bartender said as he placed a small silver plate with a receipt held down by a pen. Clifton scribbled his signature and handed the plate back to the barman. He sat back in the bar stool taking in the atmosphere and saw the reflection of a dark haired woman in the mirrorpassing by which caught his attention.

Her hair was just covering the corner of her face so it was impossible to read all of her features apart from her lips but there was something almost hypnotic about the way her hair bounced as she walked past. Clifton had to remind himself not to stare.

He could not see past her shoulder height over the screen between them but it looked like she was wearing a navy blue suit jacket with white piping, highlighting the cut of the collar and lapels. She had a white or cream coloured blouse which had a high collar which pleated at the neck line. He could make out a thin golden chain of some kind just showing which he assumed was some form of necklace. As fast as this phantom had arrived she was gone again and he took another sip of his drink as he found the *Irish Times* resting on the bar and began to pick through some of the headline articles of interest.

He finished his drink and tipped the bartender before making his way to the spa area. He rolled up the towel with the swimming shorts inside it that was occupying the stool next to him and placed it under his arm. He reached the spa's entrance and signed in at the reception where he was greeted by a friendly hotelier's smile.

Walking to the changing room he could not help but notice how peaceful this environment was as birdsong was being played in the background over the speaker system. Inside the changing room he quickly got changed into his swimming shorts and placed his clothes into the locker, tightening the strap of the keyring around his wrist. The changing rooms were simple but elegant. The floor tiles were a light grey and heated under bare foot. They rose up to benches fitted to the base of the light oak framed lockers. On the far wall a vanity area reflected the extent of the changing room making it appear almost double the size.

As he crossed the floor he noted that he was the only person in the changing room. He thought how nice and tranquil it was here but bizarre how quiet it was given how busy the hotel seemed to be. He thought nothing more of it and walked down the corridor with his towel over his shoulder.

He headed for the sauna thinking that the heat would sooth his aching body. Reaching for the handle he stopped and took account the bruises that were starting to form on his forearm. He began to take a quick inventory of abrasions and bruises from the day's activities. Only now beginning to realise the results of the day's activities.

He had a large bruise on the back of his left arm just above his elbow, his right elbow was turning a deep reddish brown, and there were no marks on his torso thankfully. His knees were grazed and there were various smaller bruises on his shins. He thought quickly how to explain these away should anyone ask in passing. He knew that he had to think of something plausible so that he could say it with confidence should it occur.

The injuries were mostly on his appendages so it would have to be something that involved physical activity, simply falling over would not allow for these kinds of injuries. He thought quickly, skiing came to mind but he did not know anything about skiing and it would be likely that if questioned further about where he had been skiing and how he had done it would prove difficult to improvise on the spot. He remembered what he had thought in the car with Derek, he needed to base the lie on a truth for it to be believable. Then it struck him, climbing while on holiday. It was based on a half-truth as he had sustained the injuries while climbing, only he wasn't on holiday.

He walked into the sauna, and sat on the middle bench taking in a deep breath of the pine-scented space. He sat back, rolled the towel into a makeshift pillow and closed his eyes rerunning the events of the day through his mind making sure that he had not forgotten anything or left any clues as to what he had been doing there. He started to drift off into his own world before being brought back to reality with a start as the door to the sauna had been opened.

The cool air seemed to chill the room almost instantly. Standing in the doorway, slightly in silhouette, was a tall woman wearing a black swimming suit which hugged her slender body. She tilted her head and flicked her long brunette hair over her left shoulder and smoothed it with her hand. He recognised the soft flowing hair as it cascaded down around her neck as the woman from walking past at the bar. She smiled and apologised for letting all of the hot air escape.

Stretching, Clifton asked her to join him in a playful tone with a short chuckle at the end. As she stepped into the sanctuary of the pine sauna she looked up at the thermometer and joked how cold it was. She threw her towel towards the top bench and set about the coal fire. She scooped up some of the water from the small wooden bucket with the wooden ladle and the coals hissed as the droplets evaporated straight away. She was looking down at the coals, a strand of her hair was hanging down in front of her and she smiled and bit her lower lip. There was a moment of tension before she broke the silence looking over her shoulder towards Clifton smiled and said in a soft Mayo accent, "It's about to get very hot in here!"

Clifton chuckled and retorted, "I'm already feeling the heat. It's like a sauna in here." She could not contain her laugh as she quickly made her way up to the top bench and laid down on the wooden slats.

"That has to be the cheesiest joke I've heard in a sauna, well done." She smiled looking at the ceiling and bring one knee up into a triangle.

"I have jokes about other rooms if you want to hear them?" Clifton said as he reclined back against the middle bench resting his head on the towel once again.

"So I have to ask or it would be rude. Did you win?" came the voice from the bench above. Clifton's shoulders stiffened as he considered this beautiful woman's question. "I mean I'm guessing you were in some sort of fight or something for those bruises?"

"Oh no, haha, I did this rock climbing at my gym. It was an open day, a sort of try out something that you haven't before event and I picked the wrong thing obviously!" He was amazed how easily he had come up with the idea and how it gave enough detail leaving it difficult for any follow up questions. The excuse was delivered without much study and was a much better reason than a skiing incident. "Forgive me I should have introduced myself. My name is Alex, Alex Clifton" He offered up a hand to the bench above.

"Well you don't sound like you are from around here Alex. They call me Aideen, my parents that is! Where are you from?" She took his hand in hers and squeezed it.

"I'm from a city called St Albans in Hertfordshire, it is just north of London but just south of Luton."

"I'm Irish, of course I know Luton. So what are you doing so far from home Alex? Holiday or work?"

"Work, but this is such a pleasant place it always feels more like a mini-break. I am an architect."

"That sounds very fancy. What sort of work do you do?"

"Predominately mission critical data infrastructure. I'm with the contractor on a project for a social media organisation just down the road from here."

"Would that be the MyLife one?"

"It could very well be, although I'm not at liberty to say, but given the proximity it could not really be anything else."

"You have to admit they do treat us well at this hotel, the service here is terrific. I'm here on business too. I'm a Business Change Project Manager. Most people don't know what that is.

"I manage change through a business transformation, identify risk, develop programme delivery, responsible for strategic planning of systems and development, defining and driving new strategies and methodologies aimed at reducing project lifecycles and value for money."

"Ah I see, you are an accountant with the authority to fire people?"

"Ha, yeah in short. Yes you could view it that way but another way to look of it is that we trim off the fat off from stumbling companies and make them streamlined. To be fair it is better to let a few ineffective people go than for the whole to company to fail"

"The need of the many outweighs the need of the few."

"Dickens, *A Tale of Two Cities*?"

"Actually I was thinking Spock, *The Wrath of Kahn*"

Aideen laughed turning over onto her side to look down at Alex laying with on his back with his eyes closed. Somehow he looked very vulnerable like this as she made a study of him. He opened his eyes and caught her staring. She did not pretend that she had not been studying him.

"How does your family feel about you spending so much time away from home?" Clifton asked nervously.

"Is that your subtle way of finding out if I'm involved with someone?" Aideen responded almost accusingly.

Clifton was slightly taken aback at such a direct response and was about to back track but decided to hold his ground and answer truthfully.

"Well yes, quite so in fact."

"Ah well you see there is someone in my life. His name is Cabhan."

Clifton's chest fell slightly hearing the news.

She continued "He has distinctive markings. Stripes to be honest. He is very immature but what else can you expect for a four-year-old. Physically he's about twenty-five centimetres high and about forty-five centimetres long and covered in fur."

"Either we are talking about a very short hairy child or I take it that Cabhan is a cat, right?"

"Of course, silly!"

"What would you say to the hot tub now?" Clifton asked.

A cheeky grin came across Aideen's face. "I don't know. What would I say to the hot tub now?"

"Has life really gotten that bad to the point that I'm now talking to a hot tub," he said with a half-smile.

"That's such a dad joke. It's the worst one yet!" She giggled but agreed to join him in the hot tub.

They talked for about half an hour enjoying the warmth and the relaxation of the spa. Clifton felt a connection with Aideen even though they had only really just met. They talked about each other's work, their views on art and cuisine, and before realising it Clifton had asked to have dinner with Aideen, which she had accepted. Although the hotel was busy with people and the staff friendly dining was always something better shared than the alternative of dining alone.

The dining room resembled something out of a grand country manor house. The carpets were a deep burgundy colour with gold floral twirl pattern. Each table had full silver service set out and candles. The high ceilings brought a sense of regal splendour. As with the other rooms of the hotel the walls were festooned with striking art works in chunky golden classical frames. The chairs were upholstered in a subtle green, they were more comfortable than most dining room chairs as it was an expectation that meals here would go on for some time with quality food as well as conversation.

He sat down at the table and began to examine the menu making his careful selection from the variety of appetising indulgences. The waiter came back to the table to take the order. Aideen ordered the risotto of caramelised cauliflower with Arborio rice, shaved parmesan and shallot oil for her starter course. For the main course she ordered the wild Atlantic cod with curly kale, chick peas and yellow coconut milk. For dessert she ordered new season Wexford strawberries with Kir Royale jelly, vanilla pastry cream and balsamic.

Clifton decided to order the Atlantic Sea Bass with dingle gin watermelon, avocado puree, chilled cucumber gazpacho and toasted almonds for starter. For the main course he ordered the 10 Oz fillet of Irish beef with fondant potato, onion compote with bordelaise sauce. The beef in Ireland was some of the tenderest beef Clifton had ever had, including at his club in London, which was still delicious. For dessert he ordered the warm Valrhona chocolate fondant with Baileys ice cream and chocolate caviar.

For the accompaniment Clifton ordered a bottle of the Pinot Noir Barton & Guestier Bordeaux Reserve remembering back to the wine tasting evening which felt like a lifetime ago now.

"So, Aideen. That's a very charming name, where does it come from?"

"It's a very special name which is derived from the old Irish Legend of Fionn mac Cumhaill.

"Aideen is from the word 'aed' which means 'fire'. Fionn mac Cumhaill was a warrior with followers called the 'Fianna' who form the Fenian Cycle legends.

"Fionn was the son of Cumhall and Muirne, the daughter of the druid Tadg mac Nuadat, who lived on the hill of Almu in County Kildare. Not too far from here actually.

"Anyway one of the legends tell of how he built the Giant's Causeway as stepping-stones to reach Scotland, so as not to get his feet wet.

"Some say that he never died and that he sleeps in a cave surrounded by the Fianna. One day he will awaken and defend Ireland in the hour of her greatest need.

"One of Fionn's grandsons, Oscar who is one of the characters in the Fenian Cycle was a warrior like his grandfather. It is said that when Oscar fell at the battle of Gabhra that his wife, Aideen, died of a broken heart because she loved him so much.

"Apparently I was quite cheeky as a baby and my parents saw me as their 'little fire' and so christened me with the name

Aideen. I've been told that 'Aideen's' tend to encourage others and be creative, but if they neglect to reach their full ability then they become idealists and misuse their power."

"That is a sad story for such an enchanting name. What would you say you are, a tyrant or an idealist?" Clifton said as he swirled the wine in the glass lifting it to his nose and inhaled the aroma.

"Hmm I'd say I'm a hopeless romantic, I guess. I have quite a busy lifestyle and some people find it hard to accept that. My work comes first as far as relationships go." Aideen said looking into the candlelight avoiding the answer to the question.

"Gibran the poet once wrote that 'Ever has it been that love knows not its own depth until the hour of separation'." Clifton gave a half smile as he repositioned his wine glass on the table. Their eyes met across the table in the candle light. Aideen smiled and giggled adjusting the back of her hair and looking to one side as if to share a private confidence.

They strolled down the gravel path with the lawns running each side towards the island which the river had created. There was a stone arched bridge which continued the pathway over towards the island. Aideen took Clifton's hand in hers and turning to face him while the sun began to sink in the sky. As her fingers interlocked into his felt he felt something electric that he had not before as if he was really awake for the first time. It was as though time around them had slowed and the sounds around them became mute. There was only this warm moment. The whole area was filled with a golden glow of the setting sun. "I want to show you something special" She said looking down and biting on her lower lip. "This is a secret place that I've not shared with anyone else."

"Tell me something about you that no one else knows?" Clifton whispered taking both her hands into his. As their bodies pressed up against one another.

She looked down at the ground, smiled and then threw her head back looking at him in the eye. "Well, I always smile at old people." Clifton let out a breath. "Ok that's quite possibly the most random thing I have heard today" looking into her eyes.

"Well you see you never know what's going on inside their head. If you smile at them you know that they'll not want to kill you!" Her smile sparkled in the setting sun as she laughed. Clifton leaned in towards her tilting his head to one side, "That makes perfect sense" he whispered as their lips connected.

Clifton and Aideen watched the sun set together from the bridge. Aideen rested her head on his shoulder and said nothing but lived in that moment.

Once the sun had vanished on the horizon and the chill of the evening began to set in as they walked quickly back towards the hotel, admiring the stars in the sky as they went. Clifton could not keep his eyes off Aideen, it was as if she had him in a magic trance. They went to Clifton's room where he ordered a bottle of Château Pétrus 1992 and a cheese board. They sat together at the coffee table in the candlelight talking. The room service arrived and the waiter opened the wine for them. Aideen went to pour out the glasses and Clifton told her to let it wait a while.

"If you allow it to breath for a short time it will taste better as the wine will be allowed to oxidise and will soften the flavours and bring out the aromas, trust me, it is worth the wait!"

In the interim Clifton organised the cheese board. They have laid on a lavish spread and was truly much more than Clifton had originally anticipated. Laid out on the coffee table was a marble cheese board with a wire string cutter, waxed cheddar, Raven's Oak goats cheese, farmhouse red Leicester, Brie, Camembert, Damson cheese and traditional potted stilton. In small white cylindrical pots were a selection of pickle, peach chutney, salted butter and grapes. The crackers were arranged into a fan shape with eight different varieties including traditional water biscuits, savoury bakes, wheat bran, fibre cream crackers, cheese biscuits, flaky puffed crackers and cream crackers.

They ate two crackers between them before Aideen made an excuse to go to the bathroom.

Clifton decided the wine was now ready having waited a short time and poured out the wine into the waiting two glasses.

He was trying to remember what he had been taught about wine tasting and how to really appreciate the approach to tasting. There were four basic stages that he could recall. Appearance, aroma of the wine, taste in the mouth and the aftertaste.

He held the glass up towards the light and tilted the glass so that he could study the edge of the wine and see the tannin. "Appearance… tick" he mumbled to himself before gently swirling the glass, watching its contents create a vortex down the centre of the glass to aerate the wine. He held the glass up to his nose to take in the aroma.

No sooner had he taken a sniff everything around him fell into darkness and the glass fell to the floor.

Chapter Nine

Clifton opened his eyes, blinking rapidly in an attempt to clear the haze. There was no recognisable alarm clock ringing to stir him from his sleep, but he was awake. Something had woken him. He could just make out an argument in the distance which sounded infuriated, he definitely heard some very expressive vocabulary which was followed by "How could you not have anything useful yet? … You are a quickly becoming a constant source of disappointment, do you know that?

"I told you both that I wanted the woman so that we could interrogate her, not him.

"Well go and assist your sister then, you've been paid handsomely enough for your, so called, 'expertise', you came highly recommended but I'm beginning to wonder if you've grown soft or are you growing a conscience?

"Now go, do your job and get out of my sight!"

The argument had awoken him from what seemed a disturbed sleep. He recognised that this was not the hotel, or at least any part of it that he was familiar with. He was aware of the quietness around him apart from the throbbing in his head which seemed to grow louder as he became more conscious. He was used to waking up and feeling the effects of the night before but this was certainly no hangover.

He looked down and realised that he was seated rather than lying down. That would have explained his discomfort and why his neck felt particularly stiff. He was no stranger to falling asleep sitting in chairs. Be it out at the theatre or at home watching *Midsomer Murders*. He had watched many episodes but had probably only ever seen around 20% of the full series all the way through to the revelation of the identity of the murderer. The irony was that he would always be awakened by the theme tune blasting out of the television as the credits rolled past.

He used to get rather cross with himself. It was a nuisance when this happened as not only was it terribly embarrassing when it happened in public, but also he would often find that the odd positions that he had fallen asleep in made his muscles very tight and it would take a day or two to fully regain the flexibility of his joints.

The last time it had happened he had gone to see a show after a rather handsome dinner with Clara in the West End. It was a rarity that she was in town now so it had been an extra special treat to see Wicked at the Apollo Victoria Theatre.

It was a curse, that given a certain set of circumstances, it was very easy for him to doze off when he was not actively engaged with something. Especially when he was working towards a deadline and had been working demanding hours.

They had walked briskly through a sudden downpour from the restaurant to the theatre and had taken their seats. Both of them commented how warm it was inside the theatre compared to the spring chill outside. The theatre lights went down and the magic of the theatre commenced. Within three songs delivered by an angelic heart-fuelled female voice he was asleep. It would all start with him feeling the urge to rest his eyes but listen along. As soon as his eyes were shut his head would roll forward and he was transported to the world of slumber.

He took a deep breath trying to clear his muzzy head and began to survey his surroundings wondering where he could possibly be. There was a simple light industrial metal table directly in front of him with a metal surface probably used for packaging or some other workshop function. He tried adjusting his posture in the chair failing to find a comfortable position. Although he was seemingly free he did not think it wise to attempt to move from where he was as he could not remember how he had got there.

The intensity of the light seemed just as powerful as when he first began to come round. He put his hand up to shield his eyes and tired squinting through the gaps between his fingers to see where the light source was coming from.

On top of the table there sat an Anglepois desk lamp which was pointing directly towards him. He was now conscious of the heat coming off from the lamp in his direction. He was already relatively warm but was beginning to feel uncomfortably hot. He was beginning to feel more concerned why he could not remember how he had arrived here. He reached forward towards the lamp in an attempt to redirect the beam aware from his direct gaze. The lampshade burnt his fingers, but he did not make a sound, as he focused it to point downwards towards the desk surface. The metal desk top disbursed the light and threw it back up into the rafters because of its shiny finish. He blinked a few times trying to get some hydration into his eyes and rubbed them to encourage his tear ducts to function. His surroundings were still dark but were now haunted with a green neon effect from prolonged exposure to looking at the light source. It would take a little while for his eyes to adjust back to normal.

He ran his tongue over his bottom lip, which was dry, with what little saliva he had. His mouth was very dry and he was conscious of feeling rather dehydrated which would also go some way to explaining why he had a headache. He reached up to rubbed his chin with his thumb and index finger and felt stubble there. It was more of a comfort mechanism than for any real purpose. He judged there to be at least just over a day's worth growth.

His eyes now back to normal he began to take more of an interest in the dark room around him. It did not feel as though he was in any imminent danger although this offered him little comfort. He wondered if he had been picked up by the authorities and was in some sort of holding cell or an interview room.

Looking around he could make out what appeared to be shadows of timber pallets and shipping crates stacked up on top of each other to approximately six metres high. This would have meant that there was some sort of lifting device, maybe an automated crane system or a forklift truck. This would mean that this was no interview room or holding cell but more tailored towards storage, sorting and deliveries.

He was aware of a voice again but only a singular voice this time, not a conversation with another person. It was not possible to hear the exact words that were being said and Clifton's ears were still a bit shot from his headache. The voice sounded more like distant mumbling of a passer-by who may have been on a mobile phone. He looked around but could not see anyone around.

The throbbing pain began to grow in the back of his head. He instinctively reached to feel the back of his head where the source of the pain seemed to be coming from. He could feel that his hair was matted together with something which was not wax or gel. It was almost like it was crusty with dried cake batter. As his fingers probed a bit further and they found the source of the pain. He flinched as a sharp shooting pain overrode the previous dull throbbing. He let out a gasp and closed his eyes. He could see white flashes in his vision even with his eyes closed. It was like an electrical lightning display inside his head. He knew that the pain would subside eventually and focused on that thought until it settled down to the pulsating ache which was almost following the rhythm of his heartbeat.

He knew that he must have suffered some sort of trauma which had left a deep cut on the back of his head almost an inch long. He tried to explore the wound a bit more being cautious not to trigger another bolt of agony. The wound stung as he gently felt around the edges. There was swelling around the wound which was typical of being struck with a blunt instrument. He began to work himself into a bit of a frenzy worried that without proper medical attention he could suffer a blood clot on the brain and die or perhaps his headache was actually a bleed on the brain. He needed to get to hospital to see a doctor and he thought about calling out into the darkness for help.

He knew that this sort of thinking was not going to be conducive to helping him in this situation. Apart from basic first aid he knew very little medically of benefit. He reasoned that for the amount of pain that he felt there was a surprising lack of dried blood around the wound. There was always reason and a logic behind everything.

Whoever had knocked him out was very professional and had made sure that they took him alive. His wound would heal probably leaving a bit of a scar which could be hidden by growing his hair slightly longer at the back and sides.

He began to become more anxious about his surroundings and where he was. Who had abducted him and why he was here? Only clear thinking would help in a situation like this so he went back to making some deductions about his environment. He was certainly not in the K Club hotel anymore. He had a strange feeling that he somehow knew this space although he was sure that he had not been here before. Perhaps it would look different if all the lights were switched on.

It occurred to Clifton to carry out a quick inventory by patting down his pockets. He felt his pocket where he would usually keep his phone to discover that it was missing. He did however find that his car keys were still on his person as well as his wallet which still retained all his cards and cash.

He looked towards his wrist to check what the time was and as with his phone his watch too was gone. He was annoyed that someone had stolen his watch. He felt his empty wrist where the phantom strap marks would be. He then remembered that since going through the security at Stansted that the watch that he had been wearing was in fact not *his* watch and was in fact a duplicate of his own Mondaine white and black Evo watch with a tracking device hidden within the casing. He hoped that he would be reunited with his own watch on his return – if he did return, he corrected himself.

He straightened himself up in the seat pulling his feet towards the chair and tapped his shoes on the floor a couple of times hearing it echo slightly. He calculated that if needed he would have been able to run towards the stacked crates within a few seconds. It was not easy to run in his Oxfords but they were better than no shoes at all.

He heard the voice from before, clearer now as if it was coming into focus. Clifton was far more responsive and aware than when he first awoke. Lockridge stepped into one of the small pools of light emanating from a dull bulb high up in the rafters.

It was not hard to tell, even at a distance of four metres that he looked exhausted and drained. He managed to keep his composure surprisingly well despite the fact. Clifton noticed a quantifiable amount of facial stubble which would have suggested that he had not shaved for some time. Clifton remembered that Lockridge was someone who shaved religiously every day, this was in fact the first time he had witnessed him with any sort of facial hair and looking so unkempt.

He was wearing a grey suit, which was particularly creased around the elbows and knees showing that he had been rather active whatever he had been up to. His appearance looked slightly uncombed with a dull grubby white shirt with the top two buttons undone. He was holding a Beretta 92 Brigadier Inox at his waist level and had it trained on Clifton.

"You have exceeded all of our expectations Clifton," Lockridge muttered.

"I would have asked if you would consider working for our little organisation. After all we are old school chums and as such should look out for one another and all that.

"I did give it some considerable thought you know, really I did. But I know you and your foolish sense of ethics and morality. You really are quite ignorant to how the world really works and who holds the power.

"You see the world is no longer run by governments. The world is getting smaller and it is a mess out there. The people out there cannot stand against the powers that they cannot even see. No my friend the world is now run by the global corporations and information organisations such as MyLife.

"You will have course have seen clues leading to this but like most people you will have been blind to it, but not me. I saw the cyphers, I cracked the code and I could see what was happening. Think about it for a moment, who runs the world?

"The answer may shock you, especially if you passionately believe in trivial things like democracy." He waved the gun in the air at this point in a mocking way while he smirked.

"The effect of globalisation has put Coca Cola, Shell, Starbucks and McDonald's in every far reaches of this world. Do you really think that a single government has the ability and power to manipulate these multinational corporations?

"Of course not, because they hold vast fortunes which grows day on day through commercialism. Any one of them can tip over a governments as and when they chose. They would be as insignificant as swatting an irritating gnat."

Clifton interrupted Lockridge from his lecture. Of all the people he was not expecting to meet it was Lockridge here, especially armed.

"It would seem to me that it's tough to drum up members of your little club, John, my friend, especially if you feel it necessary to give your recruiting sermon to them at gunpoint," Clifton indicated with a nod towards the pistol being levelled at him by Lockridge.

"If it's all the same to you I would rather that you put that thing away and then maybe we could talk about this reasonably." He tried to control the fear in his voice struggling to keep it at a calming tone. He made an effort to reassure himself that things were going to be alright despite however bad they really were. So long as he kept Lockridge talking there was a chance of reasoning with him.

Clifton rationalised that after all if Lockridge had wanted him dead he would have disposed of him already without all the theatrics. There was a reason for keeping him alive for the time being. He did not have any secrets to tell so there must be another reason. Whatever it was Clifton knew that he was living on borrowed time and that eventually Lockridge would want to cash in on his investment.

Clifton had deliberately dropped in the word 'friend' into the sentence when he spoke to Lockridge because he had recalled something from one of the books that he had recently read while on a flight whereby the star detective of the novel had been trapped in the hideout of the serial killer after discovering who the killer was.

The detective had used the power of psychology to undermine the murderer knowing that, like all people in positions of power, they like to talk about themselves to boost their ego. There was nothing quite like the vanity of a narcissistic psychopath to divulge everything through the self-gratification of telling someone else how entirely clever and brilliant they have been.

By using reassuring and comforting language, for example using his name, using the term 'friend', it made the serial killer feel more confident and comfortable right before the detective made his critical move.

"You were rather foolish to keep the watch and phone that we supplied you with weren't you. Do you know that we have been tracking your every movement and hearing everything that you have been saying. I've been right there sitting on your shoulder the whole time and you didn't even know I was there.

"With smartphone technology everything about you is being recorded on a device just waiting for someone on the other side to click a button and extract your personal data.

"I'm not talking about names and addresses, no that's all in the past. I mean how often you go to the supermarket, what was the last song you played on YouTube, what was your most recent purchased from Amazon, what route do you take most often to get home.

"You are only now starting to comprehend the power of information. Once this data centre goes live think how much information we can harvest for the highest bidder and people will give it to us, not freely. They will actually pay to give us their information through the latest smartphone, tablet computer, even smart jewellery."

Clifton closed his eyes, his head still pounding and breathed deeply a few times to work the blood around his system gearing himself up to make his move as Lockridge was beginning to sound as though he was coming to an end of his lecture.

"I have a question for you, John, my friend. When I was taken last night I was in the company of someone that I had met earlier that evening. She does not know anything about you, MyLife, F5 or even me for that matter. Where is the girl and what have you done with her?"

Clifton spoke in a calm but firm voice making sure that what he said would be understood but attempting not to sound too commanding as if challenging Lockridge's authority.

"Whatever this is about it is between you and I. She has nothing to do with it. You can let her go and she won't tell a sole anything, where is she?"

A devilish smirk grin began to grow across Lockridge's face.

"How poetic, the dashing hero of the hour, so chivalrous, trying to save the princess from certain death in exchange for his own life. So naïve," Lockridge shook his head.

"I hate to be the one to tell you this but she has been playing you I'm afraid, old chap. She works for the Secret Intelligence Service, MI6 Special Operations Division. But I don't suppose you knew that did you?

"Her credentials are rather so-so, rather stock run of the mill, if you know what I mean. Not like when I was head of section in China."

He seemed to drift off slightly towards the end of the sentence as if he was reliving a past memory.

"I was betrayed there don't you know. By the very Service I was supposed to be working for as it happens.

"As a result I got stuck behind desk in some poxy back water. Not even GCHQ, but a subsection that no one has even heard of!"

He almost shouted the words. "Can you believe it, me, the head of section being demoted to this meagre existence, half my previous salary and decimated my pension?"

He was turning red with anger and spat out the last few words before taking pause to compose himself.

"For all of her faults, you know, she does have a certain charm, a beauty if you will, which allows her to interview any man in the most casual of ways.

"I mean come now you would have to be dead not to appreciate a fine filly like that!"

He continued talking as he ran the barrel of the gun across length of the table surface which made a metallic screech, metal on metal. "Still it was a shame really, she knew too much about me and the organisation. She was considered a threat by my employer you see. So she couldn't be allowed to leave here alive, you understand of course."

He paused allowing the last sentence to sink in.

"There is no reason to fear the organisation you know, if you are one of us. The only reason to fear us would be if you were against us. Remember we know everything about you, your life, where you live, your family, what you eat, where you go, what you think. We have assimilated ourselves into your very home, sitting at your dinner table and are a part of your way of life."

Clifton knew that Lockridge was still speaking but was totally oblivious to it. He felt sick, wanted so gasp. It felt as though someone had knocked all of the air out of him hearing that Aideen was dead. Then he began to feel anger, and anger like nothing he had felt before. A wave of tingling energy started from Clifton's fingers and ran quickly up his forearms into his shoulders. The same from his toes, through his ankles, up the calves of his legs all streams converging in his chest.

The hairs on the back of his neck were reacting as if under the influence of static electricity. His senses became heightened turning into a white rage. Everything around him seems to slow down as he could experience everything that was about him with exacting clarity.

Clifton lost his resolve and stood up at the table throwing his arms down on the table, fingers on top and thumbs wrapped around the edge. There was a loud thud which echoed in the space.

In a lowered threatening tone he looked Lockridge square in the eyes not breaking contact for anything. Looking deep into his soul for any sort of tell-tale as to what he was about to do next. "For your sake you had better be bluffing when it comes to Aideen." He spat out the words with complete venom.

"It is outside of my control old boy, besides women and interrogation are not conducive. Females are so very delicate," Lockridge said, shrugging his shoulders simultaneously.

With a quick hand movement Clifton drew up the table with all the force that he could. The table flipped up sending Lockridge into the darkness. Clifton remained in the light breathing deeply looking for some way out of the room that he was in. 'There must be emergency lighting in here somewhere,' he thought to himself, 'all I need to do is find the green LED light and that should lead me to an exit'. The room was quiet. Lockridge must be in there somewhere. The intensity of the lights made Clifton feel extremely uncomfortable. He realised that he could not have been in a critical space as there was no dancing flashing lights of the servers. He must be in the delivery area. That would make sense – the low lighting level, the echoing of the space, yes this must be the delivery area. He made to head towards the darkness in search of the personnel route which ran around the perimeter of the room, protected by a bright orange hand rail from manoeuvring forklift trucks.

He could feel the blood pumping beneath his makeshift bandage. When suddenly he heard the words "Stop right there," followed with the sound of a click, Clifton imagined that it must have been the cocking of a gun. He could not place the voice exactly but it came from the shadows around him. It definitely was not Lockridge's voice but one that he had heard recently.

There was imminent danger in the room and Clifton felt as though he was surrounded by sharks but all he could see of it was the bright light shining down upon him. There was something familiar about the voice but he could not place the soft Irish accent. Clifton instructively knew it was unwise to try to move. He slowly moved his hands away from his sides and walked slowly back to the chair which was now lying on its side on the floor.

"I going to sit down, if that is alright with you. I have a bit of a headache and it is proving to be quite a tough day already." Clifton said slowly and calmly. There was no response which Clifton took to mean that it was alright to be seated.

He reached down and picked up the chair careful not to make any sudden movements. As he bent down the intensity of the throbbing in his head grew. He sat down and placed his hands on his thighs. He wanted to instinctively fold his arms but he knew that there was a reason that he was still alive and that was because of what he knew. Any outward sign that he was not cooperating or withholding information could make things worse.

Clifton could sense movement approaching from his rear right quarter.

"Who sent you Alex? Who are you working for?"

As the voice came closer he realised it was his first contact in Ireland, the taxi driver, Derek. He tried to think quickly, any answer that he gave had to be carefully considered but he also needed to answer quickly to ensure that it did not seem that he was studying his answers. Which of course he was doing. Keep as much to the truth as possible Clifton thought, he had learnt this from his first encounter with Derek.

"I was sent here by the security services to infiltrate this facility and prevent it being taken over by an organisation known as F5 operating deep within MyLife."

"Who was it that first made contact with you?"

"Presumably the same person that sent you to follow me, Lockridge." Clifton replied. The pain in his head growing under the pressure of the situation. He could feel the throbbing of his pulse resonating in his ears like the beat of a marching drum.

"Don't play games with me now, Mr. Clifton. I'm not a patient man and I don't care for liars."

"I am not lying to you, it is God's honest truth. I was sent here by Lockridge to place a device so that they could monitor and stop F5."

"So why didn't you call me if you thought you were in trouble, you had my number in your mobile phone?"

"I don't have it. I was taken at some point last night, quite possibly it was stolen then. I don't remember much after that, only waking up here. You could have been working for Lockridge for all I knew."

"So that's what he has been up to is it? That crafty bastard has been playing both sides. I was assigned to assist and follow you but not by Lockridge.

"Lockridge has been under suspicion from MI6 after returning from China. In fact it is the reason that he was shipped home from China. We did not have anything concrete on him to be able to being him in. But now we have the evidence we will need to shut him down and his network.

"I was there this morning at the hotel to pick you up and you weren't there, so I got onto your locator and saw that you were here."

Derek lowered the gun trained on Clifton and walked around so that he could speak to him face to face.

"I see, so I have been set up here then. I was not actually working for the government at all? I don't like the thought that I have been under somebody else's control, a puppet," said Clifton.

"It's not just your Government laddo but all the countries that have been taken in by this. I work for Stiúrthóireacht na Faisnéise, Military Intelligence. It has always been a bit of a strained relationship between the Irish and the British, let's face it, we know from past experience that British agencies have been behind dirty tricks, criminal acts including making people disappear when it suited them. Things are changing though we are learning how to cooperate together and coexist.

"Your man Lockridge has been spending a lot of time over here lately, this F5 business will affect us all. We know what happened in China and he has been on our watch list for a short while now. Before you came over we were contacted by our opposite number in the UK and we were asked to keep an eye on you as you were seen talking to Lockridge on CCTV, then with your visit to here. Well you can put two and two together.

"Now let's look at your situation a minute shall we. In the eyes of the law you have possibly assisted a terrorist organisation in hacking into billions of private social media profiles, smashed the Data Protection Act and not to mention seriously pissing off this MyLife corporation. However if you assist us in bring Lockridge and his network down then I'm sure that you can go home a hero with your conscience clean."

Clifton felt as if a weight has been lifted. He now had a chance to redeem himself.

There was a three flashes of lights and the sound of three taps of a cracking breaking the low hum of the room. Derek seemed to slump while stood, his hands fell to his sides first. Clifton heard the metal clattering of his gun falling onto the concrete floor followed by Derek's body slowly folding on itself on its journey to the floor with a soft thud. There was very little blood from the exit wounds. He had been shot from somewhere just over Clifton's left shoulder. Derek's eyes remained open seemingly staring off into the darkness in front of him.

It took a moment for Clifton to react, he had never seen someone being killed. It surprised him how quickly someone could go from being a live to dead. It was less time than a light switch being flicked. Clifton started to hyperventilate and grabbed the edges of the chair searching around in the darkness.

There was no voice telling him not to move but he knew that whoever had shot Derek was in the room, knew where he was and probably had the gun trained on him.

Lockridge walked out of the shadows behind Clifton and walked up to Derek's body. Lockridge returned his Beretta 92 Brigadier Inox to a concealed waistband holster. He shot a glance at Clifton who was frozen to the chair. He bent down and went through the deceased pockets. He retrieved a wallet and a set of keys. Quickly thumbing through the wallet he threw the contents back onto the body, taking no care to be respectful. He studied the entry wounds on the body as though comparing them to a shooting range target sheet. Two shots to the chest and one to the head, the Mozambique Drill for close quarters shooting.

Looking back at Clifton he leant over the body and retrieved Derek's gun which was lying next to the corpse and tucked it into his trouser belt, stood up and paced around Clifton's chair and then removed the brown leather gloves that he was wearing and put them into his pocket jacket. Clifton remained wide-eyed staring at the body on the floor realising that he had missed the opportunity to pick up the gun.

"Now then Alex you can relax, he is dead." He said with an unexpected grin. The moment of shock was beginning to pass and Clifton needed to find a way out of here and Aideen. Unaware of how much Lockridge had been listening to the conversation he had been having with Derek, Clifton decided to do some questioning of his own. Losing his temper or lashing out was not going to resolve this but gaining an advantage through information may just.

"I thought he was one of yours?"

"No, no, nothing to do with me. He was quite right you know. I have been using my position as cover you see. I can send people on silly little errands, keep tabs on those of interest. It's like a game of chess really only I control all of the pieces."

"It must be nice to be able to see the whole playing field from your vantage point. How can you ever be sure that your masters do not become suspicious? I mean Derek here is the perfect example of suspicion."

"Yes that will be difficult to clear up however I could say that you murdered him and I killed you while placing you under arrest. As your friend pointed out, you have been working directly for a terrorist organisation. There is nothing to connect me to you."

"You were seen recruiting me at the train station of CCTV"

"Actually no, I was seen making contact with a person under suspicion of terrorist activities. You see as an insurance I have been creating a file on you and your suspicious activities. Everything that you think will protect you has actually been creating a narrative for your involvement with F5 and MyLife. You have always been dispensable you know. The whole reason for your involvement in this was to discredit any suspicion about my elegances. All I have to do now is hand over your body and file. I go home a national hero where as you go back a traitor in a casket."

"But with the one small detail that F5 will have compromised this facility – that will be your failing in their eyes surely?"

"It was never about that. Do you want to know the greatest secret before you die? F5 and MyLife are one and the same."

"You have it all worked out don't you. What about Aideen. She was with your team wasn't she?"

"Similar but different departments. If she's not dead already she soon will be by the time Gisela has finished her debriefing. They call her and her brother the Hunters don't you know. Special skills in interrogation you see. She cannot be allowed to live you see as she's seen far too much. Admittedly this wouldn't have been such a problem if Hamilton Musgrave had not gotten involved. Once I knew that he was investigating I thought that taking his daughter and holding her would give me enough leverage to prevent him doing anything. But what can I say if you pay peanuts you get monkeys and the team that I took to carry out the kidnapping were weak to put it best. There's nothing quite like German efficiency.

"Goodbye Alex."

Without warning Clifton stood up. Lockridge did not have time to put on his gloves but flicked back the side seam of his open jacket so that he could get a grip on his pistol's handle. Whatever was about to happen was already happening. Lockridge tried to draw his weapon from its holster but failed to before a kick sent him backwards, accidentally squeezing the trigger in the process firing a wild shot at the floor. He lost sight of his intended target under the pressure before regaining his composure and levelling the gun on his intended target.

Clifton dived forward and twisted into Lockridge's body so that he was standing with his back to Lockridge with both hands wrapped around his extended arm holding the gun. In a smooth movement he twisted back to face Lockridge flipping the weapon out of his hand in the process and heard it clatter off into the darkness.

There was a look of panic on Lockridge's face before they both realised that he still possessed Derek's gun in his waistband. Lockridge looked down to check it as he did Clifton punched him square in the jaw. Before Clifton could recover, he knew that he had left himself open which such a lunge, he felt a fist hammering into his shoulder repeatedly. He managed to swivel and bring his arms up into a defensive stance. Then he felt a sharp pain in his arm as Lockridge attacked. Clifton dropped to one knee in pain holding his arm.

Lockridge pulled the gun from his waistband, spat blood towards Clifton and beamed a bloody smile. "You were always bad loser Clifton, even at rugby that we used to play at school."

Clifton twitched his wrist looking Lockridge directly in the eyes and the bulb of the screwdriver he had concealed up his sleeve fell gently into the palm of his free hand.

"The difference between me and you Lockridge is that I never cheated, I always played with dignity and honour. Something you will never know anything about."

Before Lockridge could think of a pithy comeback Clifton sprang up from the floor where he was crouching and lunged forward throwing the full force behind his arm as a singular projectile.

The whole episode happened in a fraction of a second but to Clifton it happened in slow motion. He saw the flash of the end of the barrel of the gun pointed towards him. He could feel the air being displaced around him and then the sheer heat of the bullet as it travelled within an inch of his left cheek. The screwdriver homed in on its target finding Lockridge's exposed neck. He had slightly twisted away with the recoil of the gun firing revealing his jugular vein.

Clifton heard the cracking noise of the shot being fired as it reverberated around the room. The head of the screwdriver just reaching its intended target, the soft area of Lockridge's neck just behind his Adam's apple. Clifton noticed that things were beginning to speed up again to real time.

Lockridge reached to his neck as Clifton twisted it sharply down at a right angle. Lockridge attempted to stop the blood that was now cascading out from around the wound. Clifton stood back knowing that there was no coming back from this. Lockridge waved the gun around attempting to find his target and fired off a few rounds randomly in hope before succumbing, dropping the gun and falling to his knees slumping forward.

Clifton walked steadily over to Lockridge cautiously He pulled back Lockridge's head by his hair so that he was now forced to look up to him under the LED strip lighting. Blood came out of the side of his mouth as he said with all the spite he could muster, "You won't save her and you will not win," he choked and smiled.

"Maybe not, but I will give it a go if you don't mind," Clifton stated through gritted teeth. "So long John Lockridge, do not bother coming to the next school reunion" and with that Clifton pulled the screwdriver from Lockridge's neck letting him fall to the floor in the pool of his own blood as he walked away into the darkness to put things right.

Chapter Ten

Aideen's eyes opened seeing the world on its side. She realised that she was lying on a hard cold floor. Slowly she became more aware of the hunger and thirst as she awoke from her fitful slumber. She was restrained by her wrists and ankles which meant that she was unable to rest in a natural position. She could taste a metal in her mouth. Everything was hurting. She curled her body up so that her knees were up against her chest and attempted to roll herself up so that she would be at least sitting upright. As she did her head began to spin and she felt extremely dizzy.

She forced herself to take a few quick sharp breaths closing her eyes tightly trying to force the blood into her head to prevent herself from passing out. She could feel her heart beating fast in her chest and the throbbing in her ears began to fade. As she opened her eyes she began to access the situation that she was in as the stars faded away. She did an assessment of her body taking the time to make sure that nothing was broken, she even ran her tongue across the backs of her teeth to ensure that they were indeed all still there.

Aideen tried to work out how she had got there. Had someone betrayed her identity? Was this vengeance for previous missions or had her time come and the agency decided to burn her as an asset? No it could not be betrayal she knew too much and her network was far too valuable to be burned at this moment in time. That was the problem with the world of espionage you would not only have to keep looking over your shoulder for the other side but you also had to keep a trained weather eye on your own side as they were just a likely to see you dead if it suited their higher purpose.

If her network and cell was being taken down it would have to have been a large professional operation to get the whole network. She would have expected to have lost a few colleagues as they were being lifted. In such an instance the word would be put around and her colleagues knew instantly what they had to do and how to disappear. She hoped that day would never happen as much as she knew what her duty was this place had become her home and she had made a life for herself there. She would miss the long evenings and the character of the city.

She tried to search her mind fighting to reflect if any of the voices or faces were recognisable from any files or recordings she had coming into contact with. There were so many files that she had looked at and was constantly reviewing with various photos that she could easily remember, facial features were something that she would always retain. There were times when she would be somewhere and recognise someone and taking a moment would know not only where they had met last but everything about the conversation that they had. Names on the other hand was something that Aideen had always struggled with, although she had been able to muddle her way through usually. Accents, like facial features, was something that Aideen was good with. She was able to identify someone from their voice typically within a few seconds of speech. Even with all the training and searching her memory she drew a blank in this case. She had to conclude that the most convincing argument was that this was something to do with Clifton.

She had been abducted while she had been with him. She was annoyed with herself that she had allowed herself to fall into the trap so easily. She was meant to be the honeypot trap for Clifton, not the other way around.

Aideen felt that that she had misjudged Clifton and that he was not the person that she thought that he was. He had seemed so genuine, really genuine. She knew by the fact that he was covered in bruises that he was lying about how he had got them, but she had felt a connection with him that she had not felt in a long time. Maybe it was the moment, maybe it was the wine but she felt as not only as if she had let herself down but also betrayed herself. She was stronger than this, she should not have let her feeling get in the way of her job. She had learnt how to control her emotions and feelings long ago and bury them deep inside so that no one could ever hurt her again but Clifton had somehow managed to make those feeling escape, just for the briefest moment from their imprisonment.

She ran back though the evening in her mind analysing everything that had been said and action done. Nothing there seemed to suggest to her that he was a threat or working for any organisation other than his firm, he had talked about it enough to convince her that was only an architect who was very clumsy but charming. Her mind was too much of a blur of the night before to be able to tell for sure whose side he was on.

She tried to recall what she had been taught in her interrogation resistance training which seemed like a lifetime ago now. She looked around squinting at the intensely lit room. It surprised her that she had managed to rest at all. It was more likely that she had passed out from the earlier interrogation.

Aideen fought to recall her interrogators face, who had she been? Was it possible that they had met before somewhere? Did she remind her of anyone that she knew from her own past?

She tried to focus on the pattern of the dazzling clinical white square lay-in grid ceiling and at the rows of lights which omitted such a beam of strong light it almost burnt the backs of her eyes. She looked around the rest of the room attempting to lean about her surroundings while she had the chance and see what she could use to her advantage.

She could feel some sort of fabric against her back, she noted that all of the walls that surrounded her seemed to have this dense fabric panel applied to them. There was some sort of equipment in the room, not furniture that you would find in an office or but industrial machinery which did not seem to be in keeping with the rest of the room finishes. Her eyes were still trying to adjust so she could not really focus on what the machinery was exactly, it appeared as a blur to her almost as if she were subconsciously blocking it out of her mind.

The room itself was completely quiet almost completely silent. The only time that Aideen could recollect a silence so quiet that it was almost deafening was when she had climbed Binn Chaorah in County Kerry.

Wherever she was there was always some form of background noise, be it a gently hiss of a motorway in the distance, the whoosh of an aeroplane flying overhead or the noise of birds in the trees but here alone at the summit of Binn Chaorah it was like a frozen moment in time with the peace and stillness. What should have been a blissful moment Aideen found unnerving, it was too quiet, too beautiful and too perfect. For Aideen it felt as though something was very wrong, there had to be some sort of flaw, no matter how tiny it was for it to be natural. Life was not ideal and faultless so it made sense that the environment around here should also reflect that. To witness something so impeccable, so absolute demanded some sort of disturbance to restore the balance.

Aideen shuffled herself around so that she was now parallel with the wall and leaned her head against the fabric material pushing her ear deep into the textile finish and tired hard to listen for signs of movement from the outside. She held her breath so that there was no contamination. She was rewarded with silence, pure silence in return. She hated not being able to tell where she was, was there another room on the other side of the wall or was it the outside on the other side of the wall.

She wanted to shout out, make some noise, bang against the wall with her fists to create some sensation that would disrupt this numbness that she felt with the detached silence.

Aideen then began to recall what seemed like a distant echo in her mind of the grinding sound that the blades inside a jet engine makes as it is revving up on the runway just before it is about to take off getting louder and a baby screaming as well and sickening hysterical laugher. She shook her head trying to make herself stop but the noise seemed to be inside her head as if it was playing on a loop. She began to sob quietly and wondered if she was going insane. She could see white stars in her vision that danced around behind her closed eyes. She felt exhausted and was not sure how much longer she could last in these conditions or at least how much of herself she could save if she told the interrogator everything now.

She could remember being in this room but sat in a chair while her gaoler paced around her in tight circles. She had headphones placed on her head which were connected to a phone which was playing all of these terrible distressful sounds. She tried desperately to block it out by thinking about other music. Firstly something that would challenge her mind, she thought of La plus que lente by Claude Debussy but it was it did not seem strong enough to drown out the screaming child. She then tried an Oasis hit from the 1990s, '*Wonderwall*', which seemed to work for a brief time but the overriding grinding sounds were like a raging sea being held back by a concrete wall which was beginning to show signs of fatigue with stress cracks fracturing the surface.

Then the perfect song came to her. It was so mindless that it downed out the terror from the headphones. The popular children's television show *Rainbow* that she had grown up with was something that she could recite without having to give it any thought at all. She used the happy mindless sounds of her childhood as a shield from the horror around her.

As she remembered the jolly pipe of the theme tune began to flood through her mind hushing the noises that troubled her.

Aideen felt trapped and helpless, fearing the return of her interrogators for another round of questioning and torture.

No, she had to work on a way of finding a way out of this room and get word out what was going on here.

She deduced that the panels on the wall were for acoustic dampening and that this was a completely soundproof space designed to silence anything that went on inside. For a moment she wondered why so much of the room had been soundproofed. Whatever it was protecting it would have to be something far louder than someone shouting at the top of their voice. No this was sound proofing for something terribly loud and noisy like a buzz-saw in a timber mill.

There were no windows or natural light in the room so it was impossible for her to tell whether it was day or night time. She understood how important it was for rooms where people spent a lot of time needing to have some form of natural light. She remembered reading an article showing that offices with natural daylighting really did booster productivity by as much as 40% compared to offices that were purely artificially lit. She could relate to times when she was working in stuffy offices feeling depressed under the buzzing glow of the white strip lighting. In those days she was only able to mark the time of day passing by someone coming around the office to do a morning and afternoon tea and coffee run.

Being deprived of natural light for prolonged periods would affect her physiologically leaving her feeling lethargic and depressed working to the interrogators advantage by defeating her spirit.

In her previous employment Aideen had felt that if was frowned upon by senior management to leave the office during lunchtime. She had been working long hours as the Operations Manager for a small electronics distributor based in County Laois. She found herself arriving in the morning and leaving in the evening in complete darkness. Within a two months of a repetitive days she felt it difficult to go into the office and felt very melancholy towards life. After speaking to her doctor, who suggested that she was suffering from seasonal affective disorder, she began consciously making an effort to leave her desk at lunchtime and go for a walk around the block. It was not one of the most inspiring walks around what was then an industrial park but it did serve its purpose and she would return after lunch feeling much refreshed and ready to take on the afternoon. It was not long before the chucked this job in and came across the sea to work in the for the Institute for Government where she had a wonderful view out onto St James's Park and would often spend her lunch time walking between St James's and Green Park depending on what took her fancy on that day.

She took a moment to rewind and recall the last few hours in this place. All that came to her was an overwhelming sense of pain. She tried to remember exactly how she had got there, what happened next, what she had said. She was struggling to concentrate as all she could think about was the coldness of the bare grey concrete floor against her naked body.

Some of her training started to come back to her. After the initial tests in a room somewhere in Whitehall, London, she had spent the first two weeks of her basic training at Fort Monckton in Portsmouth where she learnt self-defence, strategy and all the things she needed to spy.

From the road approach Fort Monckton did not look very much beyond a series of mounds and ditches around some two-storey bricked residential apartments. From this perspective the thought of a Fort was almost ironic however it all made much more sense of course when it was seen from the air. The star like form resembled the appearance of Tilbury Fort which was built in the seventeenth century by Sir Bernard de Gomme with additions added later. The outer mounds and moats allowed the fort withstand an attack by an enemy from the sea and land.

Accommodation, classrooms and non-vital services were exposed on the surface level of the base however the more important test ranges and other facilities where hidden deep underneath the façade on the surface. The base was a series of interconnected tunnels which created corridors to larger spaces within the earth. If there was ever going to be a nuclear attack this would be the place to ride out the storm in relative comfort.

It was a brisk Tuesday morning in February. A storm had set in and was forecast to last the rest of the day. The wind howled outside and the sky was a heavy grey. Rain was drumming against the large classroom windows. The classroom resembled a 1960s chalet from a Pontins holiday camp.

The classrooms were formed two-storey flat roofed block approximately twenty-five metres long by ten metres deep. The brick bays externally were in filled with PVC glazing and spandrel panels which given their age whistled with the gale outside. The rooms were extremely cold and only heated with a small two-kilowatt electric fan heater which offered little heat against the draughts coming through the gaps in the building fabric.

The course was led by a man called Mr McGregor who spoke in a broad Scottish accent and had a great sense of humour. One day one of the students had left a pie on his desk and a small blue coat on the back of his chair as a prank in reference to the Peter Rabbit tales which he later shared out with the group along with a bottle of Famous Grouse.

Her classmates kept themselves very much to themselves. Aideen found this quite difficult as she was a very sociable person. One Friday evening she had managed to convince some of her peers to sneak out of the base and try and find a local pub to spend the evening. It was easier said than done.

Sneaking out of the base did not present the challenge that they thought it would, locating the local boozer did however. The base was fairly remote and was separated from anything resembling a built up area by a golf course. After they had walked for some time in the rain in search of somewhere she had noticed that the group of seven had reduced to a smaller group of four. It was slightly sad to think that her classmates were not really getting the whole team bonding thing.

Finally the remaining four stumbled across a pub called the Fighting Cocks which was just set back from the main road. It looked a bit provincial from the outside but at this time of night on a cold wet February evening it looked most welcoming. One of the group was concerned that it was one of those pubs only frequented by the locals and any 'outsiders' would be watched all evening but the weather got the better of them and they all went inside to escape the cold outside.

They had stayed until closing time talking about general nonsense, nothing personal or stories that could identify them or their background. It was as if deception was now a way of life for them and the only person who would ever really know them would be themselves. Aideen wondered if she would be lonely from now on.

During the introduction of the training with the meagre introductions they were all aware that the names that they were using were false given to them prior to coming here. This was of course for security reasons. In the event of them ever being caught, interrogated and tortured. When they submitted, and ultimately everyone submitted, despite what is to be believed in films, all the interrogators would have learnt from their victim would be a list of meaningless names from a network that could not be traced.

Aideen had decided it had been a good night regardless of the company. They left the pub just after last orders and began their crawl back to base trying to avoid the worst of the puddles and deluge. The others were making quite a pace and Aideen struggled to keep up preferring to take her time. Besides they could not all sneak back onto base at the same time or they would be caught. It was better to return at intervals to remain undetected. She passed one of those convex safety mirrors which had been fixed to a lamppost on a blind hairpin corner to help motorists see what was coming from the other side. They others had paid it no attention pulling their coats over the top of their heads and starting to do a light trot around the pools of water which gathered as the storm drains struggled to keep up with the amount of rain that was falling.

She stopped, the rain splashed off from her face, her hair already soaked through. The rain did not bother Aideen, she was used to going for six mile runs every morning no matter what the weather. In fact it felt somewhat liberating. In her inebriated state she walked back to the mirror and quickly grabbed the edge with both hands holding onto it to steady herself. The rain continued and droplets ran down the face of the mirror. She studied the distorted face in the mirror and wondered who the reflection in the mirror really was. Then she wiped the surface using the sleeve of her top to see if it would make it any clearer but to little effect. She looked round to see where her colleagues had got to, left the mirror to the rain and ran towards them.

During McGregor's lectures he was a stern orator, not tolerating any folly or idiocy. Before they were allowed into the room the students would have to wait in the corridor outside the room which reminded Aideen of her school days. He understood and knew that what his students learnt here today would be used to save not only their lives but quite possibly the lives of many more.

Some of the slides that were put on the overhead projector were shocking but it was important that the people in the room knew and understood the risks as well as the most common techniques for surviving interrogation. It was all about desensitising

She realised that she was being treated with a typical interrogation technique used to humiliate and intimidate as a psychological aversion to self-exposure.

She tried to get up but found that her feet were bound and her hands were tied together with several winds of a sharp plastic tape normally used for parcel wrapping. As she studied her bonds she felt a dull stinging pain and she noticed the wounds around her wrist and ankles where the plastic tape had cut into her skin. She had obviously struggled against to break free of the tape. The more she seemed to move and twist the tighter the tape felt as it cut deeper into her flesh. She manoeuvred herself from her side onto her back and swung herself up so that her back was resting up against the white fabric wall. She leaned into it and felt a slight flex in the material giving a little comfort in a very foreboding almost clinical space.

A flash of pictures came to her memory, she was finding it difficult to put it together. The memory loss must be the result of trauma and stress. It was very scary for her not being able to remember clearly. She could remember being in the hotel, she remembered meeting Clifton there, she remembered eating food and going for a walk. She was walking with someone, but who? It was as if her memory had smudged out the details. She could remember being in a hotel room, someone else was there then darkness. Then a white light, she felt unsafe, tied down. Her ankles and wrists bound with something. Then she remembered the seeing a figure, a silhouetted figure. There was something else, something that her mind was deliberately concealing from her for her own protection.

With its set up the room resembled some sort of sensory deprivation space. There was no way to mark the passing of time, there was complete silence and the lighting was constant and all she could smell was the metallic dust that filled the air. Her eyes rested on the only way in and out of the space.

An orange coloured steel double door. There was no obvious ironmongery from the inside except a rectangular stainless steel push plate on the active leaf. It was as if a form of torment, teasingly knowing that there was an exit but not being able to use it as it was only openable from one side.

The more that she concentrated on the door the mist on the rest of the room began to lift and she began to see the machinery in the room. In the centre of the space there was a white metal shredding machine surrounded by metal tables. She could not be sure but she felt the memory of being tied to one of these tables and being forced to watch the machine chew up a server blade. The machine stood proud above all else in the room. There were fragments of shredded metal and plastic littering the floor. There was not a single sound in the room, it was a deafening silence at the moment but she could still hear the phantom shredding sound that emanated from the mighty steel teeth of the machine. It was a thunderous screeching tearing noise that could only be equalled standing a band saw while it was cutting through something solid without wearing any ear protection.

Each time her captor received a response from her with the slightest hint of hesitation the machine was fired up and another hunk of metal was fed into the crushing jaws of the machine and its terrifying churning.

Then her abductor would leave the machine running while she held Aideen's head between her gloved hands directing her vision in the direction of the machine. Then in a calm voice she would insist that she only wanted information, it would all be all right so long as Aideen was honest with her and told her the truth. She did not want to be doing this but Aideen's deceit was causing her own pain. Then the back of the gloved hand would strike her across the face and she was shaken to attention. "Witness what this can do to metal, just think what it would be like if one of your hands were to be in these jaws."

More questions were asked and Aideen tied to answer them without revealing any specifics or details in order to appear, at least on the outside, to be cooperating in a desperate attempt to not only to keep the secrets safe but also to prolong her own life. She wondered how long she would have to hold out for. She assumed that the fact that she had not checked in recently would cause enough of a concern to alert her superiors. There would be a of course a grace period where they would be attempting to make contact and begin a search. Within twenty-four hours of the first disappearance though and with a cold tail it would be time to begin preparations for evacuating those within her network telling them to walk away and get out. She was not sure how long she had been there but already she was questioning how long she could realistically hold out for.

When she answered one of the questions in an unsatisfactory way punches flew against the metal desk that she was affixed to. She could feel the air between the punches and her body by millimetres, only just missing her. The inquisitors' objective was to unsettle and put the feeling of unknown fear onto the detainee.

Not knowing when the next strike will come and where was the terror in itself, keeping the detainee under constant stress and pressure. The coldness of the table made it feel as though she was lying on a mortuary slab. She hated all things medical, even a routine trip to the dentist made Aideen tense and uneasy. It was something about the unknown, not knowing what was happening. Only being able to see their eyes over a surgical mask and your inability to control what was happening around you.

More metal server blades were fed into the grinding machine the terrible tearing screeching noise filling the whole room. Aideen knew that she was running out of time. Slowly she was beginning to haemorrhage information, she had not given up her network yet but it was only a matter of time. So far she had managed to remain vague about protocols but she knew that no matter what eventually she was going to be to be fed into the machine, very slowly, until she gave them all of the information that she contained and there would be no stopping them.

Aideen tried to lose focus and take some rest bite from the interrogation inside her own mind. She had heard stories from Iraq veterans when she had completed her basic training with the Army. It was rumoured that Saddam Hussein had a 'people shredder' installed at his infamous Abu Ghraib prison. People were fed into industrial shredders used to shred plastic feet first to prolong the agony, screaming for mercy as they died. Their minced remains were gathered up and used to feed Arabian wolves. This was of course denied by the authorities however like all rumours she believed that there was a basis to those legends.

She could not remember much after that. Maybe the interrogator realised that if she was going to get anything useful she would have to let her detainee recuperate. It was possible to keep driving a detainee through questioning up until death but the last hour of information was typically useless as the captive had accepted their sealed fate and would say absolutely anything to appease their inquisitor. This was not a tactful use of torture, a really seasoned interviewer would be able to know that fine line between helplessness and strength and then to make sure that their candidate retained their illusion of hope, hope of escape and freedom, for it was hope which produced the most useful information to the interrogator.

More memories of the interrogation began to come back to Aideen as if a mist clearing. There was not just one person at her interrogation. There was only one person asking the questions but there was definitely another figure within the room staying outside of Aideen's line of sight but there was definitely someone there orchestrating the inquisition. She knew this by the way that the female with the afflicted German accent kept focusing behind Aideen as if taking instruction from another party. In her mind she imagined a silhouetted figure with their arms folded, legs set at a shoulders width apart and barking orders to the interrogator.

The German spoke very slowly, snarling every syllable allowing it to sink in deeply. She wore a tight fitting cream polo neck sweater which accentuated her body shape, black leather gloves, with pin-striped black boot leg trousers which emphasised her slenderness. To finish the look she wore black ankle boots with side straps with a shiny silver buckle to the side. Behind her black framed Ray Ban Wayfarer glasses she had piecing blue eyes which seems to look directly through you as if there was nowhere to hide from their gaze. Her golden hair was like something from a shampoo advert and was tied back with a black scrunchie.

Her spellbinding lips were bright red, Aideen recognised the colour as one that she favoured, Max Factor Ruby Tuesday. Her captor wore very little makeup and despite her chiselled features but there was definitely beauty there. She resembled somewhat the ideal of a school mistress, someone that instinctively made people want to confide in her. Aideen could see that naturally this was a good choice for an interrogator.

She could not see the other figure in the room, she listened for footsteps against the concrete floor but heard none. Every now and again she would look to the side in an attempt to catch a glance at the other person in the room disguising it as fear through tears. Unknown to her Lockridge was the other person in the room. He remained behind her admiring her as she lay strapped to the table with one hand folded in front of him with stroking his chin with his other perched hand. He remained quiet throughout the interview only making himself known when he encouraged the inquisitor to push harder as she slapped Aideen hard once more with her gloved hand.

The combination of interrogation, humiliation, tiredness and hunger would force extreme anxiety, hallucinations, and depression making Aideen suggestable. Would Jäger really be able to break Aideen? Lockridge was unsure, if it was at all possible the Jägers were the pair to accomplish it. Lockridge toyed with the idea of getting the Jägers to turn Aideen. She was very beautiful, he preyed on her vulnerability becoming fascinated by her naked body laid on the table.

She could remember sobbing uncontrollably, trying to break free of the plastic tape which held her fast against the table. Then she seemed to feel light-headed as the German accent seemed to fade into the distance. Her vision started to become tunnel like and growing darker and darker. She felt cold although she could feel the droplets of sweat on her brow. Then all she could feel was her body telling her to rest. She passed out.

Aideen knew that she had been trained for this eventuality but she also knew that she could not take anymore. The next round of interrogation was likely to be her last.

She shuffled herself over towards some of the metal shards and debris which littered the floor like wood chips in a sawmill. She searched anxiously through the fragments in her quest to discover a piece of a fragment which would have an adequate length and sharp edge with which she could use as a makeshift blade.

Aideen could feel her fingers getting tiny scraps and pinpricks as she explored the debris, then she came across an elongated triangular shred which she carefully picked up between her index finger and thumb.

She turned aligning it against the tape around her wrists and began the repetitive sawing motion by moving one hand over the top of the other. It was extremely uncomfortable and she did she winced as the tape tightened into the existing cuts on her wrists. She had to be very careful to only cut the tape and not her own skin. As she drove the crude blade into the tape she discovered that with each repletion she was cutting into the palm of her hand.

Aideen worked quickly and finally the strands of the tape were beginning to fray into thin strings. She felt more alone in those few minutes than she had done in the rest of her life. Her heart was beating fast as sweat began to form on her brow. She had to get free before her interrogator came back. It would be worse for her if she was found trying to escape. With one final stroke of the blade the tape tore enough for her to force the remaining strands apart.

She took in a deep breath and rotated her hands so that both her palms were together. In one swift movement she pulled her arms down and apart as the wrist restraints tore away. In release of her wrists with the following pain she unintentionally dropped the metal shard onto the floor. She resisted the instinct to rub her wrists and wanted to bath them to clean the wounds but there was no way of doing that here and in any case her priority was to get out of the room.

She searched the floor for the improvised blade which was now sticky with blood. She gathered the old tape around the back edge of the blade forming a crude handle so that she could use it without further injuring her hands. She leaned forward and began working on the restraints around her ankles which seemed to give way far more easily than the bindings around her wrists. She gave herself a small congratulatory smile, this was just the first step to her achieving her freedom.

Aideen looked around the room taking in everything that was around her analysis what could be used, what was of use and then she noticed the one thing her captors had neglected.

There was no surveillance cameras inside the room. There must be an opportunity in that, she thought to herself, but what? The only way out from this place was through the only orange coloured door which was teasingly sadistic. She paced up and down trying to think of a plan of what to do. What would the implication be if her inquisitors came in and found her unrestrained?

Would she be able to overpower both of them, what if more were to join the interrogation?

Would there be any element of surprise which was at the heart of the most successful battle plans?

It would be unlikely that she would be killed in any struggle with the interrogators. They would not kill her straight away on sight for she knew that there was to be a second round of interrogation to be done in order to get what they really wanted from her.

Then a plan revealed itself to her. The whole point of this room was sensory deprivation. That meant everything was based on blinding the senses. The room was filled with intense light, she had made the assumption that the adjacent hallway or room would be at a similar lighting level. This would be the key to her escape, the darkness.

Anyone entering the room would have been expecting a brightly lit room not complete darkness. It would take at least thirty seconds for their eyes to adjust to the darkness which gave her not only the element of surprise but also a tactical advantage as they would be temporarily blinded.

Aideen disconnected the shredder machine and gathered up the electrical cable to the port of the machine. She used the makeshift knife to saw through the electrical cable, at least that put this machine out of operation for a while she thought. She then set about destroying the light fittings one by one using the plug end of the lead as a simplified bola.

Using the plug side as the weight she swung the cable around in anticlockwise circular motion building up momentum until it reached its optimum speed where she would then release the plug projecting it at some speed towards the fitting watching them as they cascaded shards of glass and electrical sparks float gently down to the floor. Anyone outside of the room would be obvious to what was going on inside the room.

She systematically took out each one working her way from the back of the room to the door. She was beginning to feel much more hopeful now as she knew that her actions were getting her closer to freedom. As the final light went out her eyes adjusted to the solemn darkness. Most people would feel anxious in the dark but the opposite was true of Aideen. She liked the stealth that the darkness gave her, it was her protector. It took about ten minutes before she began to see a thin strip of light emanating from below the door leaf. This would be her tell-tale sign that someone was approaching the door. She stood there poised behind the waiting to spring the trap. She had to remain vigilant and absorb everything that she could while she still could.

Chapter Eleven

Clifton needed to find a clear way past all of the security cameras and patrols. Then the idea came to him quite out of the blue. The only place on the whole campus that was not vigorously monitored by security surveillance was the roof area. No one had considered that the roof area was an especially vulnerable security risk and so layers of security were focused on the site perimeter, the approach to the building and inside areas.

He made his way down the corridor passing various doors searching for one of the maintenance access rooms which contained ladders which reached up high allowing him to climb up onto the roof and evade the cameras. The main staircases which led up to the roof area were likely to be heavily guarded or if not they would be closely monitored by dome cameras sweeping the floors for any sign of movement.

He stayed closed to the wall as he made his way down the hallway and caught himself hunching down when he heard any noise. It occurred to him that this would probably look more suspicious and draw attention to the fact that he was someone who was not supposed to be there rather than if he were to walk normally down the corridor. So he stood up tall and carried on his journey down the centre of the corridor with the earlier mindset of if you looked official enough you could gain access to the most sensitive of areas so long as you were confident.

He was not wearing any of his personal protective equipment that he was wearing the day before when he had been walking around the data centre which would have identified who he was working for. So he felt that he was more likely to blend in with the MyLife staff at a distance as the only people who were still using high-visibility vests were the contractor staff. The transient spaces were lit but dimly, which indicated that the building was running on night time mode. It was impossible to make out any physical features of anyone at a distance just the silhouette of a figure, which would work in his favour making it harder for anyone to spot him. He recalled the argument between Lockridge and the stranger. It was possible that there were others and possibly by now what had happened to Lockridge. The building was already on high alert just by the very nature of the function of the campus.

The building was operated twenty-four hours a day, seven days a week by and army of shift workers. It was important that those working shifts did have a sense of time and nature so the building systems were designed to reflect the external environment so that those who were still working away had a sense of time and did not feel as though they were constantly asleep or awake. Being able to connect with the outside world does raise the human spirit and with a building that had very few windows it was important that the inside should mimic the external atmosphere for health benefits of those working away inside at all hours of the day. The quality of the lighting was one of the most important influences on the efficiency of workers in the office.

For critical areas the lighting was always set at the same levels to ensure that visual work could be carried out correctly and safely in comfort. For areas that we not considered critical like the office areas that focused on marketing the lights would dim towards the end of the day gradually going down like the sun until the area was only lit by emergency lighting. This not only was not only beneficial to the health of the people that worked in the space but also there were environmental benefits in reducing the consumption of energy. Of course the other benefit was financial.

Sky-wells fell through the building from the roof level teeing off at various office accommodation and stopping at the plant levels. The idea was to bring natural daylight down into the centre of the building core where there was no daylight otherwise. It was recognised that workers spent most of their day inside, even when at home, which limited their exposure to essential vitamins which we get from being outside. By introducing skylights into the various spaces via the super sky-wells natural light was brought into every part of the building commonly habited by people.

He could hear some chatter in the distance followed quickly by a roar of laughter from a group of people. He squinted at the sign on the wall making out the lettering in the semi-darkness which read 'Room 01.SF.023.CD – Canteen'. Every room on the entire campus had its own unique room number so that if security or emergency services had to travel to any room in any building on the campus they were able to quickly locate where they were going by the room number. The first number would identify which building the room was located in on the campus. The second code would identify which level the room was on, GF indicating that the room was on the Ground Floor. The next number was a sequential number given to identify the room on the floor and then the last two letters were given as a brief description of the room.

The corridor was not brightly lit being in night mode but the light pollution from the other brightly lit internal rooms where people were gathered was spilling into the corridor revealing what was happening there. If Clifton were to walk past it would have been very noticeable for anyone who was watching the opening. This was the shortest route to the nearest maintenance ladder access point anyway. A detour here would take him through a far-reaching loop where it would be more likely he would be discovered. He thought for a minute and decided that is was worth taking the risk.

If he walked briskly and with purpose, making sure not to make eye contact, it was likely that no one would show him any attention. They would probably be too distracted being on some sort of break period to be noticing the comings and goings of the corridor space. The chances were that they would all be transfixed on their smart phones updating their MyLife page and watching videos of cats pushing glasses of water off from a table.

As he strode past the opening he heard another rumble of laughter emanating from the canteen. There must have been a small group of at least four people in there. He did not flinch nor look to investigate but carried on. He found the access hatch and went to open the door. It was locked. 'Locked?' he thought to himself. 'These were never designed to be locked, there is supposed to be free egress for fire escape.' Bemused and slightly cross he took a step back to ponder what his next move would be. The security team must have been doing some retrospective fit outs over and above the knowledge of the contractor on site.

Clifton was then aware of what looked like a torch being held about three inches from the floor steadily making its way towards him. Then an amber beacon began to gently flashing at around eye level, like a lighthouse approaching him from down the corridor. Then a faint motorised whirling noise could be heard. It was gradually getting louder as the lights drew ever nearer. 'It cannot be one of the MyLife robots operating at this time of night surely?'

Clifton hated the fact that everyone referred to them as the 'robots' as it sounded somehow daft and lacking in intelligence. He preferred to think of them as mechanoids or androids although they were not designed in human form although they did had artificial intelligence to carry out tasks in the most efficient way.

The server cabinets when fully loaded were extremely heavy. In most data centres the cabinets would be fitted out either in situ once located in the data hall or in a purpose built assembly room where the racks would be fitted out and then transported to the data halls on a motorised server rack tug which was a machine that resembled a palette jack.

MyLife had however decided that it was too dangerous for humans to transport the cabinets on the server rack tugs reasoning that the risk of the fully loaded rack toppling over was simply too great. Not only that but at 120,000 euros each these cabinets were deemed too expensive to be damaged by clumsy human error. There were independent companies that offered data centre relocation and migration services however these firms were seldom used by the larger data centre suppliers as the paranoia of rival companies sabotaging equipment during down time was seen as a real danger.

In lieu of manual human controlled transportation, MyLife had developed a small legion of motorised robots which were capable of travelling at top speed of five miles per hour while carrying a load of one-point-four tonnes. The multiple arms which hugged the cabinets and prevented them from toppling along the route worked to a maximum of ten thousand psi. This equated to the 'jaws of life', a hydraulic rescue tool, which was used by the fire brigade to cut their way through the outer shell of cars to extract people from vehicles that had been involved in serious accidents. These robots manoeuvred on six driven wheels and were capable of rotating on the spot in tight corridors and around doors.

The robots were programmed to be automatous and self-learning allowed to roam the building unobstructed by security or operators. They had an array of sensors which could detect objects in its path and it could adapt if something was in its way. However like all things technological it was possible for the robots to be controlled by the Services Operations Technicians and their programming protocols overridden should it be necessary.

This was their one flaw, allowing human error to override the system. Clifton was already aware of one instance where one of the robots had been overridden by the Operative. He was using the robot to deliver some spare parts to a colleague elsewhere in the building. Unfortunately while piloting the overridden robot around the building the sensors which would normally prevent one robot driving into another were disengaged. It was sheer luck that the returning robot was not carrying a server rack so the damage was limited to superficial items that could be repaired. There had been a full investigation held and staff warned not to override the systems unless there was imminent danger or an emergency. If a human had become trapped between the two colliding robots then they would have easily been crushed to death.

Clifton recalled the master key which he had used earlier the day before. He could not remember if he had returned it to its secret compartment in the sole of his shoe or if it would have been removed along with the watch and mobile phone. There was no time to take off the shoe so he kicked it up and tried to fiddle with the catch looking at it from a distance. He scrabbled around with nails against the plastic heel of the shoe, pleading with it to open before he was discovered. He was on the verge of forgetting the master key and making a break for it when the compartment slid open suddenly.

He felt a burning sensation on the top side of this fingers, looking in the dim light he could tell that it was a graze where the edge of the catch had torn some skin away. The burning sensation subsided and was then replaced with a stinging feeling as sweat began to feed into the wound. He had no time to think about that and getting out of this place was more urgent then attending a small graze. Clifton searched within the compartment, his fingertips finding nothing but the edges of the empty vessel. Would it have fallen out as the compartment opened?

Clifton fell to his knees stretching his arms out before him and urgently began sweeping the floor with the palms of his hands in the hope of locating the key. There was no sign of it. He wondered if he may have missed a spot. He strained his eyes trying to see something in the dim light around in the hope of capturing a reflection off from the metallic object on the dull matt floor. He was unsuccessful at finding anything and felt despondent.

He was sure that it was where he left it and could not think where else it have gone. He pushed the catch closed for the compartment on the heel of the shoe and tested in out on the floor to ensure that it was properly fastened. He was puzzled as to what had happened to the key. Clifton began to walk swiftly away from the approaching robot which was almost level with him now.

He placed his hands in his pockets causally and put his head down to avoiding looking directly at the approaching machine in case there were any on-board mounted cameras, which he thought could have used some sort of recognition software relaying its movements to a control room somewhere deeply secured on the floors below.

As his hands went into his pockets the ends of his fingers discovered something metal and rough. Gripping the key tightly in the palm of his hand now he realised that he must have placed it there after its last use rather than replacing it in the housing of the shoe. By not putting it back there had probably saved it from being removed by Lockridge when he would have searched Clifton while unconscious and removing his watch and phone. He probably had looked in the compartment, found it empty and had assumed that it was lost.

He turned on the spot and sprinted back to the access point passing the robot along the way which did not appear to pay him any attention. He desperately placed the key into the lock and tried to turn it.

The lock was particularly stiff, he rattled the key around in it in hope of bumping whatever pins were being obstructive. The hum of the robot's motor was passing into the distance. He caught a glance of the beacon fading away like a distant echo down the corridor.

He felt the click of the mechanism recoiling inside of the lock and the handle twisted freely allowing the access hatch to open on the hydraulic arm. Throwing caution to the wind he climbed straight in without taking a moment to check inside before stepping through.

He put his head through the hatch to peer into the corridor. The distant flashing beacon of the robot still seemed to be visible fading into the darkness. He pulled his head into the lobby and heaved the hatch door closed. The room was only lit internally by the emergency lighting as there was no requirement to light this space outside of operational hours. He thought about his accent up the ladder in the darkness, trying to remember how this ladder climbed through the building. As an access ladder the lengths of a straight run were only allowed from floor to floor before being required to break onto a small landing to begin a new accent on another length of ladder to the top of that floor. This was done for safety so that should the climber fall from the ladder not only would they be contained inside the cages of the cat ladder but they would only fall the maximum of one storey rather than multiple. It was a very good concept although for such a long climb it was rather tiring to those unfamiliar with that much excretion. They only real benefit was being able to take a short break on one of the landings before continuing the climb.

Clifton was aware of a noise, a noise which he had heard before when the robots had first been unveiled at a demonstration to the team. It was the sound of one of the machines rotating on the spot a high pitched whining tone. The machine was now returning on the path it had just taken and heading towards the access point where Clifton was making his escape.

He began his climb feeling the coldness of the steel rungs of the ladder. He had made about two and a half metres progress from the floor before he heard the machine retracing its route down the corridor on the other side of the door.

He could hear the sound of the caterpillar tracks making their recurrent rapping on the floor. They came to a sudden stop and there was an uneasy moment of quietness before he could hear the sound of hydraulic pistons moving. He was unsure what was about to happen although he had some sort of premonition it was not going to be good. His head was urging him to continue climbing but he also felt compelled to see what was happening below. It was more chilling not knowing what was happening on the opposite side of the wall.

Clifton turned to face the ladder and hauled himself up to the first landing and was just stepping off onto the grating to begin the next ladder when he heard a thunderous thud hammering against the metal sandwich composite panel wall. The structure of the ladder shook and he instantly grabbed onto the nearest handrail to steady himself as one of his feet slipped off the edge of the rung, down into opening of the ladder well below. He pulled himself back up.

He quickly began the climb on the next ladder hearing the continuing commotion happening below him.

The roof seemed to be getting further and further away rather than closer as he hauled himself up another flight. It was very hot and stuffy in here with little air movement. He could feel the tiredness in his arms, his muscles pleading with him to rest awhile though his head was telling him to plough on to the top before the machine could break through the wall and begin tearing apart the ladder while he was still on it.

He looked down to monitor its progress and could still hear the machine hacking into the wall panels, then looking up he could see that he was nearing the end of the last flight.

As he made his way to the top of the ladder he stepped off onto the landing hearing the final collapse of the wall panel below with an almighty crash. Looking down into the darkness the only source of light gently emanating from emergency lighting, a flash of light reflected one of the hydraulic arms of the machine which began to close like a crab's claw before it seemed to become frozen.

Clifton ignored the safety warning signs printed on the wall next to the hatch and exited through onto the roof deck. The area had confined head room which meant that Clifton would have to crawl around below the services which were suspended from a walkway gantry which covered the majority of the roof area with plant material for cooling the data hall spaces. Once on in the roof Clifton recognised how he could use the highway of pipework and ducting to hide. He had managed to squeeze himself between an air supply duct and bank of two-hundred millimetre diameter cooling pipes.

He was safely hidden from plain sight although he knew that he could not stay here. It would not be long before someone would think to use thermal imaging cameras to pick up on his body heat. The cameras were typically used to detect any leakage in the pipes, showing up a rainbow of colours against a cold dark blue background. He needed to find a way to blend in and camouflage himself. He began to notice that he felt hungry and wondered how long it had been since had had been enjoying his earlier meal with Aideen.

It was a nice momentary distraction from his surroundings. He told himself that he had to stay focused. He needed to get out of here and get help from the authorities and if not them then his own embassy. The nearest place he could think of was all the way back at the site offices where there would be telephones and computers that he could use. That was too far away from his current location. The roof was a maze of containment and pipework, extremely organised, almost organic in its layout. As he moved across the pebbles on the roof he realised that although the pipes and cable trays would visually hide him, the crunching of his shoes across the ballast would inform anyone of his location. How could he move around on what effectively was a stony beach without making a sound? It was not possible he thought to himself before he heard single footsteps from some sort of patrol above him as the metal gantry grating slammed against its fixing brackets with each step.

Then it occurred to him, he would have to use what was available to him here. He began to stalk the person above by tracing the torchlight and footstep sounds above, making his way over the labyrinth of cable trays and pipes. He noticed a brief pause as all went silent and the illumination of the light was doused. Where had the person gone?

Clifton knew that the figure must still be there although why he had stopped seemed to be a mystery until he heard an extended exhale and a cloud of fog drifted in the moonlight. Clifton realised that the figure had stopped to vape, probably taking some sort of break. Clifton looked around him to locate himself with his memory of the building plan. He realised that he was in the central area just above the Point of Presence colocation room. In this part of the roof there were several volumes projecting from the main roof of the building which created a series of alleyways and corridors at gantry level. This was the very reason that Clifton had made his way to this area, to use the built form to hide his location. It was a maze to the unfamiliar but they were all routes that Clifton knew back to front spending the best part of a year designing them and seeing them in digital models. The guard was probably using the same maze to hide from his superiors so that he could take a break and have a vape which was strictly not allowed inside the buildings for fearing adding pollutants to the clean air environment.

He would have to be very stealthy with his movements so as not to alert the guard to his presence. The air handling units on the roof gave a constant dull moan in the background which would give him some sort of cover but any loud thumps or bangs and the guard would be alerted. Clifton made his way carefully over the nearest cable tray which he felt depress slightly under the palm of his hand. A bead of sweat rolled down his brow as he quickly looked up through the grating to see if the guard had heard him. He saw a light, not as bright as the torch light and then he heard the guard talking. Clifton surmised that the guard was talking to someone on a mobile phone as he had not heard any approaching footsteps. This was good as the guard will now be distracted by the phone conversation. He rolled over to an access panel set within the gantry which was used to switch the valves on the pipework. The guard above was now pacing up and down on the gantry with one hand held the phone to his ear and with the other tightly gripping the vaping device. Clifton laid on his back and pressed his feet up against the access panel. He waited for the guard to step on the grating so that as he did Clifton would suddenly force the grating up knocking the guard off balance, opening the access panel and allow him to spring up onto the gantry and subdue the guard as quickly as possible.

It worked just as he had planned. The guard placed his right foot squarely on the panel and Clifton pushed with all of his strength flipping the access panel over and the guard head first into the supply plenum. Clifton quickly scrambled to his feet and stood and using his arms quickly climbed up onto the gantry grating. He ran over to the guard who was leaning up against a return plenum holding his face moaning. He had dropped his phone and vaping device in the surprise attack. Blood was seeping between his fingers as he nursed what appeared to be a broken nose.

The guard mumbled something inexplicable before Clifton spun him around and gave him a quick but powerful right hook to the jaw. Not enough to cause any serious damage but enough to keep him quite while Clifton removed his cap and uniform. Switching clothes would make it more difficult for the MyLife security to identify him.

Once in his disguise Clifton made sure that the guard was still alive and dressed him back up in his own clothes. He did consider leaving him on the roof where it was unlikely anyone would find him until morning light. He began to walk away and it began to play on his mind that the guard, unconscious would perhaps die of hypothermia. He could not have that on his mind.

Clifton had not appreciated the how difficult it was to manoeuvre with a dead weight as he picked up the unconscious guard in a fireman's lift and carried him towards the maintenance access point taking care to lower the heavy body into the safety of the internal access platform. He looked rather peaceful but Clifton could not tell how long he would be out for so he bound his hands and feet and gagged the guard using some of the cable on a discarded coil which had been left there. He secured the access panel back into place concealing the evidence.

It would be likely that guard would be discovered in the morning by another routine security patrol or maintenance duty. Clifton's conscience would be clear.

Without warning Clifton heard a noise that he was not expecting. The guard's mobile phone started to vibrate loudly and glided slightly across the metal grating only a few steps away with each pulse. Quickly not wanting to alert anyone to his location he walked over to the phone and picked it up from its resting place on the grating. The screen was illuminated with the incoming call from someone named 'Val' which he assumed was either a girlfriend of wife calling to check up on her partner.

Not wanting to raise any suspicion he considered his options. To not answer if they had just been talking could generate a call to someone else in the building if she was familiar with his colleagues. Answering the call was not an option. Besides this Apple iPhone needed a thumbprint recognition to operate it. He would need to open the access hatch again and then use the guard's thumbprint to access the phone and by that time the person would have rung off wondering why he had not answered.

The chances of the person to not attempt to ring back after being rudely interrupted from their call would not doubt cause suspicion and even more so if the follow up call was not responded to. Then the solution came from the handset he was holding. The iPhone had pre-programmed text message responses built into the calling screen which meant that he did not need to answer the call but he could respond with a text message. Looking quickly through the options he selected the message 'I can't talk right now, I will call you back later' and hit send. The screen went into darkness.

"Problem solved," Clifton whispered to himself as he powered down the phone and threw it over towards the rain water gutter where the collecting water would inflict enough damage to the internal components so as to prevent the phone being used to transmit its location. He had read that it was rumoured that even if the phone was turned off that it could be tracked, it needed to be disposed of. He was not going to take any chances.

Clifton crouched down and felt around for the flashlight which was lying on the metal grating. It took longer than he had expected for his eyes to refocus and to be able to find the torch. He fiddled with the head of the torch twisting in clockwise and then anticlockwise. It did not seem to work so he shook it before holding it with both hands when he felt a button on the base of the torch and click it on with his thumb. He proceeded to navigate his way around the gantry from the plans in his head towards a way out of this madness holding the torch like a dagger at head height knowing that if he needed to strike someone with the torch it was already ideally placed.

Clifton came across another maintenance access shaft which would lead him down into one of the data halls. Without pausing to think he made his way down the cat ladder and into the room.

Upon arrival he found himself amongst rows upon rows of servers were humming away in front of him. The floor a monolith of polished concrete with the vibrant orange server cabinets which were a MyLife bespoke colour.

An array of flashing green and blue lights danced from panel to panel in between a nest of wires. Above the server racks sat the partition which created the hot aisle containment. Clifton knew that that main challenges for data centres was heat and how to keep the servers cool for optimum efficiency. It is the same for your PC at home, if it is full of dust and overheats this is when it is likely to become damaged. The fields of server racks generated an incredible amount of heat. The cold and hot aisle configuration allowed cold air from the supply duct to flood the data halls from low level. This cold air would then be drawn through the front of the server rack and the heat would transfer from the servers to the air heating up the cooled air. The hot aisle which sat between two rows of racks would allow the heated air to be pulled up through the return air plenum to the air handling unit where there would be a heat recovery system for the domestic hot water in place and the air was cooled, to begin the process once again.

Unlike the roof area it was easy to see from one end of the data hall to the other. The only way to lose yourself in this space was to get into the hot aisles. As Clifton made his way down the first row he knew that he had to make his way through this farm of metallic sentinels to reach the colocation room and remove the device that he had planted there previously.

He was suddenly aware of the door opening at the opposite end of the hall and he quickly darted into the nearest hot aisle for cover. He walked briskly towards the end of the row. The heat inside the hot aisle was around thirty degrees centigrade. With stress and with the pace that he had set himself to reach the end door he felt the sweat start to cling to the back of his shirt. He placed one hand on the push side of the hot aisle door then he heard a voice calling out over the gentle hum of the servers.

"Come now Alex. Come on out, vee just vant to talk to you a little. No v'one has to get hurt." Clifton crouched down and tried to look through the end server cabinet to see who was there. He recognised the face before but was struggling to place where he had seen him. It was someone that he thought that he had either seen or met recently. He knew that he would have remembered the accent and struggled to put a name to the face and voice, which could only mean that he did not actually know this person.

Clifton was usually terrible at recalling names unless prompted or associating a person with an event. When the moment was upon him however he was able to recall faces from events and places that he had been as if looking at a photograph in amazing detail.

The figure turned his head quickly and looked almost directly at Clifton. Then like a lightbulb moment, he remembered the couple at the airport the previous morning. Only now the man was not wearing the baseball cap. He was on his own and did not have his beautiful female companion who was with him the day before, was she in the room somewhere too pursuing Clifton? Was he calling out to make a distraction while his accomplice tried a flank attack?

He carefully opened the door of the hot to its full reach point keeping his eyes on the central aisle where the predator was sweeping each row as he passed. Clifton was now in the cool aisle and felt the refreshing air against his clammy skin. 'Focus,' he told himself, he would use the ends of the racks as cover and make his way to the door on the opposite side of the room.

"I see you!" cried the voice echoing down the hall. Clifton ducked down and suddenly he heard the cracking sound of gunfire followed by a hysterical mad laugh. Clifton was suddenly paralysed by fear. He had the flat of his back up against the back of the end server cabinet. Then he realised that none of the shots which were fired were anywhere near his location. Quite the opposite in fact. The shots had been sprayed towards the southern end of the hall. This man was firing blind in the hope to draw Clifton out.

"Ah, there's you are!" followed by another three round volley of gunfire from a Walther PPQ Classic 9mm semi-automatic pistol, and menacing laughing. This time one of the shots hit the back wall just in front of Clifton. He concentrated on the newly made penetrations in the wall's surface. As he did his back slid slightly on the cabinet and he placed his hand out to prevent himself from toppling over. As soon as he put his hand out he realised that he had given his position away. As quickly as he had put his hand out he drew in back in again. As he did he heard the door of the hot aisle close under the difference in pressurisation and he knew that the man was coming for him through the hot aisle.

Clifton jumped to his feet and began sprinting towards the end wall. As he did he could hear shots sinking into the servers around him. The gunman was firing through the racks wildly in an attempt to get a lucky shot through. As soon as the assailant reached the end of the row Clifton knew he would have an unobstructed clean shot down the row. Clifton calculated five more paces before he would have to duck into another aisle at ninety degrees to his current row to prevent any clear shots. He was wrong, it was only four paces before one shot caught him on the left arm. With the momentum he carried on. The shot did not spin him around however it did throw him off balance as he crashed into the door of a hot aisle. His arm felt hot and stung like it had been brushed with several stinging nettles. Clifton could see his blood spattered on the adjacent wall. He looked at his arm as he got back onto his feet and charged towards the end of the aisle. He felt the pounding throbbing from the wound as the blood oozed down towards his elbow. As he got to the end of this row he slid towards the door on the ground as several more shots made small explosions of plastic around him.

At the end of the row he barrel rolled through the doors and onto his feet. He applied as much pressure with his right hand to the wound on his left arm as he could muster at this time to slow the bleeding. As he reached the end door he jumped towards it, extending his right leg as his foot went crashing into the lever handle. The steel door flew open as he made it through and threw all of his weight against it to close it as quickly as possible. He heard at least three softened thuds against the metal door which he took to be bullets being fired at the door. He scrabbled in his pocket for the keys that he had relieved from the guard and snapped one of them off in the lock so that it was temporally secure.

The door handle twitched violently once and then in quick succession. Clifton pressed his body up against the door with all of his strength praying that it would hold. There was a slight pause and he thought that the person on the other side had given up. Then he heard a single thud against the door followed by four others as if someone was hammering on it from the opposite side followed by a muffled voice shouting "Nein!"

There were two further soft thuds in the door and then all was quiet. Clifton breathed a sigh of relief, he kicked off his left shoe and removed his sock before tying it tightly around the wound on his arm. He remembered that the security areas had been specifically specified to be ballistic rated but it seems as though the security consultant must have over specified the security to the other doors as well because they must have been bullet resistant to take that kind of punishment. It would have explained why the doors were so much heavier than the other doors that Clifton had used in previous data centres, he had first thought it was down to being exhausted.

He checked his arm once more telling himself that 'it would have to do for now', before setting off down the corridor towards the colocation room.

Chapter Twelve

Aideen did not know quite how long she had been standing there waiting there poised in the darkness like a coiled spring. Her mind was filled with anxiety and anger. At one point she was not sure if she was even still awake as her mind drifted. Her whole focus was on the thin strip of glowing light emanating from the base of the door. In the world of darkness around her it was the only thing that she could hold onto and that gave her some form of hope.

To Aideen it felt as though she had been standing there poised for hours, her muscles were beginning to ache holding the position although she dared not move. A shadow seemed to dart quickly across the base of the door. She was not sure if she was hallucinating, her mind playing tricks on her or if this really was it.

Whatever it was she knew that she could not hesitate, even if it was her imagination playing tricks on her. She took a few deep breaths and tensed her already wearying muscles for the strike.

She heard the beep from the card reader being used on the opposite side of the door. There was the sound of metal moving inside the door and bolts were being latched. The steel door started to edge forward into the darkness, Aideen close her eyes tightly not wanting to lose her advantage of night vision. Light started to flood into the room around the leading edge of the door. There was a slight pause and Aideen grabbed the edge of the door with both hands with a sudden movement jerked it hard towards her, catapulting the figure on the opposite side of it towards the room, taken totally by surprise as they took a step into the room stumbling.

Before they could recover themselves. Aideen stopped the door abruptly using her knee and thigh pushing back and leaning with all her strength forcing the steel door back on itself and smashing the silhouetted figure square in the face.

Aideen opened her eyes confident that she had taken down whoever was coming into the room, this was confirmed when she heard the figure make a dulled shriek noise before falling to the floor in a heap. Aideen jumped out from behind the door, quickly but cautiously as she peered around in the dazzling white light to see if there was anyone else there ready to drive forward an attack, expecting the second inquisitor to be there while she still had the element of surprise.

The short corridor was empty and apart from a background humming of equipment and machinery remained quiet. She let go a sigh of relief and relaxed her shoulders realising that there had indeed only been one person that she needed to deal with. She glanced down to see who the shadowy figure had been. She instantly recognised her German interrogator from earlier. The features of her interrogator remained expressionless, her head was leaning to one side as if in a deep sleep. Aideen surmised that she must have been knocked out stone cold from the striking the door so hard.

Aideen immediately leant over the body of the figure lying motionless on the floor and began going through the interrogators pockets searching for anything that could come in handy. The act seemed rather heartless, almost kicking the person when they were down but it was easier to search someone who was unconscious than someone who would resist.

She found the door swipe card and a Samsung smartphone which was tucked into the waistband of her trousers. Aideen stood up holding the card close to her eyes, studying the writing on it for any useful information to establish where she was. The phone was locked but she could still use it to call the emergency services for help. She began to consider how she was going to hide the unconscious inquisitor before an alarm could be raised, when suddenly she felt a tight grip on her ankle around where the plastic tape had cut in deep.

Aideen flinched at the stinging pain as the grip twisted at the already sore wounds. She dropped the phone and access card. The phones screen splintered as it hit the concrete floor. She looked down to see a bloodied face with wild eyes staring back at her. The nose of the almost perfectly symmetrical figure now definitely resting at a peculiar angle. It was clearly broken and two lines of blood flowed from her nostrils, over her lips and droplets were forming on her chin. Through gritted teeth the interrogator managed to spit out the words, "Bitch, you vill die!"

She grabbed a fistful of Aideen's hair and pulled it back hard making her neck jerk back. She let out a cry as the pain shot across her shoulders. She could make out the shadow of her attacker at the edge of her vision. Aideen retaliated with a short uppercut with her open palm making her assailant loose her grip.

Before Aideen could react she found herself off balance almost falling back into the darkness. Gisela Jäger had been unconscious only momentarily ago but was now fully awake, cursing, moving so fast that Aideen did not even see the kick coming towards her. All she saw was a flash in her vision from the impact and then the pain at her temple. She was stunned and dazed, taking a couple of steps back. Jäger had released her Aideen's ankle scissoring her legs and suddenly rising to her feet. Aideen made a grab towards the door as she saw it begin to close.

As it was closing Aideen saw the devil in the woman's bloody face, wild eyes transfixed on her, smiling aa her as the room was eclipsed in darkness.

Aideen recovered from the blow and instinctively raising her hands up towards her face and taking a defensive stance. She listened intently standing as still as she could waiting for some give away of her assailant's position. She heard a grunt and a step possibly two paces to her two o'clock position on the crushed glass.

She kicked her right leg out in the hope of making contact, which she achieved striking Gisela in the side of the knee.

Aideen made the assumption that Gisela would have had to have fallen onto one knee on the floor and the other bent in an almost proposal position. Aideen fired a straight punch to where she imagined her attacker would be but found only air. She quickly pulled her fist back to a protective position and was about to take a jump backwards but before she could she felt a tight grip around her throat.

She was thrown up against the cushioned wall and lifted up so that just her toes were touching the floor. She tried to bring her hands up between the arms wrapped around her neck but the other persons grip was too strong. She fought against the hands wrapped around her throat to no effect, she could feel herself starting to feel light-headed and the world starting to fade away as she fought for breath.

It was make or break time, Aideen grabbed onto her attacker bringing her fists down onto Gisela's shoulders, again and then angling her fists slightly so that they struck her collar bone. The hands around her neck loosed just enough for Aideen to break free. She spun herself around so that her attacker was now behind her simultaneously placing her leg in front of the assailant's knee and pushing down hard with her remaining strength.

The inquisitor screamed as she fell onto the smashed glass on the floor. Aideen held her grip on the woman's arm with her left hand twisting the wrist to inflict maximum pain as she brought her right hand down in a chopping like action onto the assailant's throat. It was an odd feeling, as she felt the hard tissue crush underneath her blow. She could not be sure but she suspected that she had crushed her windpipe.

There was silence as the body relaxed into a lifeless state. Aideen grabbed her attackers booted feet and dragged the body back towards the door where there as a slit of light shining through the bottom. She fumbled around in the darkness searching for the access card which she had dropped before. She began to feel panicked not being able to find it in the darkness. "Where is it, please, where is it?" she kept mumbling to herself almost as a prayer. She felt something as her fingers pushed it slightly away with their rapid movement. She scrabbled, her nails against the concrete, and managed to pick up the card. The sense of triumph and relief was indescribable. Then she heard a gargling sound from the body and then a ghastly sucking noise.

There was a cough and a spluttering noise as distorted words were hissed, "Ich werde dich töten!" Aideen impulsively raised her left forearm as she did she felt something glide across her arm followed by a stinging pain and wetness. She realised that the Gisela was using the remains of one of the smashed light bulbs as a blade. Aideen veered back and with the booted foot still within her grip she twisted the Hunter over onto her front hearing cries of nonsensical threats. The body began to convulse and Aideen drove her knee into the position of where she imagined the spine was. There was one single battle cry before the laboured breathing slowed down and finally came to a silent rest.

Aideen was not going to take any more chances so she grabbed the head and with one hand on the forehead and one on the back of the head twisted it violently back and up at an angle ensuring a clean break. She still held the plastic pass card in her hand, looked around for the foot of the door, it taking a moment for her eyes to readjust. She could not see any shadows there. She gently placed the card up against the reader on the inside of the wall tapping her fingers against the steel door and a green luminaire on the reader lit up. She prised the door open a little acclimatising her eyes to the new found light.

She picked up the phone looking at the smashed glass across the screen and pressed a button on the side of the phone which made the screen illuminate. The damage was only superficial so the phone could still be used. She tied to make an emergency call typing 112 into the keypad. She raised the phone to her ear making sure not to press the smashed screen to her ear. Three beeps from the handset followed, she looked at the screen as she pulled it away. 'No signal' flashed up between parts of the shattered screen.

She thought and realised that with all the electronic equipment and copper cabling that surrounded her it was likely that the radio waves operating by the mobile network would be blocked inside the building which was acting as a huge Faraday cage. She would need to get to the very edge of the building, maybe even to a window but more likely she would have to be outside, and possibly some distance at that. The alternative would be to find somewhere that she could broadcast from. At any rate when all things considered it would be easier and smarter to try and use a wired landline when she came across it. She tossed the phone back into the darkness also taking into account that it could be a way of tracking her movements.

She looked down at herself and realised that she couldn't walk out of there naked. She looked back to the body of Gisela Jäger on the floor to see if she could use those clothes. She had been roughly the same height and build so it may have worked. She noticed small flashes which looked like distant Christmas lights twinkling, she realised that it was not going to be possible to use those clothes as they were covered in glass fragments and other protruding metal shards which were catching the light coming from the corridor. There was a noticeable pool of blood on the concrete floor which was beginning to be visible around the body.

Aideen took her first step into the light of the corridor, as she did she felt a sensation of a sharp pain from her foot. She couldn't push it off so flipped up her sole to investigate what was causing the pain and swiftly assess it. True enough during the struggle she must have trodden on some of the broken glass fragments. She took a deep breath before pulling out what she could and tested her foot out on the floor. She could still feel pain but she was unable to feel that there was anything left in there, the pain was slightly numbed with the coldness of the floor.

Aideen's bare feet tapped against the polished concrete as she ran down the hallway which was filled with high-level cabling and pipework. She thought that she must be in some sort of basement in the plant area with all of these services running up and down the corridor. It was like the inside of a computer with cabling neatly arranged in parallel lines and splitting off at different junctions. There was something quite aesthetically pleasing about the hierarchy and discipline of the wire routing. It was useless for her to try and clean up the blood patterns on the floor as she had no material with which to do this with. All of the doors were towering orange steel. She raced past one which seemed slightly smaller in scale and backtracked the last few steps. She looked at the sign and it said 'toilets and changing'. An idea formed in her head as she used the key card to access the door and pushed it open.

She found her way to the women's changing room and found it deserted much like the rest of the spaces she had travelled through. She looked at the lines of lockers and selected one at random. She tapped the door assessing it for strengths and weaknesses. The metallic hollow ping confirmed a pressed aluminium door which relied on folds and creases for the panel's strength. All she had to do was find the weakest part of the door and force her way in. She located the hinges and the lock and then selected her target point which was the top left corner of the door. She measured the area studying it carefully and decided that an elbow jab would be the best option to create a dent in the door. She levelled herself to the target area took a couple of practice moves, concentrating on her breathing as she did, remembering to exhale on contact with the door to use the full force concentrated on the small surface area. Her movement came quick and all that could be heard was a metallic thump as the corner of the locker dented far enough for the corners of the panel to lift. She then gripped the edges tightly with her fingers and leaned back using her own weight as leverage to prise the panel off from the simple locking device. There was a click sound and the door swung freely opened and banged against the adjacent locker door. She took a step backwards catching herself from the exertion focusing on her breathing.

There was a noise of a door closing and Aideen froze.

"Hullo?" Came the call from somewhere further into the changing room.

Aideen cursed herself that she had not fully checked the whole changing area to see if anyone was there.

She did not respond and waited for the person to lose interest. She pulled off the small rounded mirror that had been affixed to the inside of the locker and crouched down using the mirror to see around the corner of the bank of lockers. There was a woman standing next to the row of washbasins wrapped in a towel and with a towel wrapping her hair into a makeshift turban. She must have been in the showers and just heard the final noise of the locker door being opened. She was finishing off some sort of routine, checked her reflection in the mirror and walked off in the opposite direction to Aideen to some other part of the changing room.

Aideen quickly sought about getting dressed as she pulled the clothes off from the plastic hanger. She took a moment to address her wounds as best she could without a first aid kit. She made sure that her wounds were at least clean, running them under the cold water of the wash basins. There was something quite cooling and refreshing feeling the water against her skin. She also took a few mouthfuls of water as she was terribly thirsty. She could not recall the last time she had any sustenance. She tore up a towel that was neatly folded in the locker and used the strips to dress the wounds. Just then her stomach began to rumble, she was hungry but the adrenaline would keep her pressing forward.

Aideen checked herself in the mirror to rate her hurried disguise. She was now wearing a pair of light blue jeans which were slightly too large for her. She used a scarf that she found in the locker to run through the belt loops creating a improvised belt. She pulled an orange polo shirt with the MyLife 'ML' motif printed across the front of her shirt at an angle over her head. There was a navy fleece-lined gilet with the same 'ML' motif on the top pocket, with the same recognisable orange colour which she zipped up to midway.

She found some trainers carelessly tossed in the bottom of the locker. They had some fresh grass cuttings around the sole, the insides still damp, which indicated that the user had probably been for a run around the site during their break. As she carefully pulled them onto her feet trying not to disturb the towelling dressing that she had applied. She could feel the sogginess of the trainers as she slipped them on. She muttered under her breath to herself 'I hope that the owner of these doesn't have athletes foot!'

Searching further in the locker she also found some hair clips which she used to fashion a different look with her hair. The intention was to disguise her image as far as practically possible. The last time anyone had seen her she was a long-haired brunette. She could not do anything about her hair colour at this moment in time however she could make it seem shorter by using the clips and rolling her hair into a low twisted bun. She also found a compact makeup which she used to tan her pale features instantly.

She placed the door back into position as best she could so that it was not immediately obvious that the locker had been broken into and sat back down on the changing bench.

She heard approaching footsteps and the hairs on the back of her neck stood up. She decided to test out her new disguise. The women from before, now fully clothed with a large bag hung over her shoulder, walked past the changing benches where Aideen was.

"Morning!?" Said a mid-west American accent. The woman seemed almost surprised to see someone else there that time of the day after the night shift.

"Hi," Aideen replied, looking up to read if there was any indication in the woman's face of recognition.

There was none as the woman continued, "Are you just starting or punching out?"

"Just starting," Aideen replied not wanting to get too deep into conversation pretending to do her shoelaces on the bench.

"Ah too bad, a few of us are going to go and get a bite to eat. I don't think we've met, I'm Grace. I love your accent."

"Ha thanks, I'm Niamh, pleased to meet you."

"That's a real nice name. I love all the Irish names, they all seem to have meanings, what does 'Neeve' mean then?"

Aideen paused momentarily before replying, trying to recall the meaning of her nieces' name, "It's daft really, it means bright or like radiant you know? I'm sorry I must be getting on, I'm running late already."

"No problem. It was good to meet you too 'Neeve'. We'll have to set something up soon to get to know everyone here. These shifts seem so antisocial."

Aideen lived on her own in a modern two bedroom apartment building with cream-coloured render and large glazed windows and ample balcony which overlooked the harbour in Howth. It was a peaceful place mixed with the excitement of the workings of the harbour. She would often watch the lifeboat being launched from the stone built boathouse in the depths of winter. There was something inspiring in the fact that they would never turn back even despite the harshest of conditions.

To ensure her own safety and the safety of her wider network she had insisted as part of the conditions of her accepting this role that a quite separate safe house would be arranged. This would allow her to disconnect from her job when she was at home. It also meant that if she was ever under suspicion at any time and her apartment was either decidedly bugged or searched there would be nothing on the premises that would link her to any organisation or any living family except for a tortoiseshell tabby cat called Cabhan who was regularly fed not only by Aideen but by the local fishermen at the harbour for keeping the gulls away from their prize catch of the day.

The safe house had been set up and rented under a false name although the bills were always paid on time and in full which meant that it went unnoticed by everyone. The house was in Harold Road in the Arbour Hill area of Dublin. It was a fine mid-terrace property and hardly distinguishable from those that surrounded it. The features such as the orange red brick single course which ran at low level along the terraces were mirrored each side of the narrow road. The rest of the elevation was awash of yellow stock brick with the same orange red brick detailing used around the windows and recessed entrance doors.

The only really distinguishable features looking down the rows of houses were the front doors, each was slightly different reflecting the character of the occupier. The street was uniform in its aesthetic which was ideal for a safe house. Aideen used the property as a base to store sensitive information with all of its secret cavities, niches and hidey-holes and a place to draft her reports. Sometimes there would be more visitors which would usually be explained as either a debriefing or a formal interview, set within the context of the causal surroundings. This was usually beneficial for those who were either unsure or scared of being interviewed. The comfortable two-seater sofa and wingback chair separated by a knee height coffee table set the scene of a modest homely environment which put most people at ease. She had also used the house to cache equipment as and when it came her way.

The road offered on street parking without designation which allowed easy visits as not many people were aware of the Volkswagen Golf that she drove. She never parked directly outside the property, preferring to find a place a few spaces along and walking back. This also allowed her to see if the property was secure or not.

The house was maintained by a house keeper only known as Mrs O'Sullivan. She was employed by the services but kept a very low profile. She was as strict as a school mistress and Aideen often wondered where this strictness was something inherited or if it was nurtured from some past tragedy. Although she was known as 'Mrs', Aideen had never seen nor heard her speak on any husband or partner. In fact apart from her professional association she knew next to nothing of Mrs O'Sullivan.

As a visual sign to let agents know that the property was approachable, Mrs O'Sullivan would place a basket of seasonal flowers on the front ground window sill. If the basket was not there then this meant that the property had been compromised and that no agent should approach it.

Aideen had only been aware of this happening once. It had been a false alarm after some light-fingered teenagers stole the basket of plants. Mrs. O'Sullivan was extremely cross about the whole matter but this was the only time that Aideen had seen Mrs. O'Sullivan apologetic, she was a very stern serious woman but in this event Aideen saw something in her that she had not seen before. A vulnerability of someone upsetting her order and protocol.

Aideen used this place to don her alter egos. For short-term assignments or one-offs she would use theatrical disguises to alter her appearance. She had multiple wigs and a wide variety of accessories including contact lenses, which she hated to use for fear of the lens travelling beneath her eye.

These masquerades were not acceptable for assignments of longer duration, the simplicity of these covers were rudimentary. For longer-term assignments she would actually have to alter her appearance either by dyeing her hair, having it styled in a totally different way, using a sun bed to keep a holiday tan, go to the gym to work on upper body strength, learning a new dialect and accent, pick up new habits. It was not too difficult to create a new character and persona as part of her cover for various operations.

The problem was becoming herself afterwards. There would always be residual traces of the previous character. She often wondered if she could ever really be herself again after playing at being someone else for so long, was she creating another character when she became *herself*. A recent habit that she had become accustomed to unintentionally was to tap biscuits on a plate before eating them. This had stemmed from a character that she had created who hated mess, to the point of an obsessive compulsive. Crumbs were not to be tolerated so not only were biscuits eaten from a plate but three taps of the biscuit before biting into it would release any loose crumbs onto the plate and not onto the surrounding surfaces.

As she walked out of the changing room she made sure to keep her head down just enough to keep out of view of the security cameras but not enough to make someone watching think that she was deliberately avoiding them. She pulled the precious swipe card with the image of the blonde-haired assassin from her jeans pocket and tried to open a door. The card reader was mounted on a stainless steel post at approximately waist height so that the opening of the door leaf was protected. She nervously swiped the card through the reader waiting for a distant alarm to sound. Nothing, the small glowing LED light remained red. A sudden panic made her stomach turn as she thought about once again becoming trapped. She collected her thoughts again, there would be time later for that sort of wobbliness but not now. Now she had to stay strong, get out of there and sabotage anything of F5 that she could along the way. She tried the card again and pulled down on the lever handle of the door. She saw the LED light turn green and the electronic locking mechanism clicked open.

She found herself in a corridor where the walls were leaden with strands of conduit carrying hundreds of individual cables. It was not as well illuminated as the other spaces that she had been in. She knew that she had to find a way out of this place. The deeper she got into the data hall spaces the more like a labyrinth it seemed. Almost every wall that she looked at looked the same. The only way that she to distinguish any progress through the building was the change in colour of a stipe which ran down the walls of the rooms. She imagined that this was some sort of 'zoning' for the building similar to a carpark. She felt disorientated but knew that there had to be some sort of hierarchy to the space. It was not designed to be a maze regardless of how it first appeared.

Nothing in her briefing the she had been told would have prepared her for this. She was on her own now and would have to work out what to do for herself. Ahead she could see someone in a high visibility vest and hard hat talking into a radio in a rather hurried fashion. She went to turn in the opposite direction and then decided that it was better to press on forward. The person was concentrating on something at the side of the corridor oblivious to anything else around them.

As she neared closer trying to look at what was causing all of the commotion with her peripheral vision she could see the man trying to pick up damaged pieces of wall. There was some kind of machine that was buried under the debris. It looked as though someone had driven some piece of plant equipment into the wall by mistake. It has caused a lot of damage almost as though it had been struck at speed.

She could see the logo of the construction company on the back of the vest clearly now identifying him as one of the contractors and not staff from MyLife. He was trying to clear the debris away from the machine carefully lifting chunks of the panelised wall system which looked as though it had been torn apart rather than crumpled in the impact.

Then a whirring noise sounded like a hydraulic piston being flexed and a new lower tone noise like a motorised engine starting up. Among the debris a flashing yellow light began to flicker. The contractor jumped back in surprise not knowing what to expect dropping the radio to the floor.

The radio hit the floor and the base where the battery was housed shattered as the rest of the device clattered to the ground with a sudden stop, now utterly useless.

Something was beginning to move from within the wall void as if the machine had come alive of its own accord. Aideen wanted to move but for some reason was compelled to stay.

Some of the debris started to become dislodged fallout from the scene of the crash. The contractor leaned in to inspect what was happening when two arms suddenly protruded through the wreckage and grabbed onto him. He was unable to escape the jaws of the machine which was now unearthing itself from the collapsed wall. The contractor who had now become aware of Aideen's presence was shouting towards her pleading for her to do something.

All she could see was an array of tentacle like arms which had entombed the worker. She could see him trying to struggle against the machine and his cries became muffled as the machine seemed to engulf him in its clutches. She looked around to see who was controlling the machine but there was no one else there nor was there any visible shut off point. Before she could do anything she heard a muffled last cry before the machine finished its compression cycle and began opening its claws, dropping the contorted body of the contractor onto the floor. She let out a little cry in horror. Nothing could have primed her for this kind of awfulness. The machine leached forward towards her and then paused as if it were making a decision. She realised it must be carrying out some sort of scan. The flashing lights continued and she held her breath unable to move.

The machine then started to rotate on the spot and continued down the corridor leaving the carnage in its wake.

Aideen felt sick but was so full of adrenaline she just took a moment to compose herself before she could progress. She wondered why the machine had not attacked her after it had attacked the unarmed contractor who was really no threat at all. She wondered as she put her hand up to her chest feeling her heart beating rapidly. Then she felt the stitching of the MyLife logo on the clothing that she had stolen.

The machine must have scanned her and seen the MyLife logo and considered her not a threat. Because the contractor was not wearing any MyLife clothing the machine had seen him as a threat to be neutralised using its artificial intelligence programming.

Clifton was now standing before the 42U high rack, there was a green hue glowing from the array for flashing LED lights that resembled the twinkling of Christmas lights, but there did not seem to be a set rhythm or pattern to them. The blinking was intelligent it was beautiful in its own right. The cabling which hung down from the trays above were tied back to vertical panels and teed off from the highway of cables into the patch panels so neatly and orderly, a shrine to the obsessive compulsive. Clifton tried to think where he had placed the device. Looking now each server blade looked the same. He tried to think, was he standing when he inserted the device, would he have been bending down trying to look for an obscure place that would be hard to visually inspect. "That's it," he said under his breath as he began to reach upwards.

There was a crisp 'beep' noise and he heard the sound of air rushing as a door opened somewhere in the room. The room was suddenly flooded with the white light from outside the room. Clifton squinted as his eyes adjusted from the semi-darkness. He froze for a moment like a rabbit caught in the headlights not knowing what to do. He could hear phantom footsteps coming towards him. They were probably in his head though. Maybe it was just a patrol rather than the German henchman.

Whoever it was it would be better if he had somewhere to hide until they were gone. He moved away from where he was standing being careful not to make any sudden movement or sounds. He tried to look through the server cabinets to see if that would reveal anyone but it did not. His heart was beating so fast now that all he could hear was the sound of his own heartbeat dumbing in his ears. His body temperature was starting to rise with the warmth of the room. His mind flashed back to the coolness of the night out on the roof top. Then he was sure that he heard another beep and a door latching.

He closed his eyes in relief, "Thank goodness whoever it was has gone," he whispered to himself.

"Wrong!" he heard from just behind him as he yelped in pain as a strong hand gripped his arm. Clifton knew it was the German just by the sound of his voice. He tried feebly to throw a punch with is free arm which had little effect.

"I zee Lockridge is dead, by your hand maybe? I doubt it. Who else is here with you?"

Before Clifton could say anything a swift blow was dealt to his abdomen and he stumbled backwards into some servers.

"Kindly, go to hell," Clifton spat the words out looking up towards his attacker.

The German smiled and laughed heartily to himself. "Now you are going to die you silly little man." Placing both his hands tightly around Clifton's throat lifting him up onto tip toes. Clifton struggled against him, beating at his assailants arms with his fists. It was like hitting rock. Clifton was beginning to quickly tire and a wave of exhaustion began to take its hold on him. His ears fell silent, his arms and legs began to feel heavy as he felt himself sinking in. As his vision began to fade he thought he was having one last hallucination. It was Aideen standing there smiling wearing some sort of hat which didn't suit her.

His ears picked up and he could hear the dull murmur of the fans. The pressure around his throat was loosening. He took in deep breathes before he was able to organise himself. He was slumped on the floor, there was another body lying near him which he inadvertently nudged with his foot. There was no movement. He began to look around the room for answers and hears a soft Irish voice speaking to him. He looked up and saw a silhouetted face with light appearing to emanate from around the figure with its hand stretched out towards him. Instinctively he offered out a hand. A bandaged hand grabbed his and hauled him to his feet. As his eyes focused he found that the hand belonged to a beautiful face. It was Aideen. He embraced her as if he had not seen her for years. He held her so tightly, he wanted this so much to be real and not in his mind. "Sorry I couldn't find you," he whispered into her ear.

"What are you talking you eejit, you're alive!" Then they kissed.

"Not that I'm not pleased to see you but we've got to get out of here."

"Wait there is something that I must do before we go." Clifton climbed up to the server and pulled back the cables in search of the device. It was not there and he began to panic frantically shifting cables until there it was. He used his thumb and forefinger to prise it out of the connection and went to drop it on the floor where he was going to stamp on it and destroy it.

Aideen grabbed his hand "No wait," she said in a very authoritative tone. "We can learn from that." She took it from his hand and stuffed it into her gilet pocket. She searched the unconscious man on the floor and found a gun on him, relieving him of it and checking to see if the safety was on it she tucked it into her waistband and covered it with her clothing so that it was concealed.

"Lockridge told me that you are an Agent, is that right?"

"I don't think that really matters at this moment in time do you? We can discuss this later once we are out of here."

This was a side to Aideen that he had not seen before. She appeared to be the same person but as if the character had been exchanged for a much harder and more assertive personality.

Chapter Thirteen

Clifton sat across the table from the two agents who were debriefing him after the events from earlier.

They had picked him up walking through the town of Clane just outside Jas Manzor's Village Inn where he had stopped for a pint of Hop House 13, having felt the need after such an eventful two days. He had just left and was making his way across the road towards the Esso garage on the corner heading towards the bus stop which would take him into Dublin, and the airport from there. He longed to be back at home in his own bed and rest his aching body. The traffic on the main road was not particularly busy for midday. He walked by the entrance to the Esso garage with the bus top in his sights when suddenly he was confronted by a white van which had pulled across the cross over in front of him sharply.

The side sliding door sprang open and two muscular men jumped out, each grabbing one of Clifton's arms and escorting him quickly into the van. It all happened so quickly Clifton could offer no resistance.

He felt plasticuffs being placed on his wrists and tightened, which cut into his wrists. The inside of the van was only slightly lit from a small led light which was fixed to the ceiling of the van and with no window between the drivers cabin and the storage compartment of the van. He was pushed down onto a wooden bench seat but before he could get a look at either of the two men. A black sacking hood was placed over his head by one of them and the two sentries sat down either side of him.

Clifton thought about pleading his innocence, trying to reason with whoever it was, but who was it who had picked him up? He decided to just sit there and wait until they got to wherever they were going. Besides in his condition there was no way he would be able to outrun or outfight two guys in the back of a van. He would bide his time and try to make an escape when he was less well guarded. He would not try and put up resistance here while in transit he would send these goons to sleep thinking that he was no trouble then once they had that false impression he would make his move.

They travelled in silence for what seemed about twenty minutes. The only noises that could be heard were those outside when the van must have been stopping at traffic lights and voices of part conversations from pedestrians outside the van carried in.

Clifton knew that they must have joined a motorway for part of their journey as the speed of the van had changed and he could hear the wind noise swirling around the van. He was concerned at this point that the wooden bench that he was sitting on did not have any form of restraint should the van stop suddenly.

Clifton let himself begin to doze, not knowing when he would get another chance to. It would also help him to conserve what was left of his energy. He was awoken with a jolt and the sentries either side of him held him in place on the bench. They must have gone over a speedbump or something similar. The van stopped and the side door was slid open. Clifton could just make out day light through his hood but nothing more. He remained seated as the two next to him stood and began moving around. Someone pulled him up to his feet by his arm. He was gearing up to spring out of the van and make a run for it. The hood was suddenly pulled back and he was blinded by the bright light. He went to leap forward out of the van into the unknown when he heard Aideen's voice telling him everything was alright. Then he felt a sharp pain in his arm and realised that he had been given some form of injection. He tried to struggle and fight it off like a cornered tiger, his arms and legs became incredibly heavy and his head longed just to sleep. He went down within two minutes as the serum worked its way around his bloodstream.

The room where he was being questioned was well lit with a central pendant light which had a glass bowl at its base. There were two crescent wall lights on each side of the wall which gave off a low buzzing noise that was barely audible. There was a modern stainless steel clock on the wall with some sort of artistic deconstructive coat-stand made out of beech wood. Clifton leaned back in the leather conference room chair and stretched before leaning forward and putting his hands on the table but consciously not crossing them. The officer sitting closest to him wore a dark navy three-piece suit with a blue shirt and red tie. He looked much older than his actual years with wrinkly vain protruding from each temple towards his eyes. He wore circular wire-framed glasses and had a stern face with short whitening hair at the sides being the only residual hair left.

Clifton was sure that he had seen him before and let his mind work on recalling where he had remembered the face from.

The female officer who had introduced herself simply as Lucinda, looked up from above her laptop computer where she had been taking notes and finished typing. Clifton did not know if this interview was being recorded but suspected that somehow his every word and movement was not just being imprinted on the minds of the officers before him. Lucinda looked at Clifton for a short time as if making some sort of judgement in her head before speaking.

"I want to go through this one more time if you don't mind," she stated rather abruptly.

Clifton had been through the whole episode with them at least twice now and was becoming considerably irritated at having to repeat the story over again and over again. He knew deep down that this must be some sort of protocol but it still annoyed him. He returned the studying stare like a poker face apart from everyone knew that he was not bluffing, what he had told them was exactly the facts as he knew them to be.

The more Lucinda pushed and questioned parts of his story the more Clifton felt her was pushing back with less response and more curt replies. Which was to be expected although he knew that he wanted to have these people on side but after all he had been through it was hard to distinguish who was telling the truth from a lie. After all Lockridge had approached him under the banner of the National Cyber Security Centre under GCHQ.

She had explained that Lockridge had been a plant at the NCSC after being recruited by F5 some months after setting up as head of section in China. F5 as an entity had spread throughout the MyLife social media platform gathering intelligence of every person that had an account. Like an undetected cancer it had spread throughout the network and was enveloping the MyLife as a host to a parasite until the parasite became more powerful than the host. The device that Clifton had been tasked to plant in the latest MyLife data centre would have given F5 access into the core of the data connection allowing them to effective have their own access into the fields of server racks held within the data halls. From a security perspective it would be like tapping a line from inside the firewall. Anyone's and everyone's data would have been available to them.

Lucinda had a militaristic air about her. She spoke well but phased things in a very matter of fact sort of way but without sounding too officious like a solicitor. She seemed to appreciate his frustration but this was her job and she would not stray from the debriefing. She had meticulously taken down his story before his creative mind rewrote his actual memory. She obviously held some sort of high rank as her colleague had remained silent throughout the whole interview. Only to rub his brow with his thumb and forefinger or to look over the top of his glasses at Clifton as he had explained how he had been told that he was actually serving his country before he unravelled the deceit and knew that he had to put things right.

Clifton then knew where he had seen this person before. At the wine tasting event at his club. He had been seated at a different table but the manner with which he rubbed his brow was an unmistakeable idiosyncrasy.

He kept his encounter with Aideen to the briefest mention that he possibly could. He did not know how much she would have told her superiors. He was trying to analyse each moment they had spent together and work out how much of their encounters had been strictly business and how much, if any at all, had been her. He knew that he had feelings for her but she had deceived him to get close. He struggled with this inner argument trying to answer the ultimate question which persisted in him mind. Could he trust her? He was trying hard to think objectively but how could he when he was smitten. He knew that any decision he made would of course be biased.

When the interview was over all of the three people in the room stood up. Lucinda shook Clifton's hand and informed him that he would be free to return home although he should expect a follow up in a few days' time from a local officer if they had any further questions that they would like to ask him. The male officer then turned and walked towards the door without uttering a single word. Tapped on the door once, twice in quick succession and then once again and stood back. The door was opened from the outside and two men in casual clothes walked into the room and stood to attention. Despite their standing to attention it was clear that these were some sort of plain clothes officers. Firstly they were trying too hard to blend in, they both wore tee-shirts and jeans. Sports jackets and very white trainers. The trainers were useful because they allowed almost silent movement and allowed for speed as required in the line of duty. It was unusual for causal trainers to be kept this clean which meant that whoever owned them made a point of cleaning them. The majority of people do not clean their trainers knowing that they are likely only going to last six months or so therefore it was more likely that the trainers would be replaced before there was ever an opportunity for cleaning them. In the services however it was bred into them that they would ritually clean their shoes to a sparkling standard.

The other give away was the haircuts – both were matching, short-cropped hair, typical of military and the police. Lucinda addressed the two service personnel. "You are to escort Mr Clifton to his room and wait there for further instructions." Both saluted and looked off into the middle distance. She then turned towards Clifton. "You will be leaving on the Ryanair twenty-twenty-five flight RF272 to Stansted. You will find your personal effects in your room. I wish you a safe journey home."

Clifton looked towards the two men standing in the room. "Will I have the company of these two to escort me home?"

"That should not be necessary, we do not believe that you are in any immediate danger however you did disrupt a major security breach which ironically you almost started. MyLife is still with us and I believe that F5 will raise its head once more. It has been inside MyLife for so long who knows how deep it goes. I believe that although you have managed to disrupt this site there are many more like it across the world that may have already been compromised. Sadly it is not a case of simply destroying the facilities – the internet is not something that has the capacity to simply be switched off. It can be used for truly magnificent things or it can be misused for terrifying things."

"What about Aideen, if that was her real name, will I ever see her again?"

Lucinda ignored the comment about the name, making Clifton think that he was right and that Aideen was clearly some sort of alias name used. Her response did not really give Clifton any sort of clear answer to his question. "She is recovering from injuries sustained in the field." And with that she sat down and returned to her laptop computer and began typing. Clifton looked over towards the male officer who still remained silent but had his eyes trained on Clifton.

Without formality Clifton left the room with the two guards who escorted him to his room. As the door closed Musgrave turned to look at Lucinda folding his arms and then spoke softly. "Well do you think that he will keep quiet?"

"He has signed the Official Secrets Act, I think that we have made it quite clear what would happen if he did think about going to the media."

Musgrave leaned back in his chair looking towards the ceiling philosophically placing a pen to the corner of his mouth. "I am not so concerned with the here and now I am more concerned about ten years from now. We have both seen it before when people find it too hard to keep the past in the past."

Without looking up from her laptop screen she replied. "Well that's for your department to keep track on wouldn't you say?"

"True of course, I do think that he could potentially be a useful resource in the future you know." Playing with his pen between his fingers. "I'm not entirely sure that I believe the circumstances of Lockridge's death. I mean it does wrap it all up a bit too nicely doesn't it, Derek kills Lockridge and Mr Jäger kills Derek?" Musgrave took his glasses off and rested them on the table leaning back into his chair closing his eyes to run through the story one more time in his own mind forming a pyramid with his fingers as he contemplated. "It was a foolish attempt to throw suspicion by kidnapping my daughter. Do we know yet how he got from the UK to Ireland? Once the site was searched did we find the remaining Jäger?"

"In answer to your first question we have Lockridge travelling on the CityJet flight WX119 which leaves City Airport at eleven-forty-five using an Austrian Passport under the name of Jakob Bauer, the flights were booked by the NCSC, the sad fact is that he used us as his resource to get around. They must have gone there straight from Barnet custody.

For your second question we have not found anything on the site yet to confirm if he is alive or dead."

Clifton sat quietly looking out of the window of his hotel room watching the flow of traffic making its way towards the airport. It was quite hypnotic waiting for a slight pause which occured when the traffic lights freed another tide of cars steaming around the roadway. He had been debriefed by someone who looked as though they belonged in a library with their bifocal lens glasses and strict posture.

There was a soft knock at the door. Clifton turned towards the door but before he could get up he could see the handle turning for it to be opened. This was a curtesy knock rather than a request. Aideen stood there in the doorway. She had changed since last time he had seen her. Her cut hand was now neatly bandaged and she was wearing a Stella McCartney slim suit with trousers. He noted that she seemed more comfortable, more confident now. Her character seemed different though. The way she stood and everything about her suddenly seemed alien to him.

There was a pause before she broke the silence. "I can't come with you, you know that." She took a few steps forward and held her hands in front of herself. Clifton could read from her body language that she had taken on a defensive stance.

Clifton stood up and indicated towards one of the two armchairs which were positioned around a small coffee table within the room. "Would you like to sit down? I can only offer you tea, water of something they are trying to pass off as coffee?"

She looked down as she smiled, some of her hair fell forward covering her face slightly. She had the same hair styling as when they had both first met. Clifton wondered if she was still in character or if this was the real her. Who was the real Aideen he wondered.

"Water please." She took a measured step forwards and sat in the chair. Clifton went to the mini-bar and retrieved a cold bottle of still water and some glasses. He placed the glasses down on the table and twisted the top off from the water bottle and began to pour out the glasses.

"You know, I was in a hotel room once dying for a cup of tea and the only water I had available to me at that time of night was the sparkling water. So I ended up with literally a sparkling cup of tea rather than purely figuratively."

She did not react to the story which in Clifton's mind was a bad sign. She took a sip from the glass and placed it carefully back onto the table. She crossed one leg over the other and Clifton noticed her black patient shoes – not an unattractive pair of shoes but tailored more for practicality than style. She leaned forward and put her hands together looking him straight in the eyes. Clifton knew this was leading to something bad, he had been here many times before.

"My life is very different to yours and although I like you I am too attached to my work to want to leave it.

"You probably wouldn't understand but this whole thing, it excites me in a way that no other profession could. You're a really nice guy but it couldn't work between us. I don't want to settle down and all that it's just not me and you would grow to resent that in me, and that would be worse." She kissed him softly on the cheek and they embraced one another.

There was an officious knock on the door before Clifton realised he was on his own staring out of the window watching the world go by. It was not Aideen this time but the two guards from before. One of them carried Clifton's dispatch and cabin bag.

Clifton was ushered into the back of a new looking white Volkswagen Passat, one of his minders sat in the front while the other sat beside him. There was no interaction within the vehicle except for the reflection of the driver's eyes as he glanced in the rear-view mirror briefly to see who he was transporting. They left the hotel's carpark steadily and headed towards Terminal one. Clifton looked out of the window looking at the silhouette of the south Dublin hills against a pale purple hue truing to a blue sky.

The sun was beginning to fall and street lights were just beginning to light. The car dipped down the ramp beneath Terminal Two which was clad in curved silver panels resembling something like a mythical sea monster brought onto land. The road then ramped sharply up onto a podium level forming the drop-off point. There were cars and taxis parked at least three cars deep. Clifton watched families excitedly getting their luggage out from the cars ready for their holidays. Parents saying tearful goodbyes to their children. Businessmen on mobiles marching around the parked cars toward the sliding doors of the entrance. All of this was happening while being observed by the airport Garda who watched the vehicles like a hawk ensuring that no car was picking up and that car were not parked there for longer than was truly necessary.

The car came to a gentle stop and the driver turned to the sentry to his right. Who then reached into his inside jacket pocket and produced a folded printed piece of paper. Turning in the chair he handed it to his colleague in the back of the car with Clifton. He passed the folded paper to Clifton who made no attempt to take it.

"This is your ticket home sunshine, boarding card and passport," smiled the guard.

As he took the folded paper he felt the thickness of the passport within. "Thank you," he said with indifference trying to avoid eye contact with the guard. He was about six foot two whose muscular physique could be read through the ill-fitting of his clothing. He was deliberately dressed down to blend in, but like most non-uniformed policemen was easily noticeable. He had a strong jaw line. Clifton knew that this was not someone to trifle with as he sensed that this was someone who knew how to kill efficiently and effectively but also enjoyed doing so.

"Out you get then," he barked to Clifton.

He did not wait to be told twice as he opened the passenger door and walked around to the back of the car, the boot popped open revealing his suitcase and dispatch bag. He was half considering leaving the luggage where it was as who knows who had been through his personal possessions or what they had bugged. The thought of someone like a burglar going through his house made his skin tingle and feel sick, to a lesser extent he felt the same about his personal effects. He noticed another piece of luggage in the large space which was not his. A large black nondescript rucksack. The bouncer-like guard from the back seat was now at the back of the car with Clifton and pulled it from its resting place.

"We wouldn't want you to get lonely on your flight now, would we?" There was a short pause while they both stared at one another. Clifton wanted nothing more than to swing for him and to test out how strong that jaw line really was but he was tired, physically, mentally and tired of it all.

Clifton turned towards the entrance door and started to make his way into the airport while the guard slammed the boot lid closed, tapped the back of the car twice and the car began to pull away from the drop of area under the watchful eye of the Garda.

As the doors parted for Clifton he extended the handle of his cabin bag and began to push it towards the security area. As he made his way along the concourse he noticed how the bag was now beginning to pull away from him as he pushed it along. He stopped and made the bag do a full three-hundred-and-sixty degree spin turn to see if it was something catching in one of the four wheels. He tried pushing it again and the same thing happened again, the bag pulled to away from him to the right. 'Sod it', he thought to himself, 'I'll have to get a new one when I get home anyway.'

He then started to drag the case behind him as the wheels locked. He slipped the passport out of the paper folds into his trouser pocket as he unwrapped the boarding card and placed it on the scanner. He looked forward at the glass barrier in front of him and there was a moment just before the doors parted that he could see the reflection of the guard behind him with the rucksack lazily hung over one shoulder. He walked through the barrier and stuffed the paper into his pocket without thinking to fold it backup. Clifton knew the airport pretty well and looked at the queues for the security checks. The one that appeared to be the longer queue next to the bank of lifts was actually the shorter queue as the security conveyer belt was only the other side of the lifts, but at a first glance to someone not as familiar with the layout it would seem a much longer queue. Clifton got in line.

Within no time he was towards the front of the queue and he was placing his items into the big grey plastic trays ready to be scanned. He did his usual airport ritual and placed his items in their positions as he had done so many times before. This time however he felt empty as if he was just going through the motions. He walked through the scanner with the minimum of fuss and waited for his tray to appear on the opposite side. He stood there leaning back on the metal table which stood between the conveyers so that people could use the table to place their tray on and get dressed once again.

The noise of the trays going into the return bin, repetitive chants of what items should go into the trays, the whirring should of the conveyer and the spinning of the rollers as the trays slid down the ramp – Clifton shut them all out while he contemplated Aideen. Why had he felt such a connection with her when realistically they had spent so little time together?

It was not logical for such a logical and cautious person. Was this what is was like to fall in love at first sight or was it purely infatuation.

He could not answer this here and then. Clifton realised his luggage had still not come and he began to wonder what was being replaced in his luggage this time and by whom. He was just about to walk away from the area before a woman made eye contact with him and in a broad accent asked him if this was his luggage behind the half height screen. She was obviously staff by the way she was dressed in the black combat style trousers, white shirt and blue latex gloves. She had an array of photo identification cards attached to a strap necklace which dangled to just above her belly button would be. She had copper colour hair and pale blue eyes.

Clifton nodded and made his way around to the counter crossing his arms.

"Ok sir, let's have a look." She tapped a screen which was mounted at eye level. She smiled reassuringly "No bother it's just a random swab test." She took tray away on a wheeled trolley opened up the case so that Clifton could see her running the plastic wand over his clothing, shoes and jacket before placing the wand into a machine which did not look very scientific from this distance. The light on the machine went green which Clifton took to mean as a good thing. She replaced the wand into its holder and wheeled his luggage on the trolley back over to him. "Just one last thing." She scanned the side of the tray and tapped some more on the screen before pushing the tray over towards Clifton. "Have a pleasant flight," she said. "I will try," he replied, with the irony lost on her.

He made his way through to the duty free area. He would usually spend some time looking at all of the colours of the whiskeys and the colourful displays which changed with the seasons. He dutifully visited the Butlers chocolate shop but rather than buying chocolate to take back home for friends and family on this occasion he just ordered a mint hot chocolate. Walking through the shopping forecourts sipping on the hot chocolate aware of a presence somewhere behind him watching him he made his way past the food court and suddenly turned to go up the escalator which would take him to the mezzanine level which overlooked the atrium which had a Starbucks coffee at its heart.

It was interesting to note that no matter what time of day he went past that particular coffee store it was always just as busy. He walked the last third of the escalator quickly reaching the top and walked straight into the Garden Terrace bar and ordered a pint of Hop House 13 and some chips. As a rule he would not usually eat within four hours of a flight for fear of being travel sick on the way home but he was hungry and thirsty. He watched the escalator waiting for his minder to ascend from the floor below but it did not happen. Clifton wondered if he had lost him, surely not as this was a trained professional. But it was busy in the food hall and he had darted around quite a bit so maybe, just maybe he had lost him. At least this gave him some alone time to think. All he really wanted to do at this moment in time was to speak to Clara and tell her everything. She always knew what the right thing to say to soothe any anxiety that he had.

Clifton checked the boarding time, it was twenty minutes away. He watch the sun slowly sinking into the horizon and the sky became a wonderful canvas view through the glazing of the terminus. He finished the last sip of his pint and then got up to leave. Checking that he had everything with him that he should by patting his pockets down he took one last look at the table where he had been sitting and proceeded towards the escalators which would take him downstairs towards the awaiting gates. On his way down he caught sight of his minder sitting in the

Starbucks reading a folded newspaper, with one leg crossed over the other. Clifton looked down gingerly not wanting to make direct eye contact. There was still a small chance that his minder had not seen him leave.

As he got to the bottom of the escalator he looked at the departure board and found his flight number leaving from Gate 102. He quickly made his way to the gate making use of the travellators. He used to like the sound of his footsteps on the metal flooring but now it only made him think of when he was hiding on the roof and below the raised access floor.

As he walked down the polished concrete concourse with its glittering quartz reflecting under the spotlights above he looked at the gate desk where an informal queue had started to form already. There were a few seats left next to the gate. The airport was in the process of upgrading the seating so half of the seats were cold perforated metal formed seats while the other half were cushioned black foam. He pulled the folded paper out of his pocket and checked his boarding card to see if they had thought enough of him to add priority boarding. They had not, so he took a seat and decided that he would join the queue once enough people had gone through as he hated waiting, to him the pointless queue seemed dogmatic. There was no point hurrying to join a queue, especially when they had allocated seats.

Clifton sat there and people watched the almost constant flow of people walking down overladen with bags, some being dragged behind. Every so often he would hear the wheels of a cabin bag being dragged over the grilles of the travellator which ran between the gates. It was an irritating noise. He considered closing his eyes and try and rest but he wanted to know where his minder was and if he was already there. He gingerly looked around scanning the queue, the last chance gift shop and the Soho Coffee shop before his eyes rested on the WH Smiths in the corner.

He opened his dispatch bag but could not find his book so he decided to go in and see what they had available for the trip home, he had concluded already that it was pointless trying to sleep. He would wait until he had got home, to his own house, to his own room, to his own bed. He browsed the shelves studying each of the titles, occasionally picking one up and reading some of the blurb. He picked up a spy thriller which was his usual travel companion and scoffed to himself after reading the back as he placed in back on the shelf.

Clifton had certainly had his fill of espionage, lies and death in the last forty-eight hours and would not want to read about them on the way home. There was a book with an eagle on the cover, he read the back and decided to find his escapism in a book about ancient Rome and Julius Ceasar. As he was purchasing the book he glanced back over the queue as the tannoy announced that boarding had commenced. The queue started to move quite quickly. He made his way leisurely over to the check-in desk and proceeded to board the plane.

As the took his seat half way down the plane he was not aware of the other passengers nor the one with a baseball cap pulled down low as he sat curled up against the window signalling to the rest of the world that he did not want to be disturbed.

Clifton reached up and placed his cabin bag in the overhead compartment, positioned his dispatch under the seat in front and folded his jacket over his knees. After the last two days it was painful to stay in the seat. There was no position that he could find where he was not distracted by the pain of a bruise. Eventually he found a way to ignore the pain and immersed himself in ancient Rome.

The flight seemed to be over before he had even got to chapter five. The plane touched down abruptly and the Ryanair fanfare seemed to flood the cabin from nowhere. Everyone started to take off their seatbelts, sending text messages to loved ones and updating their MyLife status. Clifton remained in his seat with his head buried in his book until people started departing the plane.

Clifton did not see the attacker moving quickly down the aisle towards him but he recognised the voice instantly. Clifton was standing facing the front of the seat, reaching into the overhead compartment to retrieve this cabin bag. He was pulling the bag out of the locker as he heard the voice. Startled he caught the bag as it fell from the compartment.

"Because of you she'z dead, I told you I vould kill you!"

He did not see the weapon that was used but he felt the force of the impact as it penetrated the plastic outer casing of his cabin bag with little resistance. Instinctively Clifton pulled the bag down abruptly, twisting it as he did. The bladed weapon remained stuck in the cabin bag as it was driven from the attackers grip.

Clifton used his other hand to drive the cabin bag at a ninety degree angle to break the grip of the angry assailant. He swung the bag around so that it travelled over to the other side of the cabin with the weapon still embedded in the case so that it was out of the reach of either of them.

At least this now made it a fair fight. He did not anticipate the first left hook punch which made him hit his head on the open hold door. Everything went black for a moment as the pain from his earlier head injury began to thump through the painkillers before he started to see stars in his vision. He instinctively put his hands up to protect his head from any further shots. He had an instant headache and but before he could take a swing he heard some sort of commotion followed by someone shouting "Taser, taser." Clifton could not be sure what followed as his vision was severely impaired and he was not able to honestly differentiate what was his memory and what his mind had created.

He remembered being sat in a quiet room in a comfortable reclining chair. He was unclear how long he had been here or how he had gotten there. At his point it did not really seem to bother him. He felt comfortable and strangely safe. He relaxed into a sort of daydream and then became aware that there were other people in the room. Someone was tending to his head with some sort of dressing. There was not any pain although he could feel the soft fingers on his skin. There was an aroma of apricots in the air, some sort of feminine scented perfume.

He dozed a little while longer before becoming more aware of his surroundings and the nurse in the room who had tended his wounds. He realised that he was in some sort of first aid room. The comfortable chair was actually a treatment couch. The room had a safety vinyl flooring, a warm grey colour, the walls were treated with a white plastic lining for hygiene reasons.

Clifton recognised the face from one of his debriefs. The solemn looking fellow. He seemed less intense than the last time Clifton had seen him. There was a woman standing next to him making a study of him as he lay there. She had a prettiness about her but as she stood there with her arms folded Clifton made the assumption that she was strictly business only. Musgrave made the introductions around the room. Before perching himself on the end of the treatment couch.

"Trouble seems to follow you around Mr. Clifton. I take it you are aware of Lutz Jäger, the man that attacked you on the plane?"

"I know that he has been trying to kill me for the last forty-eight hours but short of that I know absolutely nothing about him."

"The Jäger's were a brother and sister mercenary team out for hire. They were known across Europe. They originally came from the East side of Germany before the Berlin Wall came down. Originally they worked for the Stasi in the Party's Youth Wing infiltrating the West and gaining information from tourists.

Later on they were transferred back to East Germany when one of their joint operations went south. It soon became known that they had a certain passion and talent for debriefing Western agents involving some of the most inhumane torture you can imagine. When the wall came down things began to change. The strangle hold that the Stasi had over the people was beginning to wane and the support that they once had from the Communists was evaporating rapidly as the motherland was beginning to self-implode. When the crowds stormed the Stasi headquarters on the night of the fourth of December 1989, millions of files, letters, tapes you name it was made public. Many were lost, burned or shredded. Those who collaborated with the Stasi wanted to make sure that there was no incriminating evidence.

Stasi officials wanted to make sure that there was nothing linking themselves to any of the cases but it was hopeless.

"With the collapse of the Wall and the imminent collapse of communism in Russia, former Stasi agents being threatened with criminal charges and retribution it left the Jäger's without a cause or a war to fight. They found refuge in the Nordic countries, Denmark, Sweden and Norway, being able to slip between countries with some ease. They started off on small scale but became well known for their assimilations by torture. It was not so much about extracting information but for the sick pleasure of it.

"Our agent Aideen as you know nearly did not walk away from her encounter with Gisela Jäger. It was a shame that she was unable to bring her in as we would have really liked to talk to her. Thankfully we now have her brother in custody because of his hatred of you."

"But I had nothing to do with his sister's death, how could I?"

"Yes, well sometimes disinformation helps to draw someone out you see. We knew that it was likely that he would be listening into our communications once he knew we were there. It is what he was trained to do after all."

"You mean you used me as bait?"

"That would be one way of interpreting it, another would be a calculated risk. You were not alone one the plane. You had protection when you needed it."

Chapter Fourteen

It was a late August Saturday morning and the beach was beginning to get busy with holiday makers. Children were playing in the shallows, racing one another to see who could out run the next wave to lap upon the shoreline. The lifeguards were sitting outside on the deck of their elevated beach-hut which looked out over the bay. It would likely be a slow day for them as there was no rip current and people were generally using the designated bathing area which was identified with red and yellow flags which flapped gently in the wind. There was a small café at the top of the beach with people sitting outside nursing cups of tea while children ate ice creams from wafer cornets. They sat on bistro chairs watching the beach and the people passing on the promenade who strolled by hand in hand.

There were a few people on bicycles riding along the boardwalk which connected Highcliffe with Mudeford who were easy to spot with their brightly coloured clothing. The shoreline at the base of the cliffs was easily identifiable by the rhythm of the pattern of the pastel painted beach huts which ran along Christchurch Bay. The cloudless sky which could be seen above the green screen of the tree canopies above the cliff was a dynamic brilliant blue. It felt as though today would be full of opportunity and it was exiting. With one look at the sky thing suddenly did not seem so bad, mountains became hills and the light triumphed over the darkness.

There was something comforting about being surrounded by nature on such a glorious day. Clifton recalled that in China the colour red represented good fortune and happiness but the colour blue was associated with timber and springtime, starting afresh after a cold long winter. The Ancient Greeks saw blue as a colour to ward off evil and was often worn as a charm to bring good luck. From the design world blue is often associated with stability, faith, wisdom and truth. The colour blue is often used in packaging and in logos to play on these preconceived settings. Blue also seems to have a calming effect on humans, calming the metabolism and generally fills people with a feeling of tranquillity.

Clara had suggested they get together at the coast after some recent telephone calls which extended well into the night. Clifton had come across as being rather a recluse since his return from Ireland. He did not seem to answer his mobile telephone anymore. The only time that Clara was able to speak with him was when she had called the landline to the office phone.

She had hoped that the visit would bring him back out of himself, at any rate it would get him out of that stuffy office, which he had referred to jokingly as his man cave. She could tell that something had happened in his life which had put him into this kind of despair. Typically of Clifton his solution to most things was to keep working away at it until he could find a solution, almost obsessively single minded. He had thrown himself deep into his work, which was all he seemed to be doing at the moment. Whatever it was that was troubling him exhausting himself with work was not going to give him the answers that he sought.

Sometimes when they had been speaking she had felt as though he had wanted to tell something but was holding back. She did not want to push it, feeling that he would tell her in his own time and when he was ready. When Clara had proposed meeting up at the beach Clifton had suggested that they took out the boat. It was something that he and Clara had always talked about but were yet to do. Clifton could not reason quite why he had raised it on this particular occasion to take out the boat with Clara as there had been other opportunities before now. He seemed to be living his life a bit differently now, he seemed to plan less for the long-term future as he had always done previously realising that no matter what your plans are something can come along and knock you completely off course without any warning. He found himself being a lot more spontaneous and living more for the day. Work had helped him though the last few months in his realisation and he was slowly coming out the other side a slightly different person than when he had gone in for Lockridge.

The sunlight danced across the water as Clifton pulled in the main sheet slightly, trying to find that sweet spot where the tell-tales would run horizontal, indicating that the sail was set correctly. The wind indicator at the head of the mast showed that they were on a broad reach heading across the bay. The conditions were perfect and the warm sea breeze hinted of warmer climes, just enough for some exciting sailing without it being overly laborious. There was something about being out on the water which seemed to put the world to rights.

Sailing was a something honest and truthful which relied totally on skill and mastery of the elements. There was no deceit or treachery it was you working in harmony with the elements rather than battling against them.

After his experience he had lost his faith in people. He had been sent there under false pretences finding out that he had been used as a stooge. He hated the thought of not being in control of his own destiny and that there were forces around that could take away your life based on a convenient lie. As far as he was concerned everyone was out for themselves, everyone had an angle. The more time he spent alone engulfed in his work the more these feelings began to take root. The only person that seemed to understand him at the time was Clara. It had felt that she was the only person who did not seem to want to use him for their own benefit.

He had wondered about Derek, the man that Lockridge had killed, would his family have been looked after? Would they have ever known what their husband, father did and how he had inadvertently saved Clifton's life? How would a spy be remembered if their deeds went unknown? He wondered what Aideen was doing now. Would she remember him or would he be forgotten about as just another detail to a long career in deceiving other people?

"That's it, let the jib out just a little bit… there. See how the wind scopes up the sail reflecting the main sail?" Clifton nodded towards Clara who he had managed to convince to come aboard with him as crew. She seemed to be enjoying her first time sailing on a proper sailboat.

"This is much more civilised than that RIB I went on when I was in the Mediterranean. It is almost as warm today as well!" she smiled back to him.

They were using Clifton's J70 to sail around the bay from Poole to Christchurch in Dorset. It was a fine-looking vessel which cut through the water effortlessly. The pair were able to comfortably sit on deck Clifton was sitting at the tiller making gentle adjustments trimming the sails as they made their way across the water. He had started sailing on dinghies but disliked the fact that he equally spent as much time in the boat as in the water. After complaining about how hard it was to right the boat in rough conditions he decided some years ago to invest in a keelboat which by contrast was far more stable. He boasted that it was the most comfortable boat that he had the pleasure to helm.

A gust of wind took the tip of the mast and the boat leached slightly over. Clifton moving his weight over quickly to correct it and keep the boat a flat in the water as possible so that Clara had a smooth ride on her maiden voyage. "Are we nearly there?" she asked.

"Not too far off now, why?" Clifton replied.

"I was just getting a bit thirsty that's all." She tugged slightly on the jib rope and the sail began to flutter slightly.

"Let's see." Twisting his wrist over so that he could read the time from his new Daniel Wellington Classic Cambridge watch with its tricolour Nato fabric strap. "Yes, it's 10.43, time to resupply methinks." It was not the sort of watch that he would have typically gone for but there was something appealing about the adaptability of the strap and the classic elegant face which was comforting. He had thought about just replacing his old watch with one that was exactly the same but had decided against it.

Something in him had changed now and there was no point living in the past. The future would be whatever he would make it and the dogma of routine and sticking on the same course would change. He was not exactly sure how yet. He did not have all the answers and nor did he want to, he would discover them as he went along. This would be the time of exploration of finding out who this new person was and what they were like.

"Ready about!" he called out.

"Erm .. YES… sorry I 've forgotten it already, but I know what you mean!"

"Lee ho!" and with that command Clifton pushed the tiller away from him and the boom began to swing towards the middle of the boat. Clara knew how to control the jib and then Clifton turned the boat directly into the wind causing them to come to a gently stop. He quickly lowered the mast and furled the jib moving forward to the cockpit of the boat. He produced an anchor from the forward compartment which he carefully lowered over the side point out that it had to be done at a certain angle or the chain would damage the fibreglass hull. He looked towards the shoreline to take a transit. Clara asked him inquisitively what he was looking for.

"Well see, to make sure that the anchor is secure and that we do not accidentally drift off into the distance, as romantic as that thought is. When you are anchoring to can check your positioning by taking something called a 'transit' or 'range'. Take that lighthouse there." He pointed towards the shoreline. Clara adjusting herself in the boat setting her shoulder just under his arm.

"Yes I see it," she replied.

"Okay good, see how it is in alignment with that flagpole flying the blue flag?" She nodded in response. "If they fall out of alignment then the anchor has not worked and we are drifting, if they stay in alignment then the anchor is secure and we can eat."

"It looks good to me, all secured!" She turned and smiled towards him as he returned to the forward compartment where he revealed a large wicker picnic basket which he had secretly stowed away in the cockpit.

Clara was delighted as he produced a flask of hot coffee, butter, jam, a small red and white chequered table cloth which he draped over a small the fold out table which had appeared on deck and croissants.

It was only now that Clifton really started to notice Clara. She wore a striped blue and white Ralph Lauren shirt tucked into a pair of white shorts which looked particularly bright in the sun light, with some matching plimsoll shoes. Her exposed arms showed a slight chill as a gust of cool air drifted past. She had her Musto baseball cap pulled down low and Dior sunglasses beneath. Clifton thought how cute she looked wearing his spare Crewsaver Crewfit that she had adorned around her neck and waist that he had insisted she wear when she came on board. Although the design of the lifejacket was to be as streamline as possible and allow for maximum movement, Clara still managed to make it look awkward.

"Don't worry there is more, that was just the first course," he said reassuringly as he pulled out a further surprise in the form of eggs benedict royale with Martini Asti Spumante to accompany it. Clara put up her hands to her chest and gave a small applause. "Oh this is definitely the way to travel!" she said, "especially with such delicious meals, I could do this every weekend!"

They carried on their discussions and debates on solving the problem of the City, design, Kevin McCloud and his put-downs on *Grand Designs*. "Do you remember the *Grand Designs*' drinking game?" Clara asked

"Of course," Clifton said. "I do not think that my liver has ever quite recovered after that particular episode. What were the rules again? Oh yes now I remember; one shot when you hear the word or part word 'eco', a double if the money ran out, a treble if the design team was sacked, a double if the client decided to manage the project themselves, a shot for every time Kevin was not optimistic and a double if he ended up having a go at building something!"

"Ha, you remembered," she laughed as the boat bobbed gently with the tide.

They finished the last bite immersed in conversation about the finalists for this year's *Shed of the Year* programme. "I'd like to stay here," Clifton said carelessly looking out towards where the shoreline met the sea.

"Me too!" Clara growled as she stretched up from her reclined resting position pushing out her arms and feet across the deck.

As if a silent snap of the fingers had brought about a sudden alertness, Clifton sparked into action standing up and beginning to tidy up. "However if we don't move soon we will be stuck here for quite some time as the tide has turned and in no time at all this here will be dry land," indicating towards the lapping water against the fibreglass hull.

"Fair point," she replied with a short giggle at the end smiling and holding onto the rail which ran around the perimeter of the hull. "Okay just one last question then. If you were stranded on a desert island what five things would you want to take? – but remember you can only have five."

"Hmm ok simple: one, a pair of decent walking boots; two, a decent knife; three, a good warm waterproof jacket; four, string; five, sunglasses – anything else I can make."

She doubled up with laughter, "Yep I should have expected that from you… practicality all the way, of course!"

"Of course," he said with a smile.

Clifton checked his watch thinking about the tidal times that he had studied earlier that morning. In no time they were back under way and heading towards Christchurch Harbour via Mudeford. The weather was beginning to turn slightly and a refreshing cooler breeze started to whip up the top of the waves making the boat cut through the water faster. Every now and again a spray of water was thrown up into the air. Clifton saw Clara lick her lips, doing the same he could taste the salt wash. It was quite exhilarating as the boat took up was cutting cleanly through the water. They sailed through the narrow channel towards the harbour which had become noticeably slenderer from when they had first seen it while picnicking as the tide had gone out.

Clifton charted the course which would keep them carefully set within the centre of the channel between the red and green buoys. When they strayed slightly stray of the centre of the channel Clifton gently rested his hand on Clara's shoulder indicating for her to pull in the jib slightly to pull the nose of the boat back towards the centre of the channel. As they approached the opening to the harbour Clara pointed towards a wall created from lobster pots which decorated the harbours entrance and stood almost two meters high. "Look at all those cages!" Clifton just nodded in acknowledgement replacing his sunglasses to his face. He could see the Haven House Inn pub just behind the lobster pots. His mouth longed for the refreshing taste of a cool Magner's cider, he could almost taste the sweetness as they passed by.

Other smaller vessels began to come into view around the corner. A small tender being was being readied by an older man with what appeared to be his grandson. He leant over the side of the inflatable sides and untied the rope line that was holding the craft in place. Making sure that the child was safe at the head of the boat he tugged at the starter-cord and the Marine outboard spluttered into life.

Over the port bow there was a family of five, spread out in three plastic kayaks, using paddles to cruise around the harbour in. There was some rivalry between two of the three kayaks which had the children racing each other while mum and dad followed slowly behind just glad to be enjoying their leisure time.

Clifton and Clara found their mooring inside the harbour and Clifton showed Clara how to tie a running bowline knot. She found it quite tricky to remember the process so Clifton stood behind her running his hands over hers and whispering into her ear the instructions as they tied the knot.

"So we take this rope and double the end like this, then wrap this tag end over and up to side of the new loop that has been created there. Now we make a small loop on the topside of the original loop like this by twisting the rope over itself. Then you feed the tag end through the small loop, wrap tag end once around topside of large loop and then back down through small loop remembering to pull tag end tight creating like this, fixing the loop so that main rope can slip through there."

As they fondled the rope together she leaned back into his chest. He was suddenly aware of her perfume which seemed to fill the roof of his mouth. It was almost intoxicating. He was suddenly transported to thoughts of what might be but stopped himself from dreaming.

The sound of tinkering metal tapping filled the marina as the breeze swept through the harbour making any loose cables hitting the mast resonate. They passed a quiet residential area. There was a mixture of brand new four-by-fours parked up as though they were on display in an open-air showroom next to more practical family cars. Clifton sighed as he caught sight of what looked to be a wedding reception at one of the seafront villas. There was a short white wall with black iron topping rails which prevented access but left unhindered views out towards the beach and beyond.

Securing the boat they stepped out onto the pontoon decking and walked back towards the club house where they could get changed. "You mustn't run," Clifton said to Clara.

"Why ever not?" She giggled as she began to prance along the pontoon which started to rise and fall with the motion.

"That's why, you'll fall in if you're not careful!"

"You worry too much, you never used to worry as much as this. I remember you when we had that bridge building project on that stream and on the first day of the site investigation fact finding mission what did you do?" She stopped, turned with one hand on her hip and the other indicating towards Clifton.

He smiled, looked skyward. "I fell in the river, it was definitely a river and not a stream."

"Hmm ok we'll use the term 'river' in its loosest possible form then. You spectacularly fell in the river!" laughing before putting her arms around him in a friendly hug.

"Right this is where I'll have to leave you I'm afraid."

"What?"

"That's the ladies changing rooms, the men's is over there. I will meet you in the club lounge."

"Okay see you in a bit."

Clifton was quite quick at changing but made sure before he left the changing room that his hair was styled properly. After wearing a hat out on the water he did not want it to stay completely flat. He made his way to the lounge and took a seat on one of the comfy armchairs waiting for Clara.

Clara was someone who took great pride in her appearance and Clifton knew that he would not see her again until she was absolutely convinced that she was ready. 'This could take a while' he thought and picked up the *Times* newspaper which happened to be on the coffee table next to him. Sifting through the stories he stopped at the headline. "MyLife Top Exec admits to not doing enough to control the monster that has become social media.

The social media site MyLife was founded with the goal of linking individuals together from there its founder became obsessed with connectivity and information gathering.

Oliver Manning told the *Times* that "We were deliberately reached into the human psyche as programmers we used this to manipulate people. We needed the advertisers and the only way we could guarantee their message of getting through to the users was to get them hooked on MyLife, like alcohol, gambling or a drug.

We worked on the premise that by overwhelming people's senses they would get withdraw when they weren't connected.

Every time someone got a 'like' or received comments on their posting it was like a small hit for them which drove them to crave more. Strategic product placement between postings meant that subconsciously advertisements were being almost streamed directly to the users, who in turn for another hit would add more and more personal information about themselves. We even had software which would read product branding from photos they would upload so that the users could be targeted by those advertisements.

It was sick really and I don't know what sort of generation we will end up with.

The next story was almost more important but only occupied a discreet section towards the centrefold "MyLife's Ethan Thomas admits that mistakes have been made," read the heading:

In his first comments since the reports earlier this year that personal data was being harvested by rouge developer applications grafted into the MyLife platform, Thomas recognises that there has been a breach of trust between his social media empire and its users. It is reported that well over a billion MyLife pages have been accessed over a four year period and personal information ranging from dates of birth, locations visited, photos actively harvested from users accounts.

Although it is believed that this is an historic breach of privacy and should not happen with the current security measures in place many feel that it is too little too late.

Former cybersecurity analyst for Google Judy Simpson commented on Twitter, "Admitting there have been mistakes at MyLife is a start. More importantly, users will be expecting an apology at the very least. It can be seen from the share prices of MyLife today, which are down 5%, that investors are simply not going to accept this sort of breach of trust.

Clifton folded the paper and pushed it to one side thinking deeply. The enjoyment of the sailing across the bay seemed to have been purged from him as solemnity over took him. Clara came out of the changing room and could read on his face that something had changed from the time she had left him.

Clara talked Clifton into walking down the sea front towards Highcliffe. Tall trees shaded the marina from the warm summer sun.

As they passed the marina Clifton noticed a white Ford Transit van packed up on the kerb. What first drew his attention to it was how the brilliantly white van contrasted so with the blacked out tinted windows. On the roof of the van it was possible to make out what first appeared to be some sort of roof box, which was brilliant white too, with what looked like four black metal limbs stretching out from the sides of the roof box. At the end of each arm was a silver canister device. It looked as though a rather large drone had landed on top of the vehicle. There was also a well-concealed camera pointing out the side of the roof box.

There was some writing in just below the sliding door panel which read, "MyLife Maps… coming soon *maps.MyLife.com."*

"Oh wow" Clara said as she caught side of the vehicle. "Smile, we're going to be on MyLife maps!"

Clifton looked towards the ground and put his hands in his pockets muttering beneath his breath. "He was right after all, they really are everywhere." Whatever else Lockridge had said to Clifton it was clear to him now the he knew the secrets behind the magician's tricks as the veil fell. Life would never be the same again as he would see everything in a different way from now on understanding the tricks of the trade, the lies and propaganda being pumped out of all media orifices not being challenged but simply accepted. Why? Because that was the done thing, you conformed, you did what you were told and you believed what you were told to be the truth.

Clifton now understood that the truths which he had believed in the past were far from the reality. Truth was a fabrication spun to a particular view point, propaganda leading to the ultimate control over people and no one could see the puppeteers pulling the strings. Lockridge had said they were invisible but Clifton could see them, see them in plain sight and without masking the fact.

They walked along the seafront not speaking to one another in a comfortable silence. Clara had her arm looped into Clifton's arm. She could sense that something was bothering him but decided that it was best not to enquire. Clifton would tell her in his own time.

It was possible to hear the relaxed sounds of the sea with its steady lapping of the surf onto the shingle beach. When they reached Highcliffe they stopped at a bench where they sat looking out over the bay. Clifton observed all that was around him, taking in a deep breath. The seagulls were calling in the distance and one glided past in front of him swooping down. He seemed to be wrestling with demons in his mind.

He was frustrated and angry to have been manipulated and used in such a way. He wanted someone to blame, to be held accountable. In his mind there was no difference between Lockridge and Musgrave. They were both in the business of interfering in other people's lives, leaving a wake of destruction in their path and to what purpose? When you took away all the pretext and subterfuge the only real difference between the good guys and the bad was which corporation you worked for.

"Are you coming inside or not?" Clara said, gently squeezing his arm as she brushed her hair with her hand against the sea breeze. "You can catch me up," she said as she stood up and disappeared behind him. He took a couple of minutes to take in the beauty of the sea and the horizon and that magic secretive connection that they shared.

Whatever had happened it was now in the past. He was not going to let it brew inside of him. The only healthy thing to do was to let it go, let Aideen go and move on from the whole thing. It was not something that he would ever forget nor would he want to because it had changed him and how he saw things. His eyes had been opened vehemently and he could not go back to the way things were. He recalled someone once saying that 'ignorance is not bliss'. He had thought about it a great deal recently. Was it always better to know even if there was not anything that one person alone could do about it? He still did not have a definitive answer for that although he would let his mind continue the debate.

He got up from the bench and made his way over to the Cliffhanger Café and joined Clara in the queue for a table giving her a peck on the cheek. They were quickly seated and given menus. Clifton reset the cutlery as he would habitually do in a restaurant even adjusting the condiments to give direct sight to the person sitting opposite him so that he could read their body language and he in turn would appear to be accessible to talk to. He removed the napkin from the cutlery and considerately placed it in his lap. Looking over the top of the menu Clara said, "You can order the wine, you're becoming quite the connoisseur!"

Clifton tilted his head to one side slightly and replied. "I would not say that. What are you thinking of having to eat?"

"The lemon and thyme chicken breast, it has protein so it's good for me."

"Yes. I gather that the chips and onion rings are a good source of carbohydrates?"

"I've told you before it is all about balance and not too much of one thing!" she grinned.

"Well you've convinced me anyway. I could not come all the way to the seaside and not have fish and chips. It would be a sacrilegious. I would recommend a bottle of the Lanark Lane, Sauvignon Blanc Marlborough. The lemon and lime aroma will complement both dishes and with a hint of passion fruit it should not be as mono-tone as the Pinot Grigio." He relaxed back into the chair and placed the menu carefully flat on the table in front of him. Looking at Clara. "I have missed you. I thought that when you moved that I would not see you again."

"I told you that wouldn't ever happen. As long as we have each other we have the strength to go through anything." She reached out across the table to his hand and placed hers on top of his. He felt pinpricks of energy from the touch. His defences were receding. He took her hand in his and noticed how soft and warm her hand was.

"Listen I've been through a lot recently, you know, with work." Instinctively he began rubbing one of the remaining bruises on his forearm. "It's not something that I want to talk about, ever. It all too raw. I cannot really elaborate any more than that. I do not want to sound like I am trying to be mysterious or obtuse but I am afraid that you are just going to have to accept that as the answer. I went away some bad things happened but now I'm back. Maybe a bit wiser than before – you'll have to be the judge of that."

Clara looked deeply into Clifton's eyes and could read that he was being sincere. There sat there still for a moment before the waitress interrupted and asked if she could take their drinks order. They took back their respective hands and Clifton ordered the bottle of wine. The waitress asked if they were ready to order the food and they placed their order. The waitress disappeared as quickly as she came. Clara was looking into her lap deep in contemplation.

"You know I will always be there for you. That is the one thing that is always constant. I have known you for what seems like forever and well, I've loved you since the first time we met. I know that this may be all too soon from what you have been through, whatever it was, but I want you to know that you are loved." She looked over to him across the table trying to gauge his reaction.

He leaned forward slightly in the chair nodding slightly and gave an affable smile. He reached across the table and took her hand is his once again. He felt the same enchantment from touching her as he had always done. "Clara, you captivated my heart from the first time I saw you. I can remember that moment as if it were yesterday. There you were standing there, the sun was coming in through the window behind you illuminating you in a golden aura. You smiled your joyful smile and my stomach turn upside down along with the rest of my world. It was as if an angel had walked through the door. Normally I would have been too shy to speak to someone that I liked but I knew that if I didn't then it would be one of the biggest regrets of my life so I forced myself to speak to you. It was probably something rather silly and nonsensical but at least I had spoken to this delectable girl."

Clara blushed and looked at the table smiling. "I remember what you said to me."

"Honestly?" Clifton sat up more in his chair.

"Yes, I remember exactly what you said to me because it was so random and it is only something that you would have thought of in your own special caring way.

"You warned me that because I was wearing flat soled AllStar sneakers I was more likely to slip on the polished vinyl floor than if I had other shoes with more of traction on the sole!"

"Really! Goodness I'm sorry. Sometimes I don't even know where that sort of thing comes from" Clifton said shaking his head breaking eye contact.

Clara chuckled "Well I thought that it was cute that you actually cared. Most guys would have made a pass at me but you cared enough to warn me about the floor. In that moment I thought to myself that this is someone different, this is someone who thinks about others before themselves. And yes I had the tummy feeling too."

The waitress arrived at the table and poured out the glasses of wine returning the bottle to the cooler. They both nodded and thanked the waitress picking up the glasses.

"What should we toast to?" Clara asked.

Clifton thought for a moment and saw Clara in front of him with the sun dancing off the ripples of the sea, shimmering in the distance. He smiled and replied, "To new horizons," as made his toast raising their glasses and clinking them together. "Sláinte."